Life Committed

Life Committed

by
William Schuster

Copyright © 2017 by William Schuster
All rights reserved. No part of this book may be reproduced,
scanned, or distributed in any printed or electronic form
without permission.
First Edition: September 2017
Printed in the United States of America

*Dedicated to my Family who
continue to be my inspiration.*

Aiken, South Carolina – October 2017

Preface
(Five Years Earlier)

There's something special about Christmas time in New York City. The often brusque nature of the people is replaced by a friendlier atmosphere; no doubt fed by the elaborate window decorations, the fully decked out tree in Rockefeller Center, and overall thoughts of the holidays to come. While the weather is crisp, the warmth of thinking about loved ones and shopping for just the right present seems to make it no bother. Tourists, shoppers and those still working crowd the streets, restaurants, and stores. Overall, it's a wonderful time of year to come for a visit to the Big Apple.

These were the thoughts Dave Price had when he and his wife, Sandy, and their daughter, Becky, made their annual pilgrimage to the city. Every year when school let out, they'd travel by train to Penn Station, then make their way to a midtown hotel which would serve as their base of operations during their stay. They'd fill their days with shopping, touring various sites (including museums), and taking advantage of the spectacular eateries New York has to offer. Lastly, they'd always plan to take in a couple of Broadway shows.

This annual trip gave them something they could look forward to as they went through their hectic daily lives. It provided them with the opportunity to bond as a family, something the demands of work and school often prevented. It was fun to be away with nothing to do but have a good time...well, that was almost the case, but all too often Dave had to hold calls with his office and deal with the ever present barrage of email; however, he managed these tasks so they provided only minimal interference with the family's time together. Generally, the family would have breakfast together, then Sandy and Becky would do some window shopping or stroll around for an hour or so while Dave got his work done. They'd then meet up at a predetermined location which they'd confirm by cell phone. It seemed to work out for everyone, and often after rendezvousing Sandy and Becky would show Dave what they'd discovered. This was typically followed by lunch, then the afternoon's activities.

This year was much like others. They arrived by train just around noon. The lunchtime crowds added to the normal press of humanity. The taxi queues were prohibitively long, and the hotel wasn't that far away, so they decided to walk. The crowds made it challenging to walk together with their wheeled luggage, but soon they were at their hotel. They checked in, dropped off their luggage, and set about to find a relatively light snack, even though Becky proclaimed she was famished; from listening to her, one would have thought she hadn't eaten for a week. They didn't want to overeat, since they planned to go out for a fancy dinner that evening. Dave had done some work on the train, so there was no need to separate, and they spent the afternoon walking around Times Square, Rockefeller Center, and Bryant Park. While in Rockefeller Center, they made plans to tour the NBC Studios the following afternoon.

That evening, they went to a deservedly famous steak place and feasted on some of the best food they felt they'd ever eaten. It always seemed this way; it was likely not just the result of the food being good, but also how they felt about this special time together. Dave figured this must be the case, since he ate at many of these same restaurants while on business and the food was never quite as enjoyable. The restaurant was close to the hotel, so they walked back. They decided to turn in early, since everyone was tired from getting up early to catch the train, as well as from the journey itself.

The next morning, they went out for breakfast. They always preferred to go out in lieu of eating in the hotel, due both to price and selection. They found a nice coffee shop and enjoyed breakfast. Sandy had a lox platter comprised of smoked salmon, capers, onion, tomato, an everything bagel and cream cheese. Becky had French toast and Dave had an English muffin. They all had juice and coffee. There was excited talk about the NBC tour coming up that afternoon, as well as the Broadway show they had tickets for the next day. The show was a musical which just opened and was receiving rave reviews. Dave gave them each a hug and kiss as he headed back to the hotel to do some work, then Sandy and Becky headed off to explore; unbeknownst to any of them, this was the last time they would ever see each other.

A NYPD cruiser in hot pursuit of some criminals lost control and careened into a crowd of pedestrians waiting to cross the street. Sandy and Becky were in the front of that crowd and were killed instantly – or at least this was what Dave was told, along with assurances that they hadn't suffered; however, as is usually the case, those left behind are the ones who suffer. Dave went from denial expecting to see their smiling faces coming down the street at any moment, to feelings of total despair as they were his life and the void they left created an emptiness that could not be readily filled. Dave couldn't get over the fact that he hadn't been with them, all for the sake of his job. He kept blaming himself, telling himself things somehow would have been different had he been with them. Only now did he reason his job wasn't so important, when up to that point it had been the center of his life.

    Dave didn't blame the police officers, though the City paid a very large sum of money to the victims' families. He blamed himself, and he blamed the criminals that plagued the country. Dave, who was an engineer by training, had always applied himself towards improved national security through the work he did for large government contractors; now he felt he needed to do something more. While it may have been the grief speaking, he quit his job, moved from the East Coast to the West Coast, and dedicated himself to ridding the country of those who harmed it. He did so in memory of his lost family, and to give his life a meaningful focus; he felt as though he'd lost everything and needed some reason to live.

    Though Dave knew what he wanted to do, he fell short of having a real, actionable plan. Instead he occupied himself with such things as learning how to fly, becoming a marksman with both handguns and rifles, and studying martial arts. These activities didn't ease his pain, but they did provide a diversion from it and, he reasoned, might prove to be useful skills, given what he was committed to doing. Like everything he did, Dave pursued these endeavors with great intensity and became accomplished in each. Ultimately, he became the sole proprietor of a security consulting firm. He didn't need to make money, as he already had more than enough, so he was able to be very selective in the jobs he took. Despite being in very high demand, Dave only took those assignments he felt honored the memory of his lost family and all he'd lost. He felt that through his work, which was tireless, he could somehow make up for having failed his family when they needed him most.

Chapter 1

Storm at Sea

They were being violently tossed around by the storm that churned above them. Commander Park and his three-man North Korean crew were in a mini-sub just off the coast of South Korea. Their orders were to travel submerged into an anchorage just south of the DMZ. Kim, the stranger to their team, was to go ashore with a small cargo chest they were carrying. Later, someone else would be joining them for the journey home while Kim remained ashore.

The initial part of their journey had been easy enough, but then there was this storm. Commander Park cursed the meteorologists for their lack of skill at predicting such things, as this storm was far from a subtle event. Under the best of circumstances, being in the sub was unpleasant enough – but with the especially tumultuous conditions of the sea, they were unbearable. The normally cramped quarters that smelled of machine oil and sweat now had added to it the smell of fear and vomit. Even some of the seasoned seamen got sick from all the tossing and turning they had to endure. In addition, there were things flying around in the crew area. They were trying to secure everything loose in the boat, which was very difficult to do with all the motion and need to hold on. If one weren't careful, he might just become a projectile himself.

If they thought things were bad at that point, they were about to become far worse. The engine died, leaving the crew with no means to maintain steering; they were already suffering a very rough ride with steering, and the ride would only be worse if they were unable to maintain a favorable heading.

"Seaman Choi, can you tell why the engine quit?" shouted Commander Park.

"No, sir!" replied Choi, "but I'll see if I can get it running again. My guess is that all the motion ripped something loose."

"I don't want your guesses," demanded Commander Park. "I just want you to fix it; otherwise, we might not be able to survive this storm. Lee - where are we? How far from closest land?"

Lee replied, "When I last checked, we were ten nautical miles from our destination and less than one mile offshore. Given the direction of the storm, we could be going further out to sea, but as best as I can tell from the charts and the depth gauge, this would seem not to be the case; instead, I think we're just being blown along the coast, since the water isn't changing depth one way or another."

With the lights flickering, on top of everything else that was going on, it took them a moment to notice a flashing alarm light.

Commander Park yelled, "Choi, Lee, what is that light flashing on the panel?"

Choi responded first. In a voice filled with fear, and barely in control, he said, "It's the gas alarm! The boat is filling with poison gas! We're all going to die!"

"Choi get hold of yourself and take us to the surface!" exclaimed Commander Park. "Choi! Choi!"

But it was no good; Choi was frozen with fear and couldn't act. So, Commander Park commanded Lee to blow the ballast and bring the boat to the surface. They needed to ventilate the cabin, or they would indeed die. Lee promptly turned the valves, but nothing happened.

Lee shouted, "It didn't work! I opened the valves, but nothing happened!"

"Activate the emergency pumps," commanded Park.

These pumps provided a manual means to force the water out of the ballast tanks, which would make the sub more buoyant and help it rise. There were two of these pumps: one was currently being manned by Lee; the other one was near Choi, who was by now in a near catatonic state.

Commander Park yelled, "Kim, are you able to get to the other pump and activate it?"

Not being a sailor, Park was uncertain of Kim, not to mention untrusting, but right now he was the best bet. If the bow pump were operated, which was what

Lee was currently doing, the front of the boat would rise while the stern, or back, would remain down. The only chance of having the boat rise in a more or less level attitude was to have both pumps running. To Park's relief, he saw Kim reach the aft pump and begin to operate it. With the turbulent ride they were having, it was difficult to tell whether or not the boat was leveling, but Park was relatively certain the boat was rising.

"Lee, can you see how deep we are?" Commander Park asked.

"No" came the quick reply from Lee. "The needle is moving around too much, but I do feel as though we're rising."

"Keep pumping – both of you," ordered Park. "It's our only chance."

Park made his way to the instrument console. The going was difficult, and he banged his head at least once, making him see stars. He saw both Lee and Kim pumping as hard as they could. Despite the cold, both men were sweating profusely. After what was only minutes, but seemed like hours, Park thought he felt the boat breach the surface.

"Keep pumping. I think we've made it," proclaimed Park. "I'll see if I can open the hatch."

Commander Park turned the wheel that would open the hatch, all the while being slammed around by the violent motion of the boat. When the latches were free, Park tried to raise the hatch. At first he wasn't able to do it; however, he eventually got it open, and there was the sweet smell of fresh air – that was, until a wave crashed down on the boat, bringing a large torrent of water through the open hatch.

Commander Park said, "We can't stay like this. The boat is dead, and we will be too if we stay in it. The only alternative that might give us a chance to live is to abandon ship. I'll try to lock open the hatch, then you can follow me out. I'll release the life raft from its mount, and hopefully we'll be able to make it to shore."

From out of nowhere, Kim produced a pistol and pointed it at Park.

"With all due respect, Commander, there's a mission that must be accomplished," said Kim. "If we abandon ship and take the raft, we'll sacrifice our duty to our country and its glorious leader in order to save our insignificant lives. I'm going to take the package we brought and use the raft to deliver it."

"You will do no such thing," shouted Park. "We are going to save ourselves so we can support our exalted leader another day."

There was a great deal of shouting. When Lee tried to close on Kim, he was too slow due to the commotion caused by the storm. Kim fired a shot at Lee, but it went wild due to the violent ride produced by the storm.

Kim said, "The next time, I won't miss. Now both of you get over there!"

Kim had pointed at the furthest distance from the hatch. They started to move, but they soon realized these actions would result in their demise. Each sought a plan, but they were coming up empty. Both Park and Lee were beginning to come to terms that this was how and when they were going to die; they were each thinking about their families and all they'd miss by having their lives cut short. Almost in unison, they each concluded it was worth taking a risk to see if they might subdue Kim and get to live another day.

They stopped their retreat to where Kim had ordered them and started to move in Kim's direction.

Kim shouted, "I warned you."

He then raised the gun he was holding and was about to shoot Park first, followed by Lee; however, he suddenly crumbled to his knees. At first, Lee and Park didn't know what happened; however, it all became clear when they saw Choi standing over him with a crow bar in his hand. He wasn't being watched by anyone and had simply snuck up on Kim and hit him.

Feeling greatly relieved, Park said, "Seaman Choi, your timing couldn't have been better in rejoining us. Thank you."

Choi simply responded, "It was my duty."

For some reason, Park didn't want to leave Kim's corpse – if he was dead – in the sub; if he was alive, they would do what they could for him. They tethered themselves to each other by fastening a rope to their life jackets, then tied the end of the rope to Kim. They needed to get out soon; waves were sending water careening through the hatch, and the boat wouldn't stay afloat much longer. Lee went out first and liberated the life raft from its holder and immediately tied the other end of their life line to it. Choi and the commander pushed Kim's lifeless body through the hatch and onto the wildly pitching deck, then they quickly followed. A series of powerful waves forcefully washed them from the deck and away from the boat. This happened before the commander could activate the self-destruct mechanism, though he saw the boat drop beneath the waves as they were blown in the opposite direction.

Park, Choi, and Lee struggled to reach the life raft, an effort made especially more difficult by towing the dead weight of Kim. Park finally cut Kim loose. Once at the life raft, they spent a long time and a lot of energy to get in it. It was so exhausting, once they managed to get in the raft, they all collapsed.

Over the following ten days they spent in the raft, Commander Park frequently thought of his failure to scuttle the boat, but he comforted himself with the thought that he saw it go under on its own. The water was relatively deep there, so despite his not activating the explosive charge to sink the boat; it was nonetheless sunk and lost forever. He'd accomplished his duty.

Park and his two other crew members eventually made it to dry land. While their escape from the sub had been harrowing, their trip home was even more so. While staying in the South had many attractions, they were both loyal soldiers – and most importantly, the North was where their families were. It wasn't so much missing their families as it was the bad fate the families would face from the government should the crew defect. So, they persevered through heavily patrolled areas and the dreaded mine fields. Throughout this journey, and for months afterward, Park couldn't shake the bad feeling he had about not having set off the explosive charge and destroying the sub. Of course, he didn't report this; he simply said the sub had sunk in deep water. After not seeing or hearing any reports from the South that the boat had been found, he eventually stopped thinking about it.

Chapter 2

Noteworthy Airline Flight

    The main terminal at Washington's Dulles airport was buzzing with people rushing to their flights. Dave Price was one of those travelers on this particular sunny Tuesday morning; however, he was in no hurry, and despite the appearance that he was headed for a leisurely vacation, he was actually on business. His flight wasn't scheduled to depart for another 90 minutes, and the TSA pre-security line would take no more than five minutes or so; therefore, he took his time.

    Eventually, Price went through security without incident and headed for the train that would transport him out to the gate. This morning, he'd be flying business class on a brand new airplane made by Sky Bus Industries. It was the SB-500, which was the most fuel efficient and comfortable airplane in commercial service. It was also the most automated, which was why Price was on this particular flight.

    The gate area was filled with people from various walks of life, including those on business and on vacation. Regardless, none of them except the crew was making the flight their business; it was merely just a means to an end. However, much like the crew, but unbeknownst to them, this flight was very much Dave Price's business. His business was also not known to the air marshal assigned to the flight. In reality, no one knew of Dave Price's plan.

Price was on retainer as a consultant to the TSA. In this capacity, he evaluated security measures and sought to identify and nullify threats. Today he was on just such a quest, but he feared what he had in mind, while making a necessary point, would still likely get him fired. Being fired didn't matter to Price, though, as long as he did something he felt would honor the memory of his lost family, as well as the life commitment he'd made.

Not a day went by without Dave thinking about them and how things might have been. These thoughts didn't need anything in particular to trigger them, and this morning they were set off by a family waiting in the boarding area heading for a visit with relatives. His thoughts of his wife and daughter were also always there when he was doing something he felt was important to making the country safer and more secure – his life commitment.

Dave's self-initiated mission this morning wouldn't have been needed if the bureaucrats had listened to him when he postulated the vulnerability he'd exploit this morning. Politics got in the way. The SB-500 was too important both from economic and prestige perspectives to allow his concern to be acted on; so, Dave just smiled to himself, thinking about how the bureaucrats would react to what he was planning to do.

The gate area was getting crowded, and before long the first boarding call was made for those needing assistance or extra time in boarding. People were gathering their belongings and starting to get in various boarding lines. Next to be called were passengers in first class, followed shortly by those in business class. Carrying just a computer bag, Dave Price went down the jet way and boarded the plane.

Noticing it still had the new plane smell and looked new, Price made his way to his seat. It was an aisle bulkhead seat, and in front of him was one of the many lavatories on the plane. No one would be sitting in the window seat next to him, since he'd purchased both seats; however, just across the aisle from him was the air marshal.

Price settled himself for the flight by taking out ear buds and a tablet from his computer case. He also put a small box from the case into his pocket. He then stowed his case into the rapidly filling overhead compartment. Before sitting down, he went to the rest room.

The marshal, who was scrutinizing everyone who boarded, paid no mind to Price. His actions were all quite normal, and there were other characters getting on the flight who posed greater interest for him. The marshal also didn't think much about how long Price stayed in the lavatory, though he should have.

Price returned to his seat, exchanged a smile and head nod with the marshal, then sat down and buckled in. He graciously accepted a coffee when the flight attendant came by offering various beverages to first and business class passengers. As he sipped the warm drink, he thought about what he'd just done and what he was about to do.

While in the lavatory, Price had opened an access hatch and tapped into the airplane's computer network. The box he'd put in his pocket was actually little more than a wireless router of the sort homes and businesses use to connect multiple devices to a network. In this case, the connection would allow his tablet to connect to the network over which all the plane's automation was implemented. He was now a second node besides the pilot's which had access to all control and instrumentation. When he turned on his tablet, various instruments, switches, and flight controls could be seen on its display.

As the door was shut and they were readying for taxi and takeoff, the lead flight attendant announced that everyone should take their seats. She then played a safety presentation that no one except extreme novices seemed to pay attention to. The captain then came on the PA system, providing flight details and saying he'd be back to provide more information after takeoff.

As the ground crew pushed the airplane back, Price put his ear buds in, which let him hear all cockpit communications. The crew began the engine start up procedures, with first one engine and then the other. Once they were running, the plane began its long taxi from the gate out to runway one left, which was the active runway for departures on this day. There were several planes ahead of them, but ultimately they were given permission from the control tower to taxi into takeoff position. Shortly thereafter, they were cleared for takeoff.

Captain John Cox, a 25-year veteran pilot with the company, said to his co-pilot, "Rick, what a gorgeous day to fly, and especially in this fine piece of equipment."

Rick James, the co-pilot, responded, "You always say that. You just love to fly; however, I agree this should be a good trip, and with the tail winds several minutes shorter than usual."

The captain would be the pilot in command for the first leg of the trip. When he got clearance to take off, he locked the brakes and advanced the throttles. The co-pilot acknowledged the clearance on the radio with a simple "Sky Bus rolling on one left."

They were instructed to contact Washington Center, which gave them their initial instructions, including course, altitude, and speed. After reaching 5,000 feet of altitude, they were to turn slightly west to 300 degrees and continue their climb to 36,000 feet.

The runway had them taking off to the north. When the engines had attained adequate thrust, the captain released the brakes and the plane rapidly accelerated down the runway. Soon the front landing gear left the ground, followed in short order by the main landing gear, and they were airborne. With the automation this plane had, they were no more than 50 feet in the air when the captain switched to autopilot. He then sat back and relaxed.

The machine would do its job, and he was along for the ride. He recalled the old joke from back in the early days of space exploration. There was an astronaut and a monkey in the cockpit on a rocket, ready to take off. The control room was giving all kinds of commands to the monkey, who was turning dials and flipping switches. The astronaut asked what he could do and was told to stand by. In the meantime, the monkey did more technical tasks right through launch and insertion into orbit. The ground then called the capsule, saying they needed the astronaut to perform a critical task. He excitedly asked what it was and was told, "Feed the monkey." Cox laughed to himself.

"What's so funny?" Rick asked. "You're looking like you just remembered your first conquest."

"Nah, it's nothing like that. I was just remembering that old joke about the astronaut and the monkey. This machine is so easy to fly. All we really need to do is monitor performance in case there's a computer glitch. Not as much fun as hand flying," said Cox.

The words were barely out of his mouth when he noticed they were leveling off at 20,000 feet and making a course heading to the east. It wasn't long before air traffic control wanted to know why there was a change in course.

Cox replied, "Washington Control, there's some kind of anomaly that caused the plane to change heading and level off. All systems appear normal. I'm turning off the autopilot now and will affect manual control."

"Roger that," the controller responded. "Turn left to heading of three–zero–zero degrees and resume your climb to 36,000 feet."

"Roger, turn to heading of three-zero-zero and climb to 36,000 feet," said Rick, who resumed his radio duty while the captain sorted out what was wrong.

Unbeknownst to the crew, Price was busy in his seat redirecting the airplane and taking control away from the pilot. Another word for this might be hijacking the plane; however, Price preferred to think of it as proving a vulnerability before the bad guys exploited it for real. While it might be possible with other computer-controlled or fly-by-wire aircraft in service, the level of automation on the SB-500 really made it easy. In fact, Price wasn't flying the aircraft; he simply gave new instructions to the autopilot and kept the pilot from taking back control.

Cox came back on the radio. "Washington center, this is Sky Bus 500 flight 1602 heavy."

"Go ahead, 1602 heavy," replied the controller.

"I'm unable to regain control. I need to declare an emergency and request you clear the airways in front of me until I can get control - 1602 heavy," said Cox.

"Roger. We'll clear a path for you, and good luck," said the controller.

After giving a wide berth to Washington, D.C., the plane proceeded out over the Maryland countryside. Shortly afterward, it turned south and began a gentle descent.

"If I didn't know better, I'd say we just entered the downwind leg of an approach to Andrews Air Force Base," Cox said to his co-pilot.

Rick said, "I think you're right. We should alert ATC, contact Andrews, and then you better make an announcement to the passengers and have the cabin crew prepare for landing."

"Let's do it, and best to go through the landing checklist – not that we seem to be able to do anything," said Cox.

They called ATC, and then called Andrews, who wasn't at all pleased; in fact, the worried controller at Andrews went through numerous protocols with them to validate that they weren't operating under duress. He tried to get them to go elsewhere, but they convinced him they weren't hostile; just not in control.

Sure enough, when they arrived far enough south of the airfield, the airplane made another right turn onto what would be the base leg of their approach. Finally, the unwelcomed plane made a right turn, lined up with the runway, and then they were on the final approach into Andrews AFB, the home of Air Force One. The plane continued its descent, lowering its flaps and landing gear. When it dropped through 250 feet above ground, Price gave control back to the pilots.

"Rick, we have control again," said Cox.

"Better land it. I think if we were to make it a touch-and-go, they might scramble fighters to come after us," said Rick.

"Agreed," said Cox.

Cox performed a perfect landing and taxied to where the controller indicated. He then went through the shutdown procedure. The ground crew brought mobile stairs to the plane. A heavily armed team asked for the front door to open, then boarded the plane. The marshal carefully identified himself and went forward to speak with the team lead, who was about to engage the captain.

"Cabin crew and passenger should deplane. They may bring their belongings. There are buses that will take them to a holding area," said the team leader. "The cockpit crew will wait here. I fear, gentlemen, it is going to be a long day."

It was a long day indeed. After the passengers were questioned for several hours, they were released. Busses were made available to take them back to Dulles, or they could get a taxi if they wanted. All things considered, the passengers were well behaved, but patience was beginning to wear thin for many of them; however, as the busses departed, the passengers were thankful to be on their way, but mostly thankful to be alive. None of them knew exactly what had happened, but making an unscheduled landing and being held for questioning couldn't mean that whatever transpired was entirely benign.

Dave Price wasn't in the same situation as the other passengers, as he did know exactly what happened – particularly since he did it. He hadn't feared for his life. If anything, the fallout from his stunt may eventually cause him harm, but he really didn't care. The vulnerability of the SB-500 needed to be fixed, or something really bad could happen. If the powers to be couldn't accept his analysis of the problem, perhaps they'd act on what had happened. Interestingly, the thoughts he was having made him appear much like the other passengers: deep in thought and reflective, while also a little sad, but in his case for an entirely different reason.

When the bus arrived at Dulles, Dave Price boarded a plane that would return him to his sanctuary on the West Coast. The flight was uneventful, and he was able to catch some much needed sleep. After landing at San Francisco International Airport, he made his way to the private aviation terminal, where he retrieved his airplane for the short flight to Carmel, where he lived. He'd made this flight hundreds of times, and before he knew it, he was landing, securing his plane, and making his way home.

The flight crew faced a more intense day. While Price was entering his home some 8 hours after leaving the airplane at Andrews AFB, the flight crew was still being interrogated. It started with the police squad that first entered the plane after landing. This was followed by several rounds of questioning by the FBI. Then the National Transportation Safety Board got in on the act. When the NTSB was done with questioning the cockpit crew, they sought out the black boxes as potential evidence of what had transpired. Sky Bus had been notified, and they provided some technical support to the investigation. Their most noteworthy suggestion was to make a copy of the onboard computer's files to see if they would provide any insights. There was one more round of questions from yet another team from the FBI, and then the two pilots were released, but told to keep themselves available.

Regretfully, the black boxes didn't reveal anything that wasn't already known, namely that the plane took off from Dulles Airport and functioned normally through its landing at Andrews AFB. The computer memory dump proved slightly more useful in that it showed that the flight plan had been cancelled and a new one was initiated from the cockpit; however, instead of clarifying things, this only confounded them, since both pilots swore they didn't alter the flight plan. In fact, they didn't possess any of the approach information for Andrews that would be needed to reprogram the autopilot. This was substantiated by a search and the fact that they were recorded doing other tasks and wouldn't have had enough time. The cockpit voice recorder also substantiated the crew's statement. This was a real mystery, but one that needed to be solved.

Chapter 3

Told You So

When word of this made its way to the executive suite of the TSA and its technical director, Mike Mahoney, he had an idea of what had happened, even though no one else had a clue. It was Mike that Dave Price had spoken with about the vulnerability of the SB-500 and who curtailed any action on it. Mike also held the contract with Dave Price and frequently used his services.

Mike called his assistant Gene in and said, "Would you please get me the manifest for that SB-500 flight that ended up at Andrews AFB?"

"Right away," Gene replied.

In a matter of minutes, Mike had the list of passengers, and when he scanned the alphabetized list and got to the "P"s, the mystery of flight 1602 was solved. He felt both relief and anger: relief that he now understood what had happened, and anger that Dave Price would go to such lengths to prove a point. He'd put lives at risk and caused the airline and government to incur a substantial bill, and who knows what impacts were caused to the passengers. The question was, what was he going to do about it? He was concerned that he wouldn't look good for ignoring what turned out to be a warning of a very real vulnerability with the aircraft.

Mike tried calling Dave Price on both his land line and mobile number; both responded with voicemail. He tried again later in the day, and then on the following day, all without success. He finally left a message but didn't expect to hear back. He was surprised when Dave returned his call at 11 PM that same day.

"Mike, you called? How can I help you?" intoned Price without much preamble.

"I noticed you were on the flight the other day that ended up at Andrews AFB. You wouldn't happen to know what might have caused this diversion, do you?" asked Mike.

"Why would I know anything?" answered Price

"Don't screw with me, Price. You did it to demonstrate the vulnerability you forecast, and now you're being coy? I need to know what you did," said Mike.

"If someone did that, it would be a serious crime for which they could be prosecuted and sent to jail. So why would anyone ever openly admit to this?" answered Price.

"OK, I get it," said Mike. "Let's deal in the hypothetical: how might someone divert the aircraft?"

Price replied, "Like I told you once before, anyone can tap into the plane's network and use hacker skills and knowledge of the plane's software to take over its operation."

Mike asked, "How would one tap into the plane's network? It isn't wireless or susceptible to radio interference?"

Price responded, "You're correct, it's fiber optic; however, there are test ports where one can gain network access. These are needed by maintenance personnel."
"Yeah, but I'd suspect they're either in the cockpit or external to the aircraft, which wouldn't fit what happened," said Mike.

"Well, the fiber cables are routed throughout the airplane, and there are such things as optical couplers that could tap into them," replied Price.

"Thank you for being so forthcoming," Mike sarcastically said. "If I do find the culprit, or more specifically evidence to convict, I won't hesitate to prosecute."

"Good luck to you," replied Price. "It seems like you have a serious problem that needs fixing more than you need chasing down the good soul who – without serious incident – pointed this out to you." Price hung up the phone.

Price felt as though the storm would blow over and he and Mike would be able to work together again; in fact, he might someday be appreciated for having done this. Price felt good about what he'd done. Preventing what was rapidly becoming one of the most popular commercial jet liners from being susceptible to being interfered with was certainly a noble accomplishment. Bad guys could do far worse than safely diverting the plane to another friendly airport.

He thought, *This one was for you*, referring to his wife Sandy and daughter Becky.

Mike had the plane searched from top to bottom by Sky Bus, under the supervision of his department's technical staff. They almost missed discovering the small box installed onto the network, located behind an access panel in the business class lavatory. The box had no fingerprints on it. Also, the marshal did report that the man across the aisle from him did go into the lavatory prior to take off, but so did others. There was nothing but circumstantial evidence, but Mike now knew for certain what had happened. With the discovery of the box, he could now take action to remedy the vulnerability without ever revealing his knowing of the threat and ignoring it.

"Damn, that Price is one clever bastard," Mike mused to himself. He forecast the vulnerability, demonstrated that it was real and did so without leaving any prosecutable evidence that he was the culprit.

Despite Mike's efforts to the contrary, word of Price's actions made it to a few select three-letter government intelligence organizations. This escapade served to enhance Price's standing in the secret world of security, as well as place his services in even higher demand. While this was clearly not his intent, Price welcomed the opportunity to gain visibility into a larger picture of the threats facing the country and society at large. With this broader perspective, he could select those missions that would have the greatest impact for good, thereby continuing his quest and his life's commitment.

Chapter 4

A New Means

Dave Price took personally the ever increasing impact on society that terrorism, illicit drugs, piracy, theft, and the violence that came with all these were having. In fact, while most people wouldn't feel the impact of these as personally as Dave Price, everyone was affected. Businesses charged more for products to compensate for theft. Increased security caused delays and impinged on everyone's right to privacy. Then there were those afflicted by drugs and the victims they preyed on to support their habits. The police cruiser that had hit and killed Sandy and Becky Price had been chasing after an armed robber who had killed one person and injured several others. It turned out the perpetrator was a drug addict who was no doubt stealing to feed his habit. The Prices were unlucky, but ever increasingly, so were many others. Dave Price now had an even larger sense of the problem and was energized to do his best to help stem the tide of these scourges against society.

Dave Price's home in California was on the water, with a heavily treed and isolated lot. His closest neighbor was quite a distance away. He had the main house, a large enclosed boat house that went out over the water, and a large garage and workshop. Inside of the single level house was a living room, a full sized country kitchen, and three bedrooms. There was a large bathroom off the master bedroom, and one in the hall. He converted the larger of the two (non-master) bedrooms into an office. On one wall was a white board, which he used to plan out some of his activities. He had a full array of computers and associated peripherals, along with a computer desk and drawing table. He also had a world clock on the wall, which displayed the time anywhere in the world. Lastly, his most expensive gadget: a large touch screen display.

    Price kept a computer out in his workshop that was networked to his main computer. He also ensured he would never be without power by having a backup generator for everything on the property. He even had a small wind generator as a third source of power. Between his workshop and the tools in the boat house, there was virtually nothing he couldn't do. Having the right tools, and more importantly using them, gave him solace when he wasn't directly engaged on a specific mission.

    The other thing that gave Price solace was being on the water in a peaceful area. He certainly lived in the right spot for this. California was quite crowded, but where he lived along the Big Sur coastal area, just south of Carmel, afforded the chance for privacy. There were large sanctuaries to protect the area that also served to protect his solitude. This was why he had selected the area.

    Whether it was taking his boat out or walking along the coastline, he felt a certain inner peace when he was alone with his thoughts with the ocean as a backdrop. Often he would think of the happy times he and his family enjoyed and how much he missed them.

He also felt a sense of guilt for the missed opportunities he'd had with his family in the name of his job. He wasn't sure if his quest could ever make up for this or fill the hole he felt, but he knew that it was what he must do.

When Price was home, one of his favorite pastimes was to walk along the coast. From his home, he could access the hiking trails that existed in Pt. Lobos Park, which ran along the craggy, jagged coast. Its breathtaking beauty comprised of gorgeous ocean vistas, the ever crashing waves, majestic cypress and pine trees, an assortment of wildflowers, scenic trails and its rocky shoreline contributed to the sense of peace that he felt when he walked there. Price was still energized by his recent escapade and its aftermath, so a nice walk would be just what the doctor ordered. It would give him time to clear his mind and think about the future. So, he put some things in a light backpack, including some snacks and a sandwich, and set out.

The day was warm with lots of sunshine, but it felt pleasant due to the ever-present onshore breeze that served to stir up the surf. Price walked the trails, sometimes detouring to walk along the rocks at the edge of the water. He was on his way from the rocks back to the trail when he noticed something in a quiet cove a couple hundred yards away. He couldn't tell what it was, but he was certain it hadn't been there before, so he set out to see what had washed into the cove.

The walk over to the area proved much more difficult than it looked. There was no trail, and some of the rocks he had to climb over were very slippery from the ever-present wetness. He also ended up having to wade through some water where the bottom had jagged rocks, with many that were quite slick. He almost fell several times. He frequently lost sight of his objective due to big boulders being in the way. It was when he was making his way over one of these that he started to make out what he'd seen: it was some kind of a partially submerged boat. When he got closer, he realized he was looking at a miniature submarine. Further inspection proved it to be abandoned and not of U.S. origin.

But whose? He wondered. *Where did it come from?*

Price decided it would be fun to salvage the boat and see if he could make it seaworthy once again. He was so excited he gave little thought to any ramifications that could result from his taking the craft.

Who knows? He thought to himself, *maybe a new tool for work.*

Regardless, this would be a great project to immerse himself in, he reasoned – maybe more hobby than work. Now the question was how to move it to his boat house, and further whether his boat house was large enough to house it.

Reinvigorated by his discovery, Price virtually ran home. He gathered up his tools, including a measuring tape, rope, and a lantern, and went back to the cove. He'd worried (irrationally) that the sub wouldn't be there when he returned, but there it was. It turned out there wasn't much he could do except further inspect it and measure it. The boat house would be just large enough, though he would have to remove the doors to get it in. He didn't see any hull damage which was good; however, it was aground due to it being filled with water. When the tide came in, it might just have sufficient buoyancy to float off the bottom. Price figured he could assist in that regard by getting some of the water out. He had no means to do that with what he had with him, but his boat had a powerful water pump that could be rigged with some hoses, and that might do the trick.

Once again, he quickly made the trip home. He was so excited about this find, he didn't feel tired, but he did notice his stomach rumbling and realized he hadn't eaten. He loaded his boat with more rope and some hoses. During the trip to the cove, he managed to eat and drink some water. He only had three hours before the peak of high tide. Price was very familiar with these waters and knew how to navigate the surf into one of the many coves, even though he wasn't explicitly familiar with this particular cove.

He expertly navigated the rough waters, and soon his boat was in the quiet of the cove. Price tied his boat up to the sub and proceeded to rig a hose into the open hatch and hook it to his pump. It worked perfectly, and soon water was being expelled from the sub at a rapid rate. He went and looked around and inside of the sub, using the lantern he'd brought. He didn't see any obvious leaks and reasoned the water must have come in through the hatch. Once again, he wondered what had happened and where this had come from.

There wasn't much for him to do except wait while the water was being pumped from the boat, so he finished his lunch and gave closer inspection to the sub. He was looking for anything that would give a clue as to its origin – and if luck would have it, an instruction manual. He didn't find either, but between the expulsion of water and the rising tide, the sub was becoming buoyant. There would be ample time to explore it, but right now he needed to get it out of there and to his boat house. The tide had reached its maximum height, so there was no time like now for getting it underway.

Price's plan wasn't at all elegant. He was simply going to raft his boat together with the sub and then fight their way through the surf and onward to his boat house. He quickly but effectively lashed the two crafts together, then fired up the engines on his boat and set out. It was extremely awkward, and the going was slow and rough, but eventually he hit the smooth waters of the protected cove his home was situated on. He pulled up to his dock and tied both boats up. Once they were secure, he set about figuring how to get the sub into the boat house.

Even with the doors removed, there was almost no clearance at all, but it would fit. Price tied a line to the stern of the sub and connected it to the winch at the head of the boat house. He then used his boat to maneuver the sub so it was aligned to go into the boat house. None of this was easy, and it all took many tries; it was after sundown when the task was complete. Price secured the sub in the boathouse and tied his boat up in one of the slips he had on his dock, and then went up to the main house. His plan was to sit down for a few minutes to rest, and then make dinner.

It was 5:30 AM the next morning when he awoke in the lounge chair he'd sat down on to rest. Price was ravenously hungry and anxious to begin work on the sub. He realized just how exhausted he'd let himself get the day earlier and realized he needed to pace himself. He was just so excited. He never dreamed he'd own a submarine, and while he wasn't sure what he'd do with it, he was certain he'd think of something.

Price started to plan his approach to returning the submarine to operational condition. First he'd thoroughly explore the vessel to see what he could learn, then he'd go online to see if he could discover anything else about it; for example, to see if any websites could help identify the sub. Lastly, he would have to ascertain the condition of each part of the sub and determine what would be needed to restore its function.

The effort to restore the submarine proved to be a gargantuan task. Price learned the sub's origin was from North Korea; this made restoring it all the more difficult, since information – not to mention parts – were in extremely short supply. The good news was that his objective was to return the sub to operational condition, not like a collector of classic cars trying to restore it to mint factory condition. This gave him the latitude to substitute parts and install the subsystems he wanted.

It had taken well over a week to understand how the sub's various components were supposed to work. It was actually elegantly simple. He also discovered the self-destruct system and removed it. Most importantly, while it was no doubt meant to have a crew of three, Price would be able to configure it to be safely operated by a crew of one.

The hull and pressure tanks were in pristine condition, which was more than could be said for the engines, battery, and controls. Price stripped the boat down and with meticulous care started to build it back up. By the time he was finished several months later, the sub was actually better than new. He rebuilt the diesel engine used for cruising on the surface or just below it using a snorkel. It was also the means to recharge the battery. He put in a new electric motor, as well as a state of the art lithium battery, which would last much longer than the lead acid batteries he'd found in the sub. He installed modern radio and navigation equipment, including satellite communication. Lastly, he redid much of the plumbing and rebuilt the control panel.

He noted the missing life raft and bought one that would fit into the holder. He also put in a small refrigerator, fresh water, and a lavatory. He installed an electronic video camera that could see in both daylight and night on the periscope mast. The optics of the periscope were fine for a backup, but he liked the video he could view and redirect while positioned at the controls. Lastly, he put in air-conditioning to keep the boat at the right temperature. He figured there was no reason to be uncomfortable. To keep power consumption to a minimum, he recaptured heat from the batteries and propulsion system, and for cool he installed heat exchangers, which would take advantage of the water temperatures that would surround him. This was some of his most inventive work.

     Price liked being busy tinkering with things, and this project fit the bill. He would be awake from morning to night with few breaks, and then he'd sleep like a baby with none of the dark dreams that most frequently filled his nights of late. During times like this, he would think about his lost wife and daughter – but mostly about the good times, not the loss he'd suffered. If one could attribute such a condition to Dave Price – this was a happy time. He was mentally challenged in figuring out how to affect the repairs, and the work was physically demanding. He also spent some time thinking about what he might do with the sub. There were many possibilities, and he couldn't wait to try the sub out.

Chapter 5

Opportunity

When the work on the sub was complete and all its elements tested while in the boat house, he decided to begin sea trials. These were comprised of short cruises, first starting on the surface, and eventually submerging the sub. Despite the inexperience Price had in piloting a submarine, he learned quickly and the boat performed well. There were a few things Price decided to improve, but overall he was pleased.

In addition to the improvements, Price decided to add two new capabilities. The first was a mechanical arm so tasks could be performed underwater without the need to get out of the boat through its air lock. The second was the ability to remote control the boat from outside. The impetus for this was his need to keep the boat out of the boat house, and while hiding it also wanting to keep it close at hand. What better place than the bottom of the cove? He could have it sit on the bottom until he wanted it and then remote control it to surface in the boat house.

Several weeks later when he was finishing up with the improvements, Price heard a car coming down the road to his house. He put down his tools and went outside to see who it was. There was a plain sedan pulling up to his driveway with just a driver inside. When he got a little closer, Price saw it was Mike Mahoney. He wondered what he was doing coming for an unannounced visit.

"Mike, what a surprise to see you - I wasn't sure you'd ever speak to me again, let alone come for a visit," exclaimed Price

"Dave, it's good to see you, too," said Mahoney. "I have a new job and thought I'd like to speak with you. Is now a good time?"

With a degree of sarcasm, Price said, "Mike, any time is a good time to speak to my friend from the TSA."

Mike replied, "Like I said, I have a new job and am no longer with the TSA. I can fill you in if we can go somewhere other than the driveway to talk."

"Sure," Price said. "I'm being a bad host. Come in, and I can make some coffee and we can sit and talk."

Price led the way into the house and went straight to his office. Price had one of those coffeemakers that make one cup at a time, and he fixed a cup for Mahoney, as well as one for himself. When they were settled across from each other at Price's desk, they were each looking at one another until finally Price broke the silence.

"Mike, I can honestly say that seeing you here is quite a surprise," said Price. "Whatever your reason, it must be important. You wouldn't fly all the way across the country unless you were playing golf at Pebble Beach and just decided to stop in."

"I'm not much of a golfer, and civil servants can ill afford the fees at Pebble Beach," said Mahoney. "I have come for an important reason and hope you'll hear me out."

Price replied, "I'm all ears, so go ahead."

Mahoney began by asking, "What have you been up to? No one has heard from you for several months."

Price answered, "I've been busy with some projects and tinkering around the workshop."

Mahoney then began describing his new position. "I'm the Director of Special Activities, reporting directly to the President's national security advisor."

"What does that mean?" interrupted Price.

"If there's some specific threat or issue facing the country that isn't readily solvable by conventional means, it would then come under my purview," continued Mahoney. "I would then determine what the best course of action was to resolve it."

Price was genuinely intrigued and said, "Wow, sounds both important and like fun. It also sounds real hush-hush. So why are you telling me?"

Mahoney continued, "After your stunt with the airplane."

Price interrupted, "For the record, I don't know what you're talking about, and it was no stunt."

Mahoney pressed on, "I was going to get to this later, but I guess it's better if I deal with it now. There's no question you hijacked the Sky Bus plane." Price was about to interrupt, but Mahoney put his hand out to stave off the interruption. "Clearly, hijacking is a very serious offense, punishable by many years in jail; however, in this particular case you – yes, you – did it to make the point that something needed to be done, or the country would face a real security threat in the future. In part, this was because no one would listen to you when you tried a more conventional means of letting the threat be known. So rather than us continuing to play this game of you denying any role in it, I asked for and got a Presidential Order stating that this was within the scope of your contract and absolving you of any legal wrongdoing in the matter. The order has been sealed for 75 years, as we don't need this to get out in the public domain. As far as they're concerned, there was a malfunction, and we'd prefer to leave it at that. There are two copies: one that's part of the official record, and the other is in my case. I'll show it to you now."

Price was impressed, but he said, "You'll do better than that and give it to me."

It was now time for Mahoney to protest, but after just some perfunctory objections, he capitulated and gave the copy to Price and said, "Are you satisfied?"

Price nodded and asked, "Why?"

Mahoney responded, "I'll get to that if you'd stop interrupting." He went on to explain, "Your skills, courage, and ingenuity are elements I need to have access to if I'm to succeed in my new job. In addition, your demonstrated commitment to eliminating threats and selfless efforts to rid the world of issues that threaten the security and well-being of Americans make you a perfect candidate for the job."

"What job?" Price interrupted. "I already have a job. In fact, I have a business already engaged in such activities."

"We know that," said Mahoney

"Who's this 'we'?" responded Price

"I thought I already made this clear," said Mahoney. "The NSC Director and the President. Please hear me out. We'd like for you to accept assignments from us that you can carry out with a great deal of latitude. The good news is that you'll be paid and will have immunity from any criminal issues within the U.S. The challenge is that whatever you do cannot come back on the U.S. government. We must have plausible deniability. I think this will give you an even greater opportunity to do what it is you want to do. In addition, to the extent we can do so without making anyone aware of your role, you can gain access to intelligence information and other resources through me and my office. What do you think?"

Price started to answer, hesitated, then said, "I'll need some time to think about this."

Price wouldn't entertain any further discussion, instead just saying he'd let Mahoney know in one week. To be polite, Price had offered another coffee, but Mahoney declined and instead headed out, leaving Price to think this through. Price was already in deep thought before the door even closed.

Chapter 6

Quest Taking Shape

Sandy was giving that lecture to Becky that most parents give at some point, namely that not all people are good and you cannot trust strangers. Price remembered this like it was only yesterday. Not all people are good.

Price thought this over and said to himself, "If they were, maybe you'd still be with me."

He missed them so much, and despite all he'd done in their honor, he didn't feel satisfied. Perhaps the opportunity Mahoney had brought him might get him to where he might feel greater peace – if he didn't get killed.

Price had no doubt that Mahoney had offered him a chance to stop more bad guys. What Price didn't like was taking orders and reporting to someone who could second guess you. After a couple more days of agonizing over the decision, he'd made up his mind. He couldn't stand prolonging this anymore. Not only had his days and nights been filled with going over the pros and cons of the opportunity, it also reenergized his thinking about his lost family. He'd certainly not forgotten them, but they didn't fill his dreams like they did now. It was almost like reliving the first year or so after they were killed all over again. He couldn't stand that pain.

Price placed a call to Mike Mahoney and said they should meet. Mahoney suggested Price come to

D,C.; Price agreed to come the next day. Mahoney tried to get a sense of what Price was thinking, but Price wasn't going there on the call. When they hung up, Price made travel arrangements and went out to berth the sub at the bottom of the cove, as well as to repatriate his boat with the boat house.

For the first time in a week, he felt at peace and didn't have any noteworthy dreams. When he awoke from what turned out to be a great night's sleep, he headed for the local airport. He flew his plane to the San Jose airport, where he caught a one-stop flight to Washington's Reagan National Airport. If he'd been surprised to see Mahoney when he'd unexpectedly dropped in to see him, he was even more surprised to find Mahoney waiting for him at the airport when he arrived.

Price didn't even ask how Mahoney knew which flight he'd be on; he thought to himself this is the kind of power that teaming up might bring to his own efforts. Price graciously accepted the ride, and they left the terminal.

He asked, "Where are we going?"

Mahoney replied, "I thought I'd take you to your hotel, then bring you over to the White House so we can have our little talk. Is that all right?"

Price replied, "Almost, but I need to get something to eat first. I'm famished, and they don't serve food on planes anymore."

"There's a nice diner with foods of all sorts on the way. It's open around the clock, and you can get breakfast, lunch, or dinner choices," responded Mahoney.

"Sounds great," said Price.

They proceeded to the restaurant, where Price selected soup and a sandwich. He ate hungrily and didn't say much. What did get said both before and at the restaurant was just small talk, with no mention of the reason for Price's visit. The weather, the problems with air travel today, and sports all seemed to be topics that could be discussed. How Price might help the government in their quest against bad guys was something neither of them brought up.

Price felt a little like a salmon swimming upstream, as it was after five in the evening and there was a steady stream of traffic heading out of the downtown area as they were making their way into the city. The good news was that they didn't have much traffic in their direction and arrived at the White House quickly after Price finished his lunch. Mahoney helped Price through the security gauntlet at the White House, and they proceeded to Mahoney's office, which was on the lower level.

Given the scarceness of real estate in the White House and Old Executive Office Building, Mahoney had a good-sized office, revealing his stature. While it didn't seem to have a particularly attractive location, it was proximate to secure areas and the Situation Room, which made it practical for Mahoney's job. It was also easy to get from his office to the NSC head, and to the President.

When they entered, Mahoney signaled for Price to take a seat at the conference table. He preferred having discussions this way rather than having them across his desk, which always made him feel a bit imperious. Mahoney closed his door and came over to sit at the table with Price.

"So Dave, have you thought about what I said?" Mahoney started without further preamble. "I assume you wouldn't be here if you didn't. I guess what I'm asking is, what are your thoughts regarding the opportunity I mentioned to you? We really think you can make a difference, and everyone knows we can use the help, as there is no shortage of issues."

Price started to respond, but there was a knock on the door and in walked a Secret Service agent. He looked around the room, went back to the door, and in walked the President of the United States. Price instinctively stood but was signaled to sit back down.

"Mr. Price, I'm so glad you've come here," said the President, shaking Price's hand. "I can only assume you're willing to help – at least I trust that's what you're speaking about."

"Mr. President, we actually just arrived and had just sat down when you came in," Mahoney said.

Price was certain the President already knew that and wanted to make a preemptive strike to remove any doubt of his support and help sell the opportunity.

Price said, "Mr. President, please feel free to call me Dave, and I came here today to discuss this with Mike to see if there are terms that might work for both of us."

The President replied, "Great, Dave. Thank you for considering our request. Your country needs you. I have just one question, and then I'll let you get back to business: did you really highjack that plane? No need to answer; I can see it on your face. Thank you again." With that, the President was gone.

"Well, you sure know how to impress a guy," said Price. "Notwithstanding your bringing in the big guns, I cannot simply say yes to your request. The proverbial devil is always in the details, and like I told the President, there may be a formula that will work for both of us, but we'll need to discuss detailed terms."

Price laid out his thoughts regarding under what circumstances he would help out. His concerns weren't financial, and they certainly weren't with the broader objective, as that was very much aligned with how he'd dedicated his life. The issue was that he couldn't accept being micro-managed or second guessed, nor could he accept having his actions get caught up in politics. What Price was prepared to do was help, but independently on his own terms.

Price proposed that he be briefed on a menu of potential areas in which he could help. He would then pick the one he wanted to do. Price would have total autonomy in planning and execution – in fact, he might not feel compelled even to tell them which problem he'd chosen to work. Price expected some support in terms of intelligence, but little else. In terms of financial consideration, he expected a modest annual retainer and reimbursement for expenses. Regarding expenses, Price thought he had a more than fair deal for the government. He would submit his expenses, and if there was something they disagreed with, they didn't need to pay it. If there were some truly extraordinary expense, he might come to ask for preapproval, but in general regarding ordinary expenses, he was unwilling to have to play the 'Mother may I?' game.

Needless to say, Price's proposal nearly put Mahoney in an apoplectic state, but he managed to speak.

"Let me see if I got this. You want the U.S. government to share very sensitive information with you regarding problems, then you'll pick what you want to work on, not tell us, and then expect us to pay whatever expenses you incur?"

Price said, "Yeah, that's about it, but don't forget that if you don't like an expense, you don't have to pay it. Of course, I fully expect immunity from prosecution within the U.S., and I'll work to ensure that none of what I do comes back on the government."

"Well, those are very interesting terms," said Mahoney. "However, that's not how it's going to work."

Mahoney had more to say, but Price interrupted. "That's how it will work, or I'm afraid my services won't be available, as much as I want to help. There's no room for discussion regarding these terms. I didn't come here to negotiate, but instead to tell you I really do want to help, but on my terms."

"I might be able to accept most of what you want," said Mahoney, "however, at least I'll need to know what you're doing."

"I'll tell you what, I'll let you know which problem I've decided to work, but not how I'm going to attack it, and there can be no explicit or implied approval," responded Price. "In addition, I'll ask and take you at your word that you won't share what I tell you with anyone other than the NSC Director and the President, not even the Veep – and only if there's a strong need to know."

"Dave, I feel very uncomfortable with this, but I'm willing to give it a try," said Mahoney. "When would you be available for some briefings?"

Chapter 7

A Life Changing Discovery

Over the ensuing months, Price received numerous briefings on various issues and acted on a select handful of them. While Price could understand the importance of these issues, and many provided a challenge for him, none proved to be fulfilling. They just weren't providing the type of reward he was seeking; none of them gave him the sense of accomplishment he was seeking or the feeling that he was honoring the memory of his lost family.

Price was doing a great deal of travel, spending much time away from his sanctuary on the West Coast, working long hours, but just not very satisfying. So, he decided to take a break. For the first week, he tinkered around the house doing maintenance chores he'd put off. These too weren't very fulfilling, but they were necessary. He then decided he wanted to go somewhere in the sub, and he started thinking about destinations. All of the places he thought would be interesting were quite a distance off; well beyond the range of the sub.

This stimulated Price's thinking about ways to increase the range. Once again, he felt some sense of enthusiasm and energetically pursued several approaches. There were four that held the most promise: 1) a deployable solar array to recharge the batteries in the daylight; 2) a small wind-powered generator that could recharge the batteries day or night; 3) a device to capture wave energy; and 4) an exterior fuel bladder that could be jettisoned after use. After working on all four, he decided on the solar, wind, and auxiliary fuel tank approaches.

    Weeks turned into months, but soon Price had completed his work and was ready to begin his voyage. He'd bought a few other accessories to help his voyage, including a reverse osmosis water purification system to turn sea water into potable drinking water and satellite TV and Internet connectivity. He also installed a waterproof locker, where among other things he put a 12 gauge shotgun and his 9mm semi-automatic handgun, along with enough ammunition for a small war. He wasn't sure why he felt the need for arms, but he rationalized it was much better to have them and not need them than the opposite. Lastly, he filled every nook and cranny with food. Most of this he bought from camping stores or survival shops. He seemingly had every variety of dehydrated food that was made and a supply for a year. After sampling some of them, he certainly hoped he'd be able to get fresh food; nonetheless, while they weren't an Epicurean's delight, they would do, and more importantly keep him properly nourished.

    Price set out the next morning before dawn. His first destination would be the Hawaiian Islands at a distance, which Price estimated to be about 2400 miles or 3-4 weeks. His actual voyage would be a little longer, in order to take advantage of favorable ocean currents. Price's spirits were high as he set out on this adventure; in fact, he was happier than he could recall being in recent years.

Despite his auxiliary fuel capacity, Price elected to conserve diesel fuel, which he could use when on the surface or when he was just below the surface, and use a snorkel to feed fresh air to the engine; instead, he traveled using mostly the electric motors, whose batteries could be recharged from renewable versus consumable means. It turned out that this worked out well for the initial part of his trip, in that he wanted to travel submerged and not be seen.

Soon he fell into a daily routine of all that was needed. On one particularly calm, sunny day, he even surfaced for a while and took a quick dip in the ocean. The cold water felt good. It also gave him an idea that perhaps he might be able to catch a fish for dinner. It took quite a while even to get a nibble, let alone catch a fish, but he didn't care. He was in no hurry, the day was glorious, and he was using the time to recharge both his own and the sub's batteries. His patience was eventually rewarded, and he caught a fish, which he prepared for dinner.

Price checked his email on a regular basis and looked at the news; he did this several times per day. While it was good to get away, he didn't want to become isolated from the world. He was feeling relaxed and was quite gratified that all was working well. He was just a couple of days from arriving at the island chain when there was a big storm.

Price was on the surface recharging the batteries, as was his practice. He always tried to keep the batteries at full charge, since one never knew when that might come in handy. When he looked out towards the horizon, he saw it: dark clouds and rain, which appeared to be heading his way. The wind was picking up, as were the waves. Price decided to submerge and hope for calmer water beneath the surface. Fortunately, he was in deep water, so the top side conditions weren't reflected below, and at about 100 feet below the surface, he found calmer water. He figured he should go another 50 feet deeper, just for good measure. While not perfectly smooth, he was largely spared the turmoil raging above.

Mary Dillon, along with her husband Tom and 18-year-old daughter Melissa had traveled overnight from the Big Island of Hawaii aboard their 50 foot sailboat. They were all experienced sailors and planned to sail up the chain of islands as part of the last time they'd likely all be together, since Melissa was heading off to college in the fall. They were all excited about this trip and looking very much forward to it; in fact, they were so excited, they failed to give close examination to the weather along their planned route of travel.

The storm came on them fast and almost without warning. It occurred before sun up, so no one could see the warning signs of dark clouds in the distance. The first evidence they had was the seas becoming rougher and the wind picking up. All of a sudden, a wave crashed over the boat, snapping the mast, and the wind finished the damage. Tom, who'd been asleep, raced up on deck to see what the noise was and was instantly washed overboard. Mary had come up behind him and arrived just in time to see him get hit in the head with a piece of the rigging and go over the rail. Despite her horror from what had just happened, and the fear of what might occur next, Mary's instincts took over and she found her daughter and made sure they both had life jackets on. She would mourn later; for now, she needed to save her daughter.

The boat was really being tossed around by the storm; as such, it was very difficult for Mary and Melissa to get around in it. They were being battered around almost as badly as the boat. There was no place to hide from the raging sea and the debris it was creating from what was formerly their boat. Indeed, the boat was breaking up.

Mary had to yell to Melissa, who was only a few feet away, in order to be heard over the noise. She said, "Let's try to make it to the inflatable raft on the port side amidships. It has some fresh water, radio, and other things we might need to survive."

Melissa was terrified but nodded affirmatively and started to move towards the raft; Mary followed. Despite the short distance they had to go, it was a bruising trip. Mary decided they should tether themselves together, despite the risk of it getting tangled up. She reasoned they could untangle themselves should that happen, but if they separated there would be little or no chance they'd be able to find each other. Eventually, they reached the compartment that held the raft. The raft and the other gear it came with were stored in a cloth bag. Mary grabbed hold of it just as another wave came and washed her and Melissa overboard. Mary was thankful for the tether that kept them together, and she concentrated on holding onto the bag with the raft.

Together they moved as best they could away from the remnants of what was once their boat. When they'd gotten far enough away, they no longer needed to contend with being hit by debris, but they were still being tossed around by the turbulent sea. Mary held onto the raft bag with a death grip. As quickly as the storm had come, it passed. In its wake was the destruction of their boat, Mary and Melissa being stranded in the middle of the ocean, and of course the loss of Tom.

There was no time for regrets or feeling sorry for themselves, as they had things to do if they were to have any chance of survival. First, they'd need to get the raft inflated and get into it. The first part was easy; the second part proved challenging, both due to their battered bodies and the turbulence of the ocean. After tying their tether to the raft, they both managed after several attempts to get aboard. Next they located the radio and tried it, but they didn't have any luck. At least they were alive and had a chance; however, while they didn't speak of it, neither of them had any delusions of what their chances of survival really were, despite the fact that the sea and wind had calmed. They did allow themselves to have a serious crying bout and hugged each other for comfort. Soon the physical and emotional exhaustion of their ordeal overtook them, and they fell soundly asleep.

Price was largely oblivious to the turmoil of the storm, since the seas at his current depth remained calm. He figured he'd surface slowly – at least to periscope depth – and see what things looked like topside. As the sub rose, he was optimistic due to no increase in turbulence. When he finally got a look at the surface through the video camera on the periscope, he noted that all was once again calm and the sun was shining. So he surfaced, deployed his solar array, and proceeded on course to the islands.

After a few hours, Price saw something orange on the distant horizon. He decided to go see what it was, so he changed course and proceeded in that direction. As he got closer, he was able to see that it was a life raft; possibly an explanation for the increase of debris he'd observed in the water. When he got closer, he noted sharks bumping into it. When still closer, he saw that there were two people in the raft that were in real jeopardy of the sharks breaking or capsizing their raft. He noted blood on their clothes, which no doubt was what had attracted the sharks.

The bumping of the raft by the sharks had woken up Mary and her daughter, who now huddled together, terrified of what would happen next. That's when they heard two loud explosions and the bumping stopped. When they got the courage to look out, they saw a strange vessel with a man on deck holding a rifle. In the water, they saw the dead bodies of two sharks.

Price shouted to them, "Can you catch a line if I throw it to you?"

Mary replied, "Yes – please!"

It took a couple of tries, but Price eventually was able to land the line right across the middle of the raft. He had them secure one end to the raft, then he pulled them towards the sub. They scrambled aboard, tearfully thanking him and hugging him, and then they collapsed right on the deck. Price carefully took each one into the sub and made them as comfortable as space would allow. He deflated their raft and stowed it, then resumed course for Hawaii, the largest and closest island in the chain.

At his current rate of speed, Price reckoned it would take them a couple of days to reach port. That was when he started to think about what to do. He didn't want to give up the secret of his sub, but he also needed to ensure that these people would be safe. His thoughts were interrupted by the older of the two women beginning to stir.

"Where am I?" Mary asked. "Who are you? You saved us."

She began to cry. When she'd composed herself, Price asked her what had happened. She explained how they'd set out for a voyage around the islands – kind of a final family trip before her daughter Melissa went off to college.

"It certainly proved to be a final family trip," Mary said and once again began to sob.

Mary explained how the storm suddenly came upon them and how her husband Tom got hit in the head and was washed overboard. This recollection momentarily caused her to lose her composure, but she got control and resumed.

"I went and found Melissa – by the way, my name is Mary Dillon – we got the raft, and you know the rest. Not to look a gift horse in the mouth, but who are you, and what is this vessel?"

"My name is Dave Price, and I just so happened to be cruising in these waters. This is a miniature submarine that's mine."

"There must be more to say than that," said Mary. "What do you do? You seem too young to be retired."

Price replied, "We're going to have a couple of days together, with ample time to talk about things. Why don't we save the explanations for when Melissa is awake, so I can inform both of you at once? In the meantime, you might want to check on Melissa; she looks like she's banged up. Need to see if any of her injuries need tending to, and in particular whether or not she had any serious bumps on her head. I'll go on deck and give you two some privacy. I have some sweats that are dry and clean, although likely too big; however, they should suffice, and we can clean and dry the clothes you're wearing."

With that, he went topside and closed the hatch behind him.

Chapter 8

Parting with Promise

Now alone with his thoughts while mother and daughter tended to each other, Price was a mix of emotions and conflicting feelings. First and foremost, he'd just saved the lives of a mother and daughter; something he'd failed to do for his own family. In fact, Melissa was just about the age Becky would have been had he taken care of them. On the flip side of his thoughts was what to do with them and how to keep his sub a secret.

Like so often after a storm, the ocean was calm, the sun was shining, and there was a gentle breeze blowing across the deck. This was a welcome relief, and Price just tried to clear his mind, but he was having trouble not thinking about Mary and Melissa. He thought about the grief they must be feeling contrasted against the relief of their still being alive. Then there was the survivor's guilt; something he was all too familiar with. They had a lot of healing to do, and Price hoped they'd have an easier time than he'd endured; he still wasn't healed.

These thoughts were starting to take him down the dark side he'd been valiantly trying to suppress. He didn't want to go there, so he forced his thoughts to the immediate issue of what to do. Price was starting to form a plan in his mind when the hatch started to open.

"May I come on deck?" Mary asked. "Would you help me with the hatch?"

"Certainly," Price answered. "It's a beautiful day up here."

Price opened up the hatch and helped Mary come on deck. Cleaned up and rested, she was a sight to behold. Even in baggy sweats she looked lovely. Price quickly reeled in those thoughts and started to discuss the mundane but necessary subjects. He would then get to the topic of how to get them safely back to land without jeopardizing the security of his submarine.

Price began, "I trust you found everything you needed and were comfortable under the circumstances?"

Mary replied, "Oh, yes. I – we can't thank you enough. You not only quite literally saved our lives, you've also been most hospitable. In these tight quarters, you've given us space without once giving any sense that it was an imposition on you."

"I'm about to be even more hospitable," Price continued with a smile. "Wait until you see what I have planned for dinner. It could turn out to be the real test of your survival skills."

"You're not hinting that we're going to feed on dehydrated camping meals, are you?" asked Mary. "They're generally dreadful. If you have fishing tackle, I'd be more than happy to try to catch something for us to eat. I may not be the best angler, but out of necessity I can learn fast."

Price broke out the fishing gear, and Mary used it in a manner that suggested she knew more about fishing than she was letting on. Price let her go about this task and remained quiet so she could have some time with her own thoughts. He watched her for a while, then decided he needed to do something, so he deployed the solar array to recharge the sub's batteries. When he was done, he returned to where he'd been sitting.

Mary broke the silence. "Please tell me a little about yourself, like what you're doing out here in such an exotic boat all by yourself. What do you do for a living? Where do you live?" And then the dreaded question: "Do you have a family, a wife, a child?"

Price thought a minute and said, "I'm an engineer by training. I do some consulting, and would you believe me if I told you I found this sub and fixed it up myself?" Choking back his emotions, Price continued. "A long time ago, I had a wife and daughter. They were killed, and I've been alone ever since."

"I'm very sorry," Mary interrupted.

"Thank you. It's in part how I know some of what you're feeling now with your sudden loss. I'm very sorry and truly hope both of you find the strength to move forward," Price said. "However, know that it won't be easy and will take some time. For me, it's been a difficult road. Part of the answer you're seeking regarding what I do and what I'm doing out here relates to how I cope with the loss. My family was a casualty of those in our society who don't obey the law. I try to honor my wife and daughter's memories by working to make the world a safer place. Part of my struggle has been feeling that they died because I let them down. While deep sea rescues aren't my norm, saving you has made me feel the way I want to feel – valuable, and not the person who couldn't protect his family."

"So what do you do to make the world safer? And did you really find the sub?" Mary inquired.

Price was momentarily saved from having to answer by Mary hooking a fish. She carefully reeled it in, and Price helped land it. Mary recognized the fish and said it was excellent to eat and that this one looked to be ample food for the three of them. The reprieve continued as Price erected the outdoor grill and Mary scaled, gutted, and filleted the fish. It was very clear this wasn't the first time she'd done this.

"Please go ahead and grill the fish, and I'll go see about Melissa," said Mary. "Maybe then you can continue your story."

Mary went below, and Price set about grilling the fish. He was glad he'd bought this grill at a marine supply house and installed it on the sub. When he'd finished preparations and was mostly in waiting mode watching the food cook, his thoughts went to what he should say in response to Mary's questions. He felt he'd already said too much, but then again he found Mary so easy to talk to.

As Mary and Melissa made their way on deck, they both immediately smelled the cooking fish and realized how hungry they both were. Price asked Mary to look through his stores of dehydrated delights to see what there might be that would go well with the fish. Mary returned with some mashed potatoes, which Price prepared. They all sat around on the deck and ate hungrily. There wasn't much talking other than about the food or what a nice day it was.

When they were finished, Mary said, "Dave, why don't you pick up where you left off? I'll fill Melissa in later."

"Funny, I was just going to ask you to tell me about you," Price commented.

"No fair! I asked first," Mary said.

Price capitulated and started with telling them how he'd found the sub. He told them how he spent months restoring it and explained the many features he'd built in it. It was obvious to Mary this had been a fun project for him, but it was also serving as a great diversion to keep from answering her other questions; still, she didn't press.

"In order to tell you some things I think you really want to know, I'll need your word that you'll never speak to anyone about them," said Price. "Can I count on you?" They both nodded in agreement, and Price continued. "I consult mostly to organizations involved in our national security."

"Are you a spy?" Melissa interrupted.

"Not exactly," replied Price. "I work on very special problems facing the country that existing official organizations cannot readily address. When I can solve one, I feel I've made an incremental improvement and done something to honor my family. I've been doing this for a while, so when I found this sub I felt it might come in handy someday for one of my escapades; however, I'm actually out here now just taking a break. I thought it would be neat to take a cruise in the sub and make things up as I go along – like coming to the rescue of two lovely women."

"Can you tell us some of your escapades?" asked Melissa.

"No, they're very sensitive in nature," responded Price, "but this gets to something we need to talk about. I'd very much prefer that no one find out about this submarine and any connection I may have with it. So, I can't just sail you into some marina; that just wouldn't do."

"So what can we do?" asked Mary with some concern in her voice.

"The highest priority is your safety; even higher than the secrecy of the sub," said Price. "I'm trying to come up with a solution that lets me have my cake and eat it, too; namely a plan that allows you to be safe while we keep the sub a secret. When I come up with something, we'll discuss it. Also, if you have any ideas, please bring them up. Now it's your turn to tell me about you."

"Why don't you drop us off at some isolated beach, and we can find our way from there?" said Mary.

"I don't like that plan, because I want to make sure you're safe. Besides, it might be difficult to explain how you got there," answered Price. "However, you've triggered a thought. What if you got back in the raft – I saved it – and I watched until you were rescued? Well, that's crazy; it might take forever." Then a thought occurred to Price, and he said, "What if we did that and ensured you'd be discovered in short order?"

"That would be fine with us, but how are you going to do that?" asked Mary.

"The consulting work I do has me working for people at the highest level of government," answered Price. "Maybe they'd be willing to do me a favor and have the Coast Guard discover you not long after you get into the raft. I can hang around submerged, just to make sure all goes well."

Mary responded, "That sounds good if they'll do it."

"I'll make a call right now and let you know," said Price.

He then proceeded down the hatch and made a satellite call to Mike Mahoney. He didn't want to tell Mike about the sub either, so his request was made without any details or substantiation. It was simply to have the Coast Guard show up at a particular location at a particular time and that Mike should find some premise for them doing so that didn't imply knowledge of anything happening or existing at that locale.

Mahoney's initial response was, "You're kidding me? You want me to mobilize the Coast Guard on some unspecified premise, and you won't tell me what's going on?"

"Yeah, that's about it," replied Price. "Look, this would be a big favor. You won't be wasting their time. Declare some sort of training exercise. I promise I'll tell you what this is all about someday, but not today. Will you do it? I know they will if you call, so will you? Please?"

"OK," Mahoney grudgingly agreed.

So, Price gave him the coordinates and set the time at mid-morning the following day. He then told Mary and Melissa the plan: they should tell the story about the storm and of their boat breaking up, as well as the loss of Tom.

"Tell it just like it happened, and how you got in the raft," said Price. "Now this is where your story will depart from what actually happened. You'll say that the storm calmed and you drifted in the raft to where they pick you up. Please don't mention the sub, me, or anything other than you making it to safety in the raft. Show them sincere gratitude and relief in being found. Can you do that? In the meantime, I'll keep watch and make sure you're rescued before I depart the scene."

"I'm sure we can do that," answered Mary. "Will we ever see you again?"

"Not if you don't tell me a little bit about yourselves," Price quipped.

So Mary and Melissa took turns giving them the short version of their lives. They lived near Santa Barbara, and Melissa would be starting college at Stanford in just two months. Tom had been an attorney, and Mary was a stay-at-home mom, though an accountant by training who still did some work from time to time. Their boat was normally moored near Santa Barbara, and they had it ferried to the islands for this special family trip. At that point they started to tear up, so Price suggested they finish the story at some other time and instead make preparations for their rescue the next day.

After Melissa went below, Mary said, "I'd really like to see you again." Then with a smile she said, "Maybe I'll even finish our story. Will you let me know how I can reach you?"

Price said he would like an email from them when they reached home so he'd know they were truly safe. He gave them an email address and his sat-phone number in case of emergency. He then suggested they get some rest, as the next day would require them to be at the top of their game.

    Night came and went quickly. Mary and Melissa changed back into the clothes Price had rescued them in. He had them remove any bandages they'd put on after they'd reached the sub, implored them to keep his secret, then into the raft they went. There were still a few hours to go, but Price wanted to be on the safe side.

    As they drifted away, Mary yelled, "I'll look forward to seeing you soon."

    They waved, and with that Mary and Melissa readied themselves to be rescued. They didn't need to do much acting to look frightened and sad; being back in the raft brought much of the horror back.

    Price submerged the submarine and kept the raft in sight on the periscope's video camera. He could see they looked really scared, and it tore at him to have put them through being rescued a second time. He was happy when right on schedule he spotted a Coast Guard helicopter in the area. Soon it spotted the raft and put divers in the water. Before long, Mary and Melissa were hoisted aboard. If they'd looked scared before, their faces showed real terror now while they were on the hoist. This further stung Price's conscience, but once they were aboard he began to plan the next phase of his trip. He also wondered if and when he may ever see them again.

Chapter 9

Regrouping

Price was more than ready to spend some time on dry land, where he could get a real meal, sleep in a real bed, and have a nice shower; this posed a challenge, however, given his desire to keep the submarine a secret. He opted for a variation of how he stored the sub at home, only in this case he wouldn't exit the sub at a dock and remote control it to a submerged berth; instead, he'd settle the submarine in a safe place on the bottom of some cove, then swim out through the airlock and go ashore. The question was where to do this?

He settled on a cove adjacent to a resort hotel and a marina. The water was deep enough for his purposes and had the added benefit of having a large buoy at its entrance. Price didn't care about the buoy itself, but would use its anchor to secure the sub in case currents tried to sweep the sub away from its berth.

With the sub tied to the anchor and settled onto the bottom of the cove, Price put some clothing and his wallet into a waterproof bag. He then donned his diving equipment, went into the airlock, and exited the sub. He swam to shore, landing at an isolated spot, and made his way to the resort, stopping first to drop off his air tank for recharging. He then walked into the resort and made his way to the front desk, where they had the reservation he'd made earlier from the sub. He checked in and immediately went to his room and showered. He luxuriated in the warm water for quite a while, then got dressed and went down to have dinner.

Price found it interesting how much he thought about Mary and Melissa, wondering where they were and how they were doing. He wasn't sure if he'd hear from them, but he sure hoped he did. These thoughts seemed to take precedence over his typical ones. Where he usually thought about his loss and what actions he could take to make up for having failed them, today was different. He felt great, and he was encouraged by positive thoughts about the future. He looked forward to continuing his voyage, but he also knew there were other things to contemplate; however, for now he was just going to enjoy this small respite on dry land before he continued his journey.

Price stayed in the resort for three days; by then, he was ready to move on. Before he left, he decided to check his email. His spirits were lifted when he received an email from Mary on the day he was leaving that indicated she and Melissa had made it home all right. She inquired about Price and what he was up to and said she looked forward to meeting up with him when his travels brought him back home. Price responded and attached a picture he took through the periscope of Mary and her daughter being hoisted onto the helicopter. The picture was priceless in both its quality and in having captured facial expressions that portrayed the sheer horror they must have felt.

Price followed up the email with a telephone call. He didn't reach Mary, who'd gone out, but he did speak with Melissa for a while. He heard the story of their rescue and the investigation into her father's death. While the subject was painful, it sounded like the law enforcement officials were very gentle and considerate. Having had an uneventful trip home, what was difficult was facing all the reminders of Tom and the fact that he was gone. Then there were the myriad tasks that needed to be done in connection with his passing. Price could empathize with them – more than they could know. Price asked Melissa to pass along his regards to her mom, and he told her he was moving ahead with his journey.

Another message in his inbox was from Mike Mahoney. It simply said to please call. Price hated to ruin his mood, but he was also curious, so he made the requested call. He dialed Mike's private number, and Mike picked up on the second ring.

"Hello?" said Mike.

Price responded, "Hello to you. I got your note that said to call. So, ever the faithful servant, here I am. How can I help you?"

Mike replied, "You're hardly a servant. I haven't heard from you for weeks. I went looking for you, and you were nowhere to be found. Then imagine my surprise to find you're at a resort in Hawaii. I don't begrudge you the vacation. I just would have liked to know how to reach you in case I needed you, not to mention knowing you're OK."

Price said, "How do you know where I am? Never mind, I think I know and will have to start using cash in lieu of my credit cards. So why the urgency to find me? I doubt it was to see how I was doing."

"You're being too harsh," said Mike. "However, it's true that I wanted to speak with you about a couple of – let's call them opportunities. Interestingly, you're currently closer to a couple of them than I am, which could prove convenient. Would you be able to make your way to the naval base at Pearl so you can get a proper briefing?"

Intrigued, Price responded, "Sure, Mike. How about 9 AM the day after tomorrow? Is that soon enough?"

"If that's the best you can do, these matters can wait," said Mike. "I'll take care of getting you in the front gate, and there will be a package waiting for you when you arrive, letting you know where to go."

They said goodbye, and Price immediately started to wonder what it was Mike had in store for him. Obviously, there was something special; although he did say there were several "opportunities". While he might choose not to act, it was always good to hear what issues were facing the country and to see if he could help.

Later that day, Price exchanged what he was wearing for his dive gear and made his way out to the sub to resume his voyage. He found the sub to be all in order, except the batteries were low; this resulted from having berthed the sub without first recharging the batteries, compounded by leaving it in that state for several days. Price raised the sub to snorkel depth and ran on diesel. This was the first extended use he made of it, and it worked fine; however, he'd have to think of a plan to refill his tank without disclosing the sub's existence. For now, he needed to get to Pearl Harbor for his meeting. It was going to be tight. He had just under 200 nautical miles to travel. He estimated that between winds and currents, he would be traveling at about 8-10 knots; that meant he'd arrive in the area in approximately 25 hours. This would give him time to berth the sub, make his way to dry land, get a room, have dinner, and get a good night's sleep.

Once he was away from land, Price rose from snorkel depth and rode on the surface, using his wind turbine to charge the batteries. It was getting dark, so he couldn't use the solar panels. It was critical to get back to running on batteries and not on diesel, or he'd run out of fuel. The next morning, he brought the solar panel on line and was able to run on the batteries, as well as keep them charged. He'd have to find a way to refill the fuel before he left Hawaii.

Other than his concern over fuel, the trip was uneventful. Price decided that staying near Honolulu was safer than getting too close to the military installations. He was afraid their defenses might detect the sub and that this could invite an unpleasant response – at least for him. Price was once again lucky to find an ideal spot to berth the sub that was proximate to a resort. He repeated what he'd done previously and made his way to shore.

    After taking a room for two nights, he decided that readying himself for dinner would be too much, so instead he ordered room service. He had a nice steak, some salad, and a nice bottle of cabernet sauvignon from Alexander Valley – his favorite. He chose to dine on his balcony, which overlooked the water. As he ate, his thoughts drifted to Mary and Melissa, wondering what they were doing. He laughed to himself in that he knew what they must be doing – given the time difference, they'd most likely be sleeping. He thought about his previous life, his failure, and whether he was making up for it. Lastly, he thought about his upcoming meeting. These thoughts followed him right into slumber.

Chapter 10

Mission Identified

The next morning, Price made his way to the meeting. He'd expected a secure video conference, but to his surprise Mike Mahoney had flown out to Hawaii to meet with him in person. They greeted each other, exchanged some small talk, and then Mike began his briefing.

"While there's no shortage of issues facing our country," began Mahoney, "there are some whose origins aren't yet clear that we could sure use your help with."

"That's why I'm here," Price interjected. "How can I help?"

Mahoney continued. "Of late, we've been detecting a number of intrusions into various computer systems that seem to have no purpose; however, we've also suffered an increase in missing inventory at both government and commercial sites. We surmise that these two observations are linked and the seemingly innocuous intrusions are just probes or reconnaissance trying to determine defenses. Sometimes these probes get caught; other times they don't. Computers control the flow of inventory, thus a compromise of them could be responsible for the losses; however, a loss has never been observed with a flagged intrusion. Theft of inventory is worrisome, but on the government side these same computing systems control a wide variety of activities whose compromise could wreak havoc and threaten our defenses, or even instigate a war."

"Is that all?" quipped Price. "What does this have to do with Hawaii and your reason for coming out here?"

Mahoney replied, "The answer to your second question is that to the extent we can localize the problem, it seems to be here in the south Pacific; however, there's an additional matter, namely that a couple of key individuals who live or were visiting here just disappeared. Those individuals were connected to the entities hardest hit. Recently, a government contractor connected to one of our most critical computer systems has also gone missing. These missing persons add to the sense of importance we place on getting to the bottom of what's going on and resolving it."

"Not to downplay the attack on computers, but tell me about these other problems, then I'd like to hear more about these missing people," said Price.

Mahoney provided a brief outline of the issues he'd identified. He then explained that almost all of the people who'd gone missing may have been last seen going boating, though it's not absolutely certain. In a number of cases, marinas complained about not getting the boats they'd rented returned. Mahoney explained that the missing boats varied from small speed boats to moderately sized sailboats.

Price had a few more questions, in reply to which Mahoney furnished him with a rather large folder overflowing with paper and said, "Read the papers in this file over. Everything we know is in there. By the way, how did you get out here? I didn't see any plane reservations in your name."

"Serves you right for snooping," said Price. "It'll just have to be one of those mysteries that keeps you up at night. Maybe I did whatever I did just to frustrate you. Regardless, I'm not telling. I'll read over what's in the folder and get back to you."

"You can't just take the folder with you!" exclaimed Mahoney. "Its contents are classified. You can stay here and read it. I'll get you a nice office for the duration."

"I just said I'd look over what's in the folder. I didn't say I'd act on it," Price responded. "OK, I'll read the folder's contents here and see if there's a play for me here."

Mahoney just shook his head, as he realized there was no point in arguing. He showed Price to a nice office that overlooked the water, then he decided to leave. Based on past experience, he knew this was the point to leave Price alone if there was hope for any action. He said goodbye and left Price in the office with the file.

Price quickly grasped the severity of the problem and its potential to create real harm. What

Mike hadn't pointed out, which Price quickly ascertained, was a possible connection between all the issues Mahoney had briefed him on. Mike had separated the issues of the cyber attacks and the missing people from the other issues he identified, namely illegal drugs, terrorism, piracy, weapons, and people trafficking. Price's review of the materials suggested all of these misdeeds could be tied together to a common source. All these issues not only had making large sums of illegal money in common, they also seemed to have other attributes in common, suggesting common leadership and direction.

He thought to himself, *Now that's intriguing.*

Price spent the next several days getting to the office before sunup and leaving well after sundown. He requested and received additional information. He felt he was truly onto something that resembled a cancer, which had been growing since before the episodes Mahoney had highlighted. Despite being convinced he was right about this, he was unable to pinpoint the origin or articulate the specifics that underpinned his feeling. He knew he'd never be able to convince anyone else, let alone even explain it. He'd need some more specifics, but they were eluding him. Price felt a little like he was hitting his head against the wall, so he decided to take a break.

As always, it was a beautiful day in paradise, so Price figured he'd take advantage of this break to check on the sub, and perhaps figure out a way to fuel it. He went to a marina not far from where the sub was lying and looked into renting a boat. He felt lucky when he was able to find a boat that was diesel-powered. If he could find a suitable location, he'd be able to transfer fuel from the boat to the sub. So, he rented the boat.

Price departed the marina and circled into the cove where the sub was. He anchored the boat, and then dove into the water. He found the sub just where he'd left it, detached it from the buoy's anchor, and connected a line to it from the boat. He went into the sub through its airlock and adjusted the sub's buoyancy so it would float off the bottom, but not surface. Price then returned to the boat and, towing the submerged sub, set out to find a suitable location to refuel.

There was a great deal of traffic on the water, so he decided it wouldn't be safe to refuel until after the sun went down, when the sub would be less visible to passing boats. He also hoped the number of boats moving about after dark would diminish. Not to waste the day, Price once again berthed the sub on the bottom and anchored it using a spare anchor from the boat. He very carefully and precisely determined its location using the on board GPS so he could find it later, then cruised around, just enjoying the sunshine, fresh air, and scenery.

His thoughts drifted from the problem at hand to thinking about Mary and her daughter Melissa. He wondered whether he'd see them again, and if so, what would become of it. His exact feelings were somewhat confused, as he still loved the family he'd lost and wondered what he was feeling with regards to Mary and Melissa. He also wondered what their thinking and feelings might be, given the loss they'd just suffered.

Price's reverie was interrupted by a ship's horn. He turned to see a relatively large white ultra-modern looking ship with lots of antennas heading for land; however, it wasn't headed to the port and harbor area. He wondered where it could be going this close to land. He decided to keep a discreet eye on it. When he was able to view it from a different angle, he noted it had the name Ocean Commander written on its stern. There was also a sign that said Khan Industries. Price decided he'd learn more about Khan Industries later, but for now he broke off his surveillance and returned to the sub's location.

When Price returned to the sub's location, the sun was almost down and he was able to surface without it being noticeable. It also helped that there was little traffic about. He tied the sub alongside the rented boat and proceeded to empty the boat's full tank into the sub's tank. When he was done, the sub was full and the boat was virtually empty. He hoped he'd left enough to get him back to the marina.

On the return, Price decided to leave the sub surfaced so he could top off the batteries using the wind turbine. When he arrived at the cove, he once again submerged and tied the sub to the buoy's anchor. Price then made his way to a different marina than he'd rented the boat from, as he would have no way to rationalize how much fuel he'd used compared to both the number of hours he was gone and the number of engine hours recorded. This way, he'd bring the boat back full and avoid any difficult questions. As it turned out, he just made it to the fueling dock when the engine started to falter due to lack of fuel. He filled it to about ¾, then proceeded to the marina from where he'd rented the boat and returned it without questions.

As he made his way back to the resort, he kept thinking about Khan Industries and the Ocean Commander ship he'd seen; however, when he got back to his room he saw the message light on his telephone flashing. After some struggle, he managed to retrieve his voicemail and listen to it. It was a message from Mary, at which point all thoughts about Khan Industries left his mind. She apologized for missing his call. She said both she and Melissa were doing well under the circumstances, but they were struggling with both their loss and the myriad tasks it had spawned. Mary sarcastically commented on how much she liked the pictures he'd sent. She ended the call by saying she hoped to hear from him and that he could call at any hour.
  Price looked at the clock and decided it was far too late and that he wouldn't disturb her sleep.

Chapter 11

Intriguing Target

The next day, Price began his research into Khan Industries. Several things were evident: first, there wasn't much information; second, what he could find hardly substantiated the enterprise he'd observed; lastly, there was absolutely no explanation for the role of the Ocean Commander. All told, he got only the vaguest description of their business, and not much else. Price contacted Mike Mahoney to see what other information the government might have. Mike asked why he was interested, but he was obviously busy with other things, so he accepted Price's lame response without challenge. Mike said he'd have someone pull whatever they had together and get it to him.

Given that he'd run out of things to do in the office until he got the promised files, Price decided to go take a closer look at Kahn Industries. Price chose a water approach using the sub. He retrieved the sub and headed to where he'd seen the Ocean Commander going. When he arrived, he saw a deep channel that led into a small harbor area, with docks and loading cranes on one end and various smaller watercraft on the other. The Ocean Commander was tied up on the far end of the dock area.

Price wanted a closer look, so he submerged himself and made his way to the channel. When he was only halfway toward to harbor area, he noted some equipment on both sides of the waterway whose purpose didn't immediately register with him. Then when it was almost too late, he realized it was a submarine net. He immediately pushed the sub into full reverse to stop it before he hit the net. He wondered why some commercial enterprise would need a submarine and decided to wait around and see what else he might observe.

From his vantage point, all Price could see was a number of buildings, but he couldn't ascertain their purpose. The noises the hydrophones were picking up in the water suddenly changed, and it sounded as though a boat was coming. Price pinpointed the boat and noted it was heading up the channel and into the harbor. Price looked on the video monitor, which at this time was showing what the periscope could see; sure enough, there was a small cargo boat, the kind that provisions ships at anchor, moving slowly past his position and toward the harbor.

"But the submarine net," Price said to himself.

The words were hardly out of his mouth when the net's machinery situated on both sides of the channel began to operate and the net parted.

In an impetuous act, Price decided to follow the other boat in. It proved no problem, given the depth of the channel and the net being open; however, getting out might be a different matter. Price reasoned he'd deal with that when the time came.

Price surveyed the area. Of course, there was the ship Ocean Commander. There were a couple of work boats not very different than the one that just entered the harbor. There was a moderately sized loading crane on the dock, and there was other equipment typically found in a dock area. What wasn't all that typical were several very large electrical generators. They just seemed out of place, and if anything, excessive to Khan Industries' needs. The other thing Price couldn't figure out was what the conduits were used for that came out of a bunker-like building and disappeared into the harbor. The other thing that didn't seem right was how few people were around. For this size enterprise, it should have been crawling with staff.

Price continued to survey the area to see what he could learn. He turned his attention to the Ocean Commander. It seemed like most ships in its class, except for two things: there was an abundance of radio antennas topside, and an intriguing set of doors on the bottom of the hull. Price was able to observe them with his underwater cameras. He wondered what they were for, as they certainly weren't in an ideal place from a boat design perspective. The doors could only be there to hide something from observers on or above the surface of the sea. Nothing else about the boat's exterior – or the harbor, for that matter – seemed extraordinary; just the submarine net, the excessive power generation, the conduits, and of course the hole in the ship's bottom.

Price decided that since he was unsure of how long he might be stuck in the harbor before the nets were reopened, and he could exit through them, he'd better recharge the batteries. Surfacing was out of the question, at least until nightfall, which was many hours away. So instead, he decided to use the diesel engine vented through the snorkel, which he raised to the surface. No sooner had the engine started than he observed a whole flurry of activity around the dock area. Several of the boats left the dock in a hurry, and it seemed as though they were headed his way.

It occurred to Price, albeit a little late, that someone who had submarine nets would likely employ other security measures. In this case, hydrophones could be the answer, which could listen in for any sounds that didn't belong and pinpoint the sound's origin. Price didn't waste any time shutting the diesel engine down and lowering the snorkel. He was tempted to sprint from the area, but he was afraid this would cause too much noise. So instead, he reduced his buoyancy, sinking down towards the bottom and proceeding from the area at a very slow crawl. When he was furthest from his previous position and more or less adjacent to the net, he let the sub settle to the bottom, shut off the motor, and waited.

Price was a little surprised that the boats didn't deploy divers into the water. It soon became evident why, as there was a series of explosions that shook and rattled the submarine. Fortunately, they were a distance away from him, which attenuated their affect. Additionally, the shape of the harbor and where he was hiding served to protect him. The bombardment went on for what seemed like hours, but was likely only a few minutes. Then as quickly as it began, it stopped. The boats returned to their dock and all was quiet, though Price suspected they'd be on high alert and more vigilant than they previously were. So, he sat on the bottom pondering his next action.

It was now nightfall, and Price wondered if it would be safe to raise the wind turbine to charge the batteries. They hadn't previously seen the periscope, but the turbine was bigger, and he didn't want to risk his luck too many times in one day. The sub with someone aboard would have power for at least a day and then some. Without anyone on board, it could sit for weeks. While he didn't like it, he decided to abandon the sub and make his way out swimming. Price deemed that doing this at night would give him the biggest edge – that is, unless he was caught, where it being nighttime would really impede any credible alibi. His plan was to come back later to fetch the sub, possibly when things cooled down a bit.

Price found an anchor on the sea bottom, likely abandoned due to the way it was lodged between two large rocks and used it to secure the net that closed off the harbor entrance. He connected the sub to it using the sub's mechanical arm. That way, currents or storms would not move the sub, as it was securely moored. He shut everything off and exited in diving gear. He approached the net but was careful not to touch it. He determined he could get through, but not with his gear. So, he undid the straps and slipped off the gear, pushed the gear through the net, then slithered through himself. After re-donning the gear, he swam out to sea and then around the point that sheltered the channel. Eventually, he came ashore, hid his gear, and sought to put as much distance between himself and Kahn Industries as he could. Price didn't want to explain himself, so he hid whenever he saw headlights coming and proceeded to make the very long walk back toward civilization. He arrived back at his room just after sunup.

Price was exhausted from lack of sleep, stress, and the physical exertion he'd made. So when his head hit the pillow, he was instantly asleep. He slept until housekeeping's knock disturbed him, then he slept again until late afternoon, when there was an insistent knock on his door.

Chapter 12

Foreboding Visits

"Mr. Price, my name is Officer Henry, and I'm with Kahn Industries security. May I have a few moments of your time?"

Price, who had been groggy, instantly came awake and replied, "Certain, but what is this about?"

"May I come in?" asked Officer Henry.

"Certainly," replied Price. "I don't know what happened to my manners. I was napping, and I guess I haven't fully woken up. Come in. Would you like something to drink?"

"No, I'm fine," said Officer Henry. "I'll get right to the point. Last night there was a trespasser at our facility, and we found diving gear that belongs to you in the vicinity. We're just running down all leads that might explain who the trespasser was and what they were doing."

Feigning surprise, Price said, "I leave my gear at the marina, where they clean it and keep the tanks full. I better check to see if it's gone."

"That would be a waste of your time, as I can assure you it's in our possession, having found it buried near our site," answered Officer Henry. "That is, unless you have more than one set of gear. So you're saying you have no idea how your gear turned up where it did?"

"No, how could I?" responded Price. "I've been here for the past couple of days."

"Well, you did rent a boat the other day and were gone for a considerable amount of time," replied Officer Henry. "Some folks also saw you returning to your room early this morning."

Somewhat indignantly, Price said, "Are you checking up on me? I don't like people violating my privacy. Indeed I rented a boat the other day, and this morning I was out for some exercise. There are no laws against either of those activities. In fact, they're quite common here."

Officer Henry responded, "You're correct, neither of those activities is against the law; however, trespassing on our property is against the law. We fully intend to find the culprit, understand what they were up to, and then take action accordingly."

"I've told you what I know, so if there's nothing else, I do have other things to do," said Price. "How come company security is investigating this, and not the local police?"

"Khan Industries was violated; hence our involvement," said Officer Henry. "When we need the locals, we'll get them involved. I don't have any other questions at this time, but if I think of any, I may be back." He then sarcastically added, "Thanks for your help. I'll be on my way."

When Officer Henry left, Price let out a big sigh, then kicked himself for having left the gear where it could be discovered. He then recalled that he'd buried it, so they must have searched the area with metal detectors. He'd have to be real careful with these guys; he was now on their radar, and they were thorough. Price reasoned his best plan would be to leave for a while, but not in too much of a rush.

He made plans to go fishing on a charter boat the next day, then he'd hang around the following day. The day after that, he would rent a boat for the day, and then the next day he'd depart for two weeks. He reasoned now was a chance to go check on his home, but more importantly an opportunity to possibly pay a visit to Mary and Melissa.

The days went relatively quickly, as Price was absorbed by thoughts of both his visit from Officer Henry and how his visit back home would go. He was also consumed with interest and curiosity regarding Khan Industries. There were many things that weren't consistent with their public persona, not the least of which was their security.

Price arrived home and thankfully found it much as he'd left it. The housekeeper and grounds keepers saw to that; however, it seemed somehow different…empty. Price went through his routine, but in a somewhat mindless way. His uncertainty of how his reaching out to Mary would be received had him hesitating to call, yet all he could think about was speaking with her and seeing her. He felt like an adolescent. Finally, when he couldn't stand it anymore, he called. As luck would have it, no one was home and he left a message. He explained he was back on the mainland and wanted to see how they were doing.

While it seemed like hours, it was a mere 45 minutes before Mary called back. She and her daughter Melissa were located just 4 hours away by car – about 250 miles – yet it seemed like they were on another continent.

When the telephone rang, Price answered it on the second ring. "Hello, this is Dave Price."

"Hi, this is Mary. How are you? I was both surprised and pleased to get your call. Sorry I was out and missed it."

Price replied, "Nothing to be sorry about. I'm just glad we've connected now. How are you and Melissa doing?"

"We're keeping busy, in part because there's a lot to do, and in part because it helps keep our mind off things," replied Mary. "Melissa has been coming home from school most weekends to keep me company, which isn't really fair to her, but I think or at least rationalize she needs the time together also."

"How does Melissa get from Palo Alto to Santa Barbara?" asked Price. "She can't be driving that every weekend."

Mary answered, "She takes a commuter flight from San Jose Airport. It's a short flight, but still a significant multi-hour ordeal."

"There's a small airport in Palo Alto," said Price. "What would you say about me picking Melissa up after her classes this week and flying her down to Santa Barbara? I'd love to visit with you; both of you. The airport is only a couple of miles from her school, versus the 17-mile distance to San Jose Airport, and there's no security hassle."

"I guess it shouldn't be a surprise you have an airplane, given that you have a submarine," said Mary. "Let me check with Melissa and see what she thinks about it, and when she'd be available. It would be great to see you and catch up on things. I'll get back with you later tonight after I speak with Melissa."

"It's been great speaking with you," said Price. "I'll look forward to your call later on."

They said goodbye, and Price's pulse was racing. Despite his apprehension, they spoke like old friends. He couldn't wait for her call back later that day. He spent the rest of the day doing busy work. Every time the phone rang, he would leap to get it; however, most of the calls were of the nuisance variety, except for the call from Mahoney.

"Hi Mike, nice of you to call," said Price. "To what do I owe the pleasure of your call?"

"Cut the crap, Price," said Mahoney. "I provide you with some information, and then you disappear without providing so much as an email? What's going on?"

"I've been looking into the issues you briefed me on," replied Price. "I didn't know I was supposed to report when I had nothing to say."

"You can fill me in on exactly what you've been doing and whether there are results or not," exclaimed an exasperated Mahoney.

Price knew he didn't want to explain about his little excursion into Khan Industries' docking area. In fact, he didn't want to bring up the submarine at all; however, it would be fair to mention Khan Industries as long as there were other explanations for his observations.

As Price was thinking, Mahoney came back and said, "Have you fallen asleep? I made a simple request, so how about it? Let me hear what you've been up to."

Price responded, "The file you sent me on Khan Industries was rather thin. It seemed not to have much information at all."

"We don't keep track of every U.S. business. That's not our job. That's the job of other government agencies. The only time a company would appear in our files is if there was some intersection with other national security interests," said Mahoney

"I've been looking into the company and am perplexed by any number of things. The company's physical plant, power plants, their ship Ocean Commander, the electronics on it, as well as the antenna farm on their buildings and their overall security posture are inconsistent with their alleged line of business," replied Price. "In addition, for all of their facilities, they seem to have very few employees that come and go from the property. I'm not certain yet, but I believe they receive food supplies that could feed a population 100 times more than the number of employees one sees coming and going on a daily basis."

"I admit this sounds intriguing, but what has it got to do with the problems I set before you?" asked Mahoney.

"To be honest, I don't know," replied Price. "My reasoning is that your main problem seems centered in the islands, and I find Khan Industries to be an anomaly in those same islands. I realize that connecting those two 'dots' is somewhat of a stretch, but I think it's a worthwhile pursuit in the absence of any other leads."

"Stretch? It's well beyond that. It's more like fanciful conjecture," exclaimed Mahoney.

"Call it what you wish," said Price. "Until I can explain the incongruities surrounding Khan Industries or discover a more promising line of inquiry, I believe it to be the best lead we have. In that regard, I'd like some more information from you. I'd like any information you may be able to get regarding the Ocean Commander, including where it may have been seen over this past year. I'd also like any overhead imagery you may have of their island facilities and harbor. Blueprints from permits for these facilities would also be helpful. Lastly, I'd like any information you may be able to get, like tax filings and/or corporate filings."

"Are you sure that's all?" said Mahoney. "Now you're not only chasing after a fantasy, you want to make me a party to it – and break a few laws along the way. You are truly a piece of work."

"Recall that you sought out my help," answered Price. "You can provide aid, or just leave me alone; however, I'm letting you know I'll be pursuing Khan Industries until I understand what they're up to."

Price knew Mahoney would help, despite his bluster, and chose not to press the matter further. They said their goodbyes, and Price started to consider his next steps. Once again, the telephone ringing broke his concentration. He excitedly answered it, but he was disappointed it was just some telephone solicitor. He thought that being on the no-call list would prevent such interruptions, but thus far he'd seen no evidence of this. It was particularly annoying when one was doing something important, napping, or as in his present circumstance, waiting for a particular phone call.

That telephone call came just before 9 PM.

"Hi, Dave," said Mary when Price picked up. "Sorry it's so late, but I wasn't able to connect with Melissa any earlier."

"That's OK," said Price. "I'm just glad you called. It's good to hear your voice. What did Melissa have to say?"

Mary responded, "Melissa would be thrilled if you brought her home for the weekend. Quite frankly, I'm excited about seeing you myself."

"Well then, we'll make it a plan," said Price.

Mary continued. "Her last class is over at 3 PM on Friday, and she could be to the airport by no later than 4 PM. She wants you to have her cell phone number to finalize the plans. I'll email it to you. We can have a late dinner when you arrive, and you'll stay with us in the guest room."

"It sounds wonderful," replied Price. "I'm looking forward to it myself. I estimate we should be landing in Santa Barbara by no later than 6 PM. Should we grab a taxi, or will you come pick us up?"

"Are you able to call when you get close? If so, we can finalize the plan when you call," said Mary.

"We can call when we're less than 30 minutes out," said Price. "I'm truly looking forward to seeing you. Is there anything I can bring?"

"Bring yourself and Melissa," answered Mary.

Price subsequently got Melissa's cell phone number from the email he'd just gotten from Mary. He then contacted Melissa, and they finalized their plans.

Chapter 13

Flight to New Life

The rest of Price's week went quickly. He had his plane cleaned up and serviced. He gathered up some things to bring with him, and he did what research he could on Khan Industries. There was precious little he could find on the company, but he really didn't care that much, as his mind was on the upcoming weekend. So instead of forcing himself to work, he focused on the flight plan and the weekend ahead.

Friday arrived, and Price was actually nervous. He hadn't slept much the night before, and he now found he couldn't sit down and relax. Price hoped to take a short nap before he left. Normally if he read for a while, he'd be ready for sleep, but in this case he could neither concentrate to read nor be sleepy enough to nap. So he just packed up the things he was bringing with him and left for the airport about 2 hours earlier than he needed to. Once at the airport, he stowed his gear, pre-flight checked his airplane, started the engine, and taxied out to the runway for takeoff.

The flight to the Palo Alto airport was relatively brief and uneventful. Price taxied his plane up to the temporary tie down area and shut down the engine. He was just advising the ground crew he'd be departing shortly when he saw Melissa coming his way. She was carrying a backpack and wearing a huge smile. Price now knew he wasn't the only anxious one, as she was also quite early.

Price greeted Melissa with a brief hug and said, "I'm so glad to see you. You're looking great."

"You, too," replied Melissa. "I can't believe you're here and going to fly us to Santa Barbara. This is so cool."

"Well, I guess we can be on our way," said Price. "Why don't you put your backpack in the back seat, then you can strap into the right seat." After they were strapped in, Price said, "You can put on the headset, which will help us talk and allow you to hear my communications with the ground. Have you ever been in a small plane before? If not, you're in for a treat."

"No, I've never been in anything smaller than a commuter plane," said Melissa. "I'm really looking forward to it."

They taxied out to the end of the runway, with Melissa just absorbed in all that was going on and quiet, so as not to distract Price from what he had to do.
After takeoff, Price asked, "Why so quiet?"

"Just enjoying the new experience," replied Melissa.

"You don't need to worry; we can speak, and I won't be distracted," said Price. "If I need quiet, I'll let you know – and don't worry, our internal communications aren't being broadcast. Would you like to try flying the plane?"

"I couldn't," said Melissa. "I don't know what I'm doing."

"I'll help you," offered Price. "It's actually quite easy. When the plane is all trimmed, very little control is actually needed. Put your hands on the wheel in front of you. When I push in, the nose of the plane moves downward, and when I pull up, the nose comes up. When I turn the wheel to the left, the wing on that side drops down, and likewise when I turn the wheel the other way, the right wing drops."

"So to go down, you push the wheel in, and to go up, you pull the wheel back?" asked Melissa.

"Not exactly," answered Price. "Movement of the yoke in and out or side to side only controls the attitude of the aircraft. To actually go up and down, you have to add or reduce power. If you want, I'd be happy to teach you, but for now just keep your hands lightly on the controls and get the feel of them."

Price went on to point out the different instruments and explained what they do. He kept up a running monologue about the plane and the scenery below. It was as though he wanted to avoid any other discussions. Before long, they were entering the Santa Barbara area.

"Do you recognize where we are?" asked Price. "Can you show me where your home is?"

Melissa worked to orient herself, then said, "That's our neighborhood over there. I recognize the shops and the school. This is awesome."

Price placed the promised call, saying they were about to land. He then contacted the control tower for instructions. There wasn't much traffic, so he was immediately put on approach and landed shortly afterward. He taxied to the private aviation area, where he was met by a flag man who helped guide him into a parking spot. He shut down the engine and opened the door.

"No speeches like you get on commercial airliners – we're here," proclaimed Price. "Let's get our stuff and go wait for your mom."

They didn't have to wait long, as Mary pulled up in front of the terminal in short order. Melissa ran up to her mother and in lieu of a more traditional greeting went into a litany of how cool the flight was and how she'd flown the plane. Mary hugged her, then shyly said hello to Price and thanked him for bringing Melissa. They put the bags in the trunk and piled into the car. During the drive, there was some small talk, but mostly Melissa dominated the conversation, all excited by the flight.

They arrived at Mary and Melissa's home. It was a single story "U" shaped home set back from the street on a relatively large lot. The middle was where the common areas were; living room, kitchen, dining room. The sides were where the bedrooms were. The house framed a courtyard, which had a swimming pool and hot tub. There was access to the pool from the bedrooms and from the kitchen. Mary showed Price the guest room where he would be staying. It was in a separate wing of the house from the other bedrooms. It looked like it shared the wing with a man's office. This was confirmed when she mentioned that the office next to his room was Tom's – her deceased husband.

"Why don't we meet on the pool deck for drinks in a few minutes, and then if you won't mind, I'd ask you to barbeque some steaks I have for dinner," said Mary. "While you're doing that, I'll prepare a salad and try my hand at making a risotto."

"Sounds wonderful," Price said. "I just so happen to have brought a couple of bottles of a wonderful cabernet sauvignon that will pair nicely with steak."

"You needn't have brought wine, but it sounds yummy," replied Mary.

It was 6:15 PM when they met up on the pool deck. Price was wearing shorts and a collared pullover shirt with sandals. Mary was wearing a so-called "skort" and blouse. She looked wonderful. Melissa joined them but explained she was only going to be able to eat and run, as she was going to a movie with her friends.

Dinner was a relatively quiet affair, except for small talk and compliments to the chef, the griller, and the sommelier who picked the wine. Melissa left and said she'd be home by midnight. Despite her protestations, Price helped Mary clean up from dinner. It was about 9:00 PM when they sat out at the pool. Price poured them each some wine. It felt awkward for each of them, as they really didn't know each other, but soon the wine did its work and conversation began to flow more smoothly.

Price said, "That's quite a daughter you have. She's smart, energetic, and very well mannered. She really got a kick out of flying in the plane."

"You think?" responded Mary, laughing. "That's all she could speak about all week, and it's all she's talked about since you guys arrived."

"I think some of the chatter since we landed is her coping with a strange man who came into your lives under stressful circumstances, not knowing what to really say," replied Price. "I'm a lot worldlier than her, but I have to admit that while I'm absolutely thrilled to see you and be here, I'm not exactly sure what to say myself."

"You're doing just fine," said Mary. "We met under truly extraordinary circumstances, and you saved our lives, but somehow I feel the fate that brought us together wasn't the end, but perhaps a new beginning. However, for now I like it when you're speaking, because I too am not sure what I should say, and I'm afraid of embarrassing myself – you know, in vino veritas."

They spent the evening talking about their pasts, where they grew up, their schooling, careers, and finally about their family life. Despite it being a painful subject, Price found that speaking about his family and their loss with Mary was actually comforting. She was an extremely good listener. Mary had pretty much caught Price up on what she'd been doing since she got back home. It was Price's turn, and he wasn't sure how much to say, but he was spared for the moment when Melissa came home.

"Is everything all right?" Mary asked Melissa. "You're home early."

"Well, actually Mom, I'm 30 minutes late. It's 12:30," said Melissa.

"I can't believe it," said Mary. "Dave and I have just been catching up, and the time just flew by."

Melissa asked, "Did you tell him about the cool rescue? Being hoisted out of the water, and then the helicopter ride?"

"No, we actually skipped that part," said Mary

"Mom, how could you?" asked Melissa. "It was maybe the second or third coolest thing I've ever done."

"What was the first?" inquired Mary.

"Being rescued by Mr. Price and flying in his plane today," replied Melissa. "I got up early today and didn't sleep much last night, so I'm going to turn in. Goodnight, and thank you for coming here and for bringing me with you, Mr. Price."

Price was able to postpone discussing what he'd been up to, as they spent just a few minutes more talking, mostly about Melissa. They then agreed it was late, so Price helped carry in their glasses and they each retired for the evening. Price had gotten ready for bed when he heard a machine sound coming from the courtyard. He opened the door and noted that Mary was in the hot tub with the jets running on high. He stood just outside his room and watched. Mary didn't hear him, due to the noise of the water. He didn't know how long he stood there before Mary spoke his name.

"Dave, you may stand there, or you're more than welcome to come and join me," said Mary.

"But I don't have a suit," exclaimed Price.

"There's one that should fit just inside the closet on the shelf," replied Mary.

The hot tub was wonderful. At first they said nothing and just savored being together, the warmth of the water and the tingle of the bubbles. They continued talking, and it was like they'd known each other their entire lives. Before long, they were sitting next to each other. When Price put his arm around Mary, she melted into him and put her head on his shoulder. They sat like that for a long time, each lost in their own thoughts, not wanting to ruin the moment.

Finally, it was Mary who said, "It's OK."

Price wasn't quite sure how he should interpret this, but he ultimately turned and faced Mary and asked, "It's OK that I hold you? What about if I were to kiss you?"

Mary's answer was that she turned, held his face, and kissed him gently on the lips. Price felt all the excitement, uncertainty, and insecurity he did as a teen when he'd had his first real kiss. They parted, then kissed again with greater passion. After a while, they parted again and looked into each other's eyes. They each had tears and didn't want to discuss the matter at just that moment, so they held tightly onto each other, lost in their own thoughts.

Price broke the silence. "Are you OK? I'll give you a penny for your thoughts."

With an arm around Price's waist and her head on his shoulder, Mary answered, "Yeah, I'm fine. In fact, I'm more than fine. I never thought I could feel this way again."

Price responded, "That is exactly what I was thinking myself. My life was torn from me all those years ago when I lost my family. I thought I could never have feelings for another, and if I did, I worried it might feel like some form of betrayal. When I first saw you and Melissa, I knew I needed to come to grips with this. Tonight, I know that I can have feelings for you without in any manner diminishing the feelings I have for the family I lost. My tears were both from happiness and from coming to this realization."

    Mary responded, "That echoes what I'm feeling. It's getting real late, and it's been a long day. I'm really glad you're here and that you came into my life. I know Melissa's happy, too."
    With that, Mary kissed Price again and got out of the hot tub without saying another word, then went to her room. Price stayed in a moment longer, then he retired to his room. He practically fell asleep before his head hit the pillow. Gone was the turmoil he'd been feeling, and his outlook on the future held promise. He slept soundly until nearly 8 AM, which was much later than his 6 AM norm. When he was dressed and left his room, he smelled coffee and something cooking. He arrived in the kitchen to see what almost amounted to a full breakfast buffet and a positively glowing Mary.

Chapter 14

Courtship

Not sure how far to go with their familiarity of the night before, Price simply said, "Good morning! I slept great and hope you did, too."

"I slept like a log," replied Mary. To avoid any awkwardness, Mary said, "Get yourself some food, and we can eat it out by the pool."

They each seemed not to be sure of what to say, or even how to act, as they wondered whether or not they'd said too much too soon. They were saved when Melissa joined them. She was non-stop chatter. She spoke of her plans for the day, which included going to a concert that evening, followed by a sleepover at her best friend's house, with whom she was going to the concert. Price was amazed that with all of her talking she was able to eat; however, before long she'd finished eating, kissed her mom, and left.

Now Price and Mary would have the day to themselves, both a pleasant and somewhat intimidating thought to both of them. They were both certain Melissa had planned her day this way intentionally, to give them this time alone.

Price asked, "Mary, what do you like to do on weekends? Is there someplace you'd like to go, or are there errands you need to do?"

"Let's not do what I've done, but instead I'd like to do something that can be ours," replied Mary.

"Have you ever visited your local wineries or the Botanical Gardens?" asked Price.

"I've not been to either," responded Mary. "Sailing was just about all that we pursued, so there is much I haven't seen or done. Why don't we go to the Botanical Gardens? We can have a light lunch somewhere, then spend the afternoon visiting a couple of wineries."

"Sounds good to me," replied Price. "What about dinner? I've heard there's a real nice French restaurant downtown. Have you eaten there? I can make a reservation."

"No, I've never eaten there, but I've heard good things about it," replied Mary.

"Good, I'll get us a table for 7:30 tonight," said Price.

In a bit, Price and Mary got in her car and headed for the Botanical Gardens. No one spoke a word on the way. As they toured the place, they spoke about what they saw, but they avoided anything too personal; however, as the day advanced, so did their closeness. Periodically, they held hands and started to speak about personal topics.

Mary said, "Last night…"

Price cut her off. "I've been meaning to talk to you about that."

Mary interceded, "What I'm trying to say is that last night I told you what I'd been doing, and we got distracted when it was your turn to catch me up on what you've been up to."

One couldn't be certain, but it appeared as though Price was relieved, but then it occurred to him that he wasn't certain what he should tell her or how far he should go. So he started at the beginning, telling her how he gave meaning to his life and the memory of the family he lost by dedicating himself to ridding the country of those who harmed it. He told her about a couple of his exploits and how when he'd found the submarine, he figured it might be a good platform to help him with his quest.

Mary listened intently and was amazed at how Price turned his loss into a mission to do good. Mary considered what she'd done from her loss but quickly realized that being even closer with Melissa was her mission. But even though it sure kept her busy, she questioned if that was enough.

"So what has your most recent project been?" asked Mary.

Price told her about his "high jacking" of the commercial airliner and how he'd met Mike Mahoney. Mary was astounded by this but said nothing. Price explained how Mike's job had changed and that he was now in a much more powerful position, aimed at addressing issues facing the country. Price related how Mike had identified some issues for him to consider and how he'd stumbled across Khan Industries. Price went on and told her about his escape from Khan's harbor and his meeting with the person from Khan Security. Lastly, Price shared with Mary some of his theories and overall sense that Khan Industries wasn't what they claimed to be and were quite likely behind some (if not all) of the activities Mike had briefed him on.

"Wow," was all Mary could think to say. "Is there anything I could help you with?"

Answering the question was delayed by the arrival of their third wine sample to taste in this, the second of the wineries they'd visited. Actually, the discussion of Price's exploits had started just before lunch when they left the Botanical Gardens, and then on the trip to the first two wineries. The time had really flown by. It had been a glorious day they both enjoyed. Price and Mary also felt much closer now that their life stories had been told. They decided two was enough and that they'd head back home so there was no rush in getting ready to head to the restaurant for their 7:30 PM reservation.

Price asked, "Is 7:15 a good time for us to leave?"

Mary nodded and headed off to her room. Price went to his. He reckoned he had enough time for a quick nap. He got on the bed and almost nodded off when there was a light tap on his door. He reflexively said, "Come in," and Mary entered.

"I just wanted to thank you for a marvelous day," said Mary. "I had a great time, but I see I disturbed you."

Price quickly sat up and said, "I had a great time also, but the day isn't over. We have to leave for dinner in just over 2½ hours. I was just going to take a brief nap."

"Would you mind if I joined you?" asked Mary

Price answered, "Certainly, you may join me."
He moved over on the bed and patted the place next to him. Mary took her shoes off and climbed onto the bed. Price put his arm around her shoulders and gently pulled her to him. They both were lying on their backs, facing the ceiling, occasionally looking at each other. Whatever else might be on the agenda, napping was not. They turned and faced each other, looking into each other's faces. Price gave Mary a very gentle kiss. This was followed by ever more passionate kissing and touching. Mary was every bit as adventuresome as Price. She explored his body outside of his clothes, then proceeded to remove them and explore beneath. Price took her lead and proceeded in the same way. Soon they were down to their underwear. Price removed the rest of Mary's clothes slowly, kissing each new area that was exposed.

Soon, Price's efforts were rewarded by Mary's soft moans. Her motions intensified, and her sounds became more urgent. She went rigid for a moment, then was totally relaxed. Price touched her again, she shivered, then he began his ministration again. The same thing happened, only with greater intensity, and a little quicker.

Out of breath, Mary said, "Enough!"

"Are you saying you're ready for a nap?" asked Price.

"But what about you?" Mary asked, still panting.

"Just give me a kiss and put your head on my shoulder and close your eyes," said Price.

Mary did just that, and soon Price heard her rhythmical breathing. Despite his arousal, when he closed his eyes he fell soundly asleep. He wasn't sure where he was or what exactly was happening, but he slowly came awake with the most pleasant of sensations. Mary was giving him pleasure with her mouth, and he was in no condition to resist. He let her continue until he was starting to thrash around, and he realized the end was near. Even though there could be little doubt, he let Mary know, but she was unperturbed, and when she finished with him he was as relaxed as he'd ever been. He pulled her up to kiss her, but she hesitated, then allowed him to kiss her passionately. They finally settled down and napped.

When Price awoke this time, Mary was gone, and he saw it was 7:00 PM. It registered that they planned to leave at 7:15, so he hurriedly got out of bed, showered, and dressed. He waited in the family room, feeling absolutely wonderful. When Mary came out of her room, she looked ravishing, with an inner glow that had her beaming.

"Wow! Don't you look great," said Price.

"Well, I'm just glad you woke up. I was worried I'd have to go eat alone. I'm famished," replied Mary.

They exchanged a brief kiss, then off to the restaurant they went. The wine and food were great but mostly went unnoticed. Their continued admiring each other, and their discussion diminished their capacity to truly value what they were eating. On the other hand, they both ate ravenously. After the earlier wine and what they drank with dinner, Price thought it prudent to take a taxi home.

Except for a brief kiss in the back seat of the taxi, they controlled themselves; when they entered the house, though, that control evaporated and they were all over each other. They kissed each other passionately while they disrobed each other while on the way to Price's room. There, they made love. A little while later, they went out to the hot tub for a spell, then came back in and made love again. This time, they went to sleep in each other's arms. They woke up the way they went to sleep. Neither of them had moved. They picked up where they'd left off and made love again. About 15 minutes later, Mary gave Price a kiss and left for her room; however, she returned in just a few seconds, delivering the clothes Price had dropped on their way to his room last night. She then left, saying she'd see him in an hour for breakfast.

When they saw each other, Mary said, "That was wonderful."

"What was wonderful?" asked Melissa, who had just walked in. "What happened to the car?"

Mary told her about most of their day together, winking at Price when Melissa wasn't looking. Mary then went on and told her they did the responsible thing and took a cab home, with the admonition that she hoped Melissa would do the same thing under similar circumstances. They also spoke about the concert.

"When are we leaving to go back to school?" asked Melissa.

"What time do you need to be back?" asked Price.

"Before 7 PM," said Melissa.

"Then let's leave around 5 PM," replied Price.

"I was going out for a jog, so why don't I just go get your car?" said Melissa.

"That would be very nice," said Mary, and she proceeded to tell her where it was.

When they were alone, Mary told Price how wonderful it was to have him visit and that she truly hoped this would be the start of something great. She then told him she was serious about wanting to help him with his quest, perhaps becoming his life's partner in all matters.

"So you didn't say – were you disappointed with your visit here?" inquired Mary.

"You've got to be kidding – it was the best, and I'm certain not the last," said Price.

They spent the rest of the day talking and laughing about things, and before they knew it the time had come to leave. Mary dropped them off at the airport, and Price gave her a small kiss on the cheek and thanked her for a wonderful weekend.

The flight back was uneventful and was consumed by Melissa's chattering. Her major topics were: *how great her mother and I looked together, did I like her mom, and whether I had any thoughts for the future.* To change this subject, Price got Melissa to take the controls while he instructed. While he might have avoided the one subject of him and her mom, Price didn't avoid the chatter, which now turned to how cool it was to fly.

When he dropped Melissa off, she told him she needed to stay at school the following weekend but would be available to fly with him again the following week – if he'd like to. He gave Melissa a brief hug, got back in the plane, and proceeded with his trip home. It actually seemed lonely without someone in the plane with him, and this feeling of loneliness was amplified when he entered his empty house. So after putting his things away, he called Mary. She answered on the first ring and somewhat startled him.

"Hi, were you waiting for a call?" asked Price.

"Yes, yours," answered Mary. "But if you're wondering why I picked up so quickly, I was just getting off the phone with Melissa. She couldn't say enough good things about you and how cool it was to fly back to school with you and for her to fly the plane. Is it safe for her to take the controls?"

"Not to worry, there isn't anything she could do that would cause harm when I let her take control," answered Price. "It's not like driving a car. When the plane is at altitude and all trimmed up, it really needs little or no control inputs from the pilot. Besides, I can take back control in a split second, should that be necessary. Now if you hear I've let her land the plane, that's another matter."

"Well OK, if you say so," replied Mary. "The house feels empty without you guys around. I liked you being here…perhaps better said: I like being with you."

Price responded, "Me, too! After I dropped Melissa off, the rest of the flight was too quiet, despite the relief from her continuous talking. Then when I entered my house, it felt kind of lonely. I hope we'll be able to see each other again soon."

"How about this coming weekend?" said Mary. "You wouldn't have to stop and pick Melissa up, as she'll be staying at school for the weekend."

Price told her it sounded like a plan. They spoke for nearly an hour, when Mary again brought up wanting to help Price in his endeavor. They spoke some about Khan Industries and what his immediate plans were – which were elusive. They each said how they already missed one another, then they said goodnight.

Price's days were filled with many errands and chores that were neglected during his absence. On the one hand, it made the time fly by; on the other, Price's looking forward to seeing Mary on the weekend added an aspect of time not moving fast enough. Price spoke with Mary every evening. Just some small talk and sharing thoughts, but nothing about their budding romance, nor about business. It was mid-day Thursday when Price lost patience and didn't want to wait until evening to call, and he really didn't want to wait another 24 hours to see Mary. Price figured that if it was OK with Mary, he'd be there that evening.

This time, Mary not only didn't answer on the first ring, she didn't answer at all. Price was extremely disappointed. He left a message that he'd called. For the next hour, his imagination got the better of him, thinking of all kinds of nefarious reasons why Mary didn't answer the phone. He wondered if she was OK, whether she was screening calls and didn't want to speak with him, or whether she had other company. Fortunately for his sanity, Mary called back just a little over an hour from when he'd called and said she was out shopping. When Price asked if it would be OK for him to come down a day early, Mary exuberantly exclaimed how great that would be. She ended the call by saying she had a surprise for him.

Price once again packed, left a note for the housekeeper, locked up the house, and made his way to the airport. He got his plane ready to go, filed a flight plan, and then he was off. Price had to force himself to keep his mind on his flying, as he was so consumed by other thoughts that his mind wandered. Price wasn't entirely successful, and he almost caused himself a problem. He'd skipped reading the descent checklist and began losing altitude before he performed all the necessary steps, one being to richen the fuel mixture. Despite the placarded checklist right in front of him and the bright red knob on the mixture control, he neglected to follow procedure. Suddenly, the engine started to run rough and sounded like it was going to die. Price was just about to declare an emergency and trying to figure out where to land, when as he scanned the instruments for the tenth time in as many seconds, he realized his mistake. He pushed in the big red control, and the engine smoothed out. He was embarrassed and for the rest of the flight had no problem keeping his head in the game.

The rest of the flight was uneventful, but he felt he'd learned an important lesson. When he got into the vicinity of the Santa Barbara airport, he repeated what he'd done just a few days earlier; however, this time he did it without Melissa. Mary arrived to pick him up just a few minutes later. They embraced, and then Mary asked Price to drive them home.

Chapter 15

Getting Closer

It was like Price had never left, and they seemed to find so many things to speak about. When they reached the house, it was only 3:30 PM.

Price asked Mary, "What would you like to do this afternoon, and what about that surprise?"

Mary replied, "I think the surprise will be good this afternoon and consume us."

Price thought Mary was thinking "naughty" thoughts and decided to enter the game. "Your room or mine?"

"There'll be plenty of time for that later," answered Mary, smiling. "The surprise is different – you'll see. But first come here and give me a proper kiss."

They clung to each other and hungrily kissed, but before things got out of control Mary escaped Price's clutches and said, "Later. Now let's go sit in the family room – I have something to show you."

Feigning disappointment, Price proceeded into the family room and asked where he should sit for his surprise. Mary indicated a seat directly facing the big TV screen that hung on one of the walls. Mary promptly dimmed light and turned on the TV monitor.

Apparently, she had a presentation to make to Price. His curiosity was piqued.

Mary began. "In my earlier years, I was a researcher and analyst for law firms. You heard me say several times that I wanted to help you, so I decided to apply my experience to aiding you in your mission – I truly hope this helps."

With that, Mary began to paint a comprehensive story about Khan Industries. She not only had compiled facts and figures readily available on the Internet, but in just a few days they'd been thoroughly dissected and she pulled together an extremely comprehensive dossier. In addition, Mary had done a rigorous analysis of the company, pointing out inconsistencies and alternative assessments on how to reconcile the anomalies. Price was not only impressed by what she was able to do, he was equally intrigued by the substance and story she'd assembled.

"That is awesome," exclaimed Price. "I've only been gone four days…how could you have pulled this together so quickly and done such a comprehensive job?"

"A few all-nighters – that's all," answered Mary. "Remember, this is what I did before I became a full-time housewife and mother. If I must say so myself, I'm good at this. Besides, it was fun to reengage in my old trade, and it was especially rewarding to be doing it for you. This is my surprise. Do you like it?"

Price answered, "Truthfully, I don't know what to say. I'm impressed and flattered that you'd do this for me. Lastly, there's much here to chew on that at first blush seems to uphold my feeling that all is not right with Kahn Industries."

They began to discuss the contents of Mary's report and shared ideas on what it all meant. It was 9:00 PM when their stomachs started making hunger noises and they realized they'd missed normal dinner time. They didn't want to stop what they were doing, so they ordered take out and had it delivered. It was after midnight when, yawning, they declared the work day over and time to go to bed.

After a brief moment of awkwardness, Mary told Price she would come and see him shortly, if he'd like that. Price readied himself for bed, got under the covers, and waited for Mary; however, within less than a minute he'd fallen asleep. Somewhere in his subconscious, he sensed Mary getting into bed, but he didn't wake up. Mary was tired as well, and she too fell asleep quickly. They awoke hours later, finding themselves snuggled about as close as two people could get, and enjoying the sensation.

Not wanting to wake the other, they each remained perfectly still until Mary asked, "Dave, are you awake?"

Price replied in a sleep-filled voice, "I am and have been but didn't want to wake you or spoil the feeling of being so close to you. Sorry I fell asleep so quickly last night."

"That's quite all right," Mary replied. "We were both tired. Let's stay like this for a while longer."

They stayed snuggled close to each other, but instead of remaining still, they began to let their hands explore. Before long, they were gently and slowly making love to each other. Afterward, they held each other while their respiration resumed a normal rate, only to begin again. This time, they dozed off after making love. Price awoke sometime later to find the bed empty and the smell of coffee brewing in the air. He got out of bed, shaved, showered, and with his towel around his waist went into the kitchen.

"Well good morning, sleepy head," said Mary with a bright smile. "I've been up forever."

"No, you haven't," replied Price. "It's only 8 AM, and I last saw you at 7:15. Plus your hair is still wet from your shower."

"OK, so you caught me exaggerating," responded Mary. "What are you going to do about it?"

Price came over and gave her a big hug and kiss. Mary returned the kiss. They held onto each other for several moments before breaking apart.

"That was nice," said Mary. "Having you here is nice. What would you like for breakfast? We must keep up your strength. Why don't you finish getting dressed, and I'll make you something."

After breakfast, Price said, "I was really tired last night, so I'd like to review your analysis again regarding Khan Industries. It seemed very thorough, and I want to make sure I don't miss anything."

Mary began to review her story once again. Everywhere one looked, there were interesting anomalies. For example, there were daily food deliveries; enough to feed a small army. Yet, there were less than 20 employees on the books. Taxes alone far exceeded any apparent revenue, and that didn't account for normal operating costs of a complex this size. Then there was their stated product line, which was totally at odds with the facilities, security, and the power it consumed. While one could not say for certain Khan Industries was engaged in criminal activity, it was clear they were up to something other than what they acknowledged.

Mary completed her summary with, "To add to all of the mystery surrounding Khan Industries, there's the ship Ocean Commander, whose design and maybe even existence is totally at odds with Khan's published mission – and yes, it's owner is a fellow whose name is Khan. He, too, is a mystery, with little or nothing I could find regarding his background."

"Like I said last night, this is some awesome work, and while it doesn't provide answers, it does raise many questions I'd like to get answered," Price said. "I'm going to go back to Hawaii and see how many answers I can find. I'll also give Mike Mahoney a call and see what he can fill in regarding Khan. Thank you so much."

Price didn't notice the look of disappointment on Mary's face following his comment. They were off the subject of Khan Industries and planning how they should spend the day. They decided to do some more tourist type activities; however, Price's mind was going a mile a minute, trying to make sense of all Mary had told him, and Mary was disappointed that Price was seemingly cutting her out of his quest. It wasn't long into their touring that each detected the other wasn't really there in the moment and they were just going through the motions.

Mary was the first to speak up, "Dave, you seem preoccupied and not very into what we're doing. Would you like to go back to the house?"

"I'm sorry," replied Price. "I'm just a little overwhelmed by your report on Khan Industries and can't get it out of my mind; however, I also noticed you aren't as cheerful this morning as you usually are. I hope I haven't done anything wrong or that you're having second thoughts."

"No second thoughts here," said Mary. "However, to be perfectly honest, I was disappointed that after doing this report for you, you plan to pursue it alone and not include me. I want to be your full partner. I don't doubt how appreciative you are for the work I've done, but I can do more and want to share this with you."

"I'm really sorry I hurt your feelings," said Price. "I certainly didn't mean to. I just thought you wouldn't be interested in the pursuit, and I wouldn't want you to be harmed in any way – this could be dangerous. I don't know what I'd do if I lost someone else I care for…"

Price's last comment hung in mid air; the ghost of his lost wife and daughter never being far away. Yet, he had intense feelings for Mary.
Price continued, "No, I don't simply care for you; I think I'm in love with you and want you to be my full partner in life, but I thought possibly putting you in harm's way was something I needed to avoid."

There were tears in Mary's eyes when she said, "You should have asked and not assumed anything."

"Have I upset you further?" asked Price.

"No, I'm not upset," exclaimed Mary. "You just said you love me. These are words I never thought I'd hear again, and they echo the feelings I have for you. So these are tears of joy, not sadness."

Mary and Price hugged each other for a few moments, then proceeded home. That evening, Mary invited Price to sleep in her room – at least one ghost had been dealt with. In actuality, Price's ghosts were also becoming a cherished memory, not an impediment to living. Each of them felt their loving another was a testament to their past lives, not in any way a betrayal of it.

The next day, Price and Mary worked together to come up with a hypothesis that fit all they knew about Khan Industries. The plan was to then test the hypothesis to see if they could prove or disprove it. It took the better part of the day, and by the time they were done, each point had been much debated. They were tired, but pleased with what they'd come up with, and even happier with how they could work together. They could disagree without being disagreeable, and they truly listened to each other's views. Never did they hold on to their own arguments due to ego. If one or the other put forward a better suggestion, it was embraced, but not without debate. Both the outcome and their nascent partnership had made them happy.

Price called Mahoney to inquire about Khan, as well as to share the hypothesis they came up with. Price didn't plan to share his next steps or introduce Mary's involvement. Mahoney had to call him back.

"Mike, thanks for calling me back," said Price. "I wanted to fill you in on my latest thoughts regarding Khan Industries and see what you might be able to find out about its leader, a guy named Khan."

Price started by sharing the observables and inconsistencies Mary's report had identified. He then put forward his and Mary's hypothesis and detailed how it supported the observables. Mahoney only interrupted Price a few times to make sure he heard correctly. He didn't debate while Price told the story.

"Let me see if I've got this correct," stated Mahoney. "You believe Khan Industries to be the hub of all the issues I mentioned to you in Hawaii. You believe they got involved with illegal drugs, terrorism, piracy, weapons, and people trafficking in order to fund the development of an Internet hacking system of a capability and scope that's unprecedented. It has the capacity to handle all the world's Internet traffic, mine it for information, then use that information to harvest vast wealth."

"That's a good synopsis of what I think," said Price.

Mahoney responded, "Well, if they've completed the system and are now extracting vast sums of money using it, then why continue in these other much more dangerous criminal activities?"

Price answered, "I would suppose greed. These activities produce a great deal of money in their own right and will continue under someone's tutelage, even if Khan abandoned them. So I'd imagine Khan concludes better the money in his pocket than to just give it to others."

"I'll see what I can find out about Khan," said Mahoney. "What're you going to do next?"

Price responded, "Thanks. I knew I could count on you."

Mahoney said, "You didn't answer my question," but he was speaking to a dead line, as Price had hung up. He thought to himself, *Price's story sounded plausible, and therefore Price better be real careful in whatever he chooses to do next.*

Mary and Price made plans to head to Hawaii to follow up on their hypothesis and gather more data. Mary flew with Price back to his home, where they spent some more time planning and Price packing. From there ,they flew to Palo Alto Airport and paid a surprise visit to Melissa. They took Melissa out to dinner and back to her dorm, then spent the night in a local hotel. The next morning, they made their way to San Francisco Airport and flew to Hawaii.

Mary was quite impressed with Price's piloting skills and with flying in a small plane. She could now see why Melissa was so taken with it. Mary said she wanted to learn how to fly, and Price said it would be a good idea. He said he'd teach her the basics but that she really needed to go through a formal course of study with a certified flight instructor. He would arrange for it when they got back. Price couldn't help wondering if they actually would get back.

Chapter 16

Followed

The flight to Oahu was long but uneventful. Price and Mary spent much of the time speaking about a wide variety of things, except for Khan Industries. They were just enjoying being together. Price had arranged for a condo on the beach near where he'd submerged the submarine – near Khan Industries.

They spent the first two days acclimating to the time zone and doing what lovers do when they visit the islands. They toured, spent time at the beach, and made love. Someone watching them and seeing how much time they spent in their condo might have concluded they were exhausting themselves in the latter endeavor; however, truth be known, while they didn't skimp on time for physical intimacy, they actually spent a great deal of their time trying to come up with a plan on how to validate whether Khan Industries was actually the criminal enterprise they hypothesized it was.

After a couple of days and brainstorming, they still didn't have a plan. So, Price suggested they go see if the submarine was still where he left it and whether it was in good working order. They could at least do some surveillance and might come up with some lead to follow. First, however, they'd have to get through the net, board the sub, and then see if they could liberate it by getting through the harbor entrance when the net was opened to let some other craft in or out.

"I know I haven't mentioned it before, but I had to leave the submarine in Khan Industries' harbor," explained Price. "I got trapped in there when I followed a small cargo boat in. I secured the sub to an anchor at the harbor's entrance and swam out."

Mary responded, "Is there anything else you haven't told me?"

Sheepishly, Price replied, "Did I happen to mention I was visited by Khan Security when they found my scuba gear, which I'd buried near the harbor? Not to worry – I'll go get the submarine and meet up with you. No need to risk both of us getting caught. I'm pretty sure no one is going to get caught, but if they do, then the other person will still be free to try and help."

"So what's your plan?" asked Mary.

"Pretty simple," answered Price. "We'll get a boat and spend a day on the water. At some point you'll drop me off, and I'll swim to the harbor entrance, go through the net, activate the sub, and then wait for my chance when the net opens."

"You told me you have a remote control mode," said Mary. "Why don't the both of us sit just outside the harbor and wait until we see a boat passing through, and then bring the sub out to us?"

Price answered, "Ordinarily that would be a good idea, but it's been a while since I've been back to the boat and would feel better if I could check it out before I tried to exit."

They rented a day cruiser, some fishing gear, and scuba dive equipment. They concluded they should stay some distance from the harbor, for fear of calling attention to themselves. So, they also rented a propulsion system to help move the swimmer through the water. It was a nice day, and they were looking forward to enjoying the water.

They anchored offshore and some distance from the harbor entrance. Price donned his diving equipment, got in the water, and headed off towards the harbor using the propulsion system. It sure made it easy. When he got to the net, he carefully studied it before trying to go through. He didn't want to set off any alarms. It was lucky he looked, as he saw some wires he didn't think were there the last time. They were no doubt in response to the incident he'd caused when he was last there. Now the question was, what were these wires for, and what should he do about them?

Fortunately for Price, he didn't have to answer that question, since a boat was coming through and the nets were being opened. Price swam to where they were parting, and as soon as they were open enough to admit him, Price entered and made his way to the submarine. It was as he left it. He detached it from the anchor, then entered it through the airlock.

Once inside, he checked the various systems; all was in order. The only issue was that the battery state of charge was a bit lower than he'd left it and lower than he preferred, but there was no choice. Shortly after entering the sub, the nets closed once again, and this time he was trapped worse than the first time, since he couldn't swim out without setting off some sort of alarm. He'd just have to wait. Fortunately, he didn't have to wait too long, as another boat needed to traverse the harbor entrance. As quickly as he could, he made for the gates and followed the other boat out. Price reasoned the other boat's noise would cover his own should Khan Security be monitoring the sounds in the water.

Price made it through without incident, though it was good he acted quickly, as the nets were closed immediately after the other boat made it through the harbor entrance. Price decided to let the sub settle to the bottom and wait to see whether he'd inadvertently tripped any alarms. He waited on the bottom for nearly an hour, then decided he could leave. He'd been gone for several hours, and he was concerned about Mary and not wanting to cause her any undue angst.

Price cruised to where Mary and the boat were to have been, but they weren't there. He double checked his location, which he'd written down when he left. He didn't understand what had happened to Mary, and he was now worried. Price risked putting up the periscope, which had an antenna on it that he'd use to try to reach Mary. He called Mary's phone. With each ring, his anxiety grew. Then on the fourth ring, Mary answered.

"Hello, may I ask whose calling?" Mary said.

"This is Dave," Price said. "Where are you? Are you all right?"

Mary replied, "Absolutely! I was enjoying the sun and some fishing. But then my daughter Jane called and said we needed to speak. The connection wasn't great, so I decided to head in for the day. I was having a few issues, and this gentleman noticed and came over to help. He's currently towing me to the marina. His name is Henry. Will I see you tonight?"

Price responded, "Certainly, you'll see me. I should be back from my meeting in a couple of hours."

They hung up, and now Price was really worried. Mary was obviously transmitting a message that all was not well by using Melissa's middle name – smart if people checked her daughter out, they'd find the name Jane. They wouldn't necessarily know she never used it. Price wondered whether Henry was Officer Henry from Khan Security. Having Henry snooping around wasn't helpful, and quite possibly harmful. For example, he might note the missing dive gear and then start really leaning on Mary to explain its absence. Price wondered what had triggered an interest in their boat; however, first he needed a plan for the immediate timeframe, how to get back to Mary and have a plausible explanation for where he'd been, and where the missing dive gear was.

Price guided the submarine as fast as it could go toward a beach area near a business district in the downtown area. On the way, he called Mahoney and asked for a favor. He wanted a car whose registration wasn't tied to any government agency, nor to police of any kind. Mahoney gave him a rough time, but in the end he capitulated.

Mahoney put Price on hold and made a couple of calls, then returned and grudgingly said, "There's a garage right across from the Wayfarer Hotel. On the second level in spot 22 is a blue late model Ford. It's registered to a real estate developer named John Gardner. You can find the key under the left front wheel well in a magnetic container. This better be good."

Price responded, "Thank you. I really owe you this time. I'll explain it all real soon."

Price had clothes on board the submarine, and he placed them in a waterproof bag. He then donned his dive gear and exited the submarine off shore, where he put it on the bottom. There was a big rock nearby, and Price secured the sub to the rock. He then headed at full pace towards the beach. No one paid much attention to his arrival, and no more to his departure as he headed up the beach. He quickly rinsed off with the shower at the beach entrance and promptly went across the street, heading towards the parking garage.

The car with its key was right where Mahoney said it was. Price took a chance and stripped off his swim wear and promptly got dressed in the clothes he'd brought with him from the sub. He threw the dive gear and wet swimwear in the trunk and headed towards the marina.

On the way, he called Mary. "Hey, my meeting is finally over. I went and saw the site and am now heading your way from downtown. Are you still at the marina?"

Mary replied, "Yeah, we just pulled into the marina. I'll see you soon."

Price arrived a long twenty minutes later. Mary was sitting in the shade, speaking to a man; sure enough, it was Officer Henry. Price called one of the attendants over and gave them his keys and asked that they remove the dive gear from the trunk of the car, as he was returning it. He said it worked well and that he may need it again.

Price then turned his attention to Mary and her companion. He gave Mary a quick kiss and squeezed her hand reassuringly, then said, "Officer Henry, to what do we owe the pleasure of your company?"

Henry said, "Mrs. Dillon seemed to be having problems with her boat when I was passing by, so I lent her a hand and returned her to the marina. I thought the two of you left together this morning? Is that not true?"

Price responded, "Thanks so much for helping Mary out. It's much appreciated. Indeed I did help

Mary launch the boat, but she dropped me off with some dive gear at my car, which I then took to meet up with an associate."

Henry inquired, "Does your friend have a name? What was the nature of your meeting?"

Price replied, "I'm sure he has a name, but I'm not sure what business it is of yours. Also, our meeting was confidential and commercially sensitive. I'm afraid I can't speak about it with you. Now would you mind explaining your interest in my affairs?"

"Nothing," said Henry. "It's just a coincidence that we cross paths twice while I'm doing my job. I'll be leaving now. Do have a good rest of the day."

Henry left, and Price was about to ask Mary all that transpired when an attendant came up and told them they'd found what was wrong with the boat. Someone had put a radio-controlled switch that turned off all electric power on the boat. He couldn't explain how it got there, nor why someone would do such a thing.

Price thought he knew who and why; it was no accident that Officer Henry just seemed to come along at the right time. As they walked to the car, Price advised Mary not to say anything while they were in their condo and to be careful in all indoor places and their car, as they might be bugged.

They got into the car Price had borrowed, and he said, "Mary, are you OK? Do you want to go back home?"

Mary responded, "I'm a little shaken, but I kept my cool, and no, I want to stay with you. I'll be all right. Besides, it was exciting and also reinforced my feeling that Khan Industries is up to no good."

"I'm sorry I took so long to get back," replied Price. "I got trapped inside of the net, and they've added some protection against swimmers that wasn't there the last time. They really seem to be on high alert. Let's go downtown, return this car, and have some dinner before we go back to the condo."

"Sounds good, except I have no appropriate clothes to wear, and after a day on the water, I must look as mess," Mary said.

"You look wonderful," Price proclaimed. "However, I take your point. I know of just the place to remedy this. Excuse me, and I'll make you an appointment, as well as make reservations for dinner."

The place Price took Mary was a day spa and boutique. He dropped her off, then dropped off the car from exactly where he'd found it. Fortunately, it was no worse for wear. He then called a car service and arranged for them to pick him and Mary up after dinner to take them back to their condo. With that done, he stopped by a local men's shop and bought some clothes for him to wear that evening. He then went back to wait for Mary, but instead of just sitting there, he availed himself of the facilities, shaving, having a steam bath, and then a massage. Mary was finished right around when he was. Mary looked fabulous, which Price told her. Price felt great both from his spa treatments and being with Mary.

They both temporarily forgot about their quest and the events of the day and just enjoyed being with each other. There was much for them to speak about regarding their mission, but tonight was about them. When they arrived back at the condo, they got ready for bed, then fell into each other's arms and made love. It lasted for quite some time until, spent, they both fell into a sound sleep and didn't awake until late the next morning.

Mary started to speak. "I had a wonderful evening. It was perfect. Thank you. Now the question is…"

Price cut her off. "Let's not think about such things, and just revel in how wonderful an evening we had together."

Price looked at Mary and saw she understood. She'd forgotten about the possibility of bugs; however, that thought caused her to blush from fear that such listening devices might have also heard their lovemaking. The thought passed quickly, as Mary rationalized it away by saying to herself, "Who cares – they should be jealous."

They went for a walk on the beach. Now they were in earnest conversation about what to do next. They decided not to make things too easy for Officer Henry and his associates. They planned to change where they were staying, possibly moving to a hotel and changing rooms every couple of days. They would return their car rental. Lastly, they would go to different places to rent boats and dive gear, and try to do so without making reservations. The first order of business would be to resume surveillance on Khan Industries.

Mary insisted that she wished to join Price in the surveillance. He didn't want to be seen entering the water and have some *do-gooder* notice he didn't come back and alert someone, so he devised a plan. There would be no boat this time. Price entered the water where he wouldn't likely be noticed. His plan was to retrieve the sub and bring it to a place where Mary could readily reach it without drawing attention. He figured the best way to do this was with little to no dive gear, as that would just draw attention.

Price left Mary and proceeded to the sub. It took him a couple of tries to release the sub from its mooring, as he needed to surface and catch his breath. He then navigated to where he was going to meet Mary. She was watching for the tip of the periscope, which Price pushed just to the surface. Mary then proceeded to the sub and got in without incident, and Price headed out to sea. He needed to recharge the batteries, which by then were pretty low. With that accomplished, he made his way towards Khan's Harbor. They were almost there when Price noticed the Ocean Commander coming their way. He decided that in lieu of entering the harbor, he'd instead try to follow the ship and see what it was up to. He reasoned that he could avoid detection if he stayed within the ship's wake, using the its owns noises and turbulence to mask the sub's presence.

Price waited for the Ocean Commander to approach, then followed in its wake. He and Mary had been discussing what they would do, but it was inconclusive. So, they decided to play it by ear and respond to circumstances as they presented themselves. After about an hour, the Ocean Commander stopped. It dropped anchor, and the door in the bottom of its hull opened. Price and Mary both wondered, *Now what?*

Price ensured her they'd remain as invisible as possible, then dove to the bottom some distance away from the ship. There, they waited to see what would happen next. They didn't have to wait long. Lights came on, and a robot sub began to descend from the opening in the ship's bottom. Besides its own wires used for power and control, the robot also seemed to be hauling a thick cable.

When the robot got to the bottom, it attached the cable it was towing to it. This took some time, then it ascended back into the ship, which started to move. The ship was now letting out cable as it moved, and it appeared it was going to connect this point on the sea floor with their facilities back near the harbor. After the ship had sailed far enough away, Price went to more closely investigate the attachment point.

What they found was a junction box that had several cables tied into it, and the new cable was spliced to them. Price knew he needed to investigate this further. Before leaving the area, he got a good fix on the precise location. He and Mary then left to return to where they were staying. Before leaving the sub, Price searched the shoreline for a place where they could easily leave and enter the water without being noticed. He then moored the sub near there. The next day, they planned to see if they could follow the other cables emanating from the Khan harbor-side facilities.

They were careful not to be followed or observed. On at least one occasion, Price was pretty sure they were being followed. Price carefully checked their car for tracking beacons before they went anywhere. When he found one, he simply returned the car and got a new one.

Over the next couple of days, they managed to trace each of the cables to similar junction boxes, as they'd seen that first day. Indeed they found that every line coming out of Khan's facility was similarly terminated. This finding confirmed their initial supposition that Khan had a massive wiretap operation going of the major undersea cables. These cables carried virtually all of the communications that transited in and across the Pacific region; more than half the world.

With their new information in hand, Price knew it was time to speak with Mahoney again. He asked what Mahoney had learned about Khan Industries and its leader. It was precious little. Price supplied Mahoney with the coordinates for the junction boxes that were presumably tapped. When asked about how he knew this, Price just dodged the question.

It was clear to Price that he and Mary had done about as much as they could do in Hawaii. There was no chance they could gain access to the Khan facility, so they made plans to leave. Price offered Mary the opportunity to fly back while he took the sub, but she wouldn't hear of it and said she wanted to be with him.

They were distracted from their disappointment of not learning more by all they needed to do to prepare to leave. They packed and shipped most of their belongings, many of which they acquired on the trip, back to California, since there wasn't much room in the sub. Next they had to provision the sub without raising any interest in their activities. This proved quite challenging; first in obtaining the necessary stuff, and then in getting it covertly out to the sub.

On their last day before they planned to depart, there was just one more trip out to the sub. This was to refuel it, and it entailed renting a boat, going somewhere they wouldn't be observed, and transferring fuel from the boat to the sub. Price had done this before successfully and didn't expect any complications. This would have been the case again, except for the fact that their every action was being watched by Officer Henry and Khan Security.

The boat rental and refueling all took place without incident. The problem started the next day - the day they were to depart. Mary and Price were enjoying breakfast at a local favorite breakfast place when in walked Officer Henry. He headed straight for their table, making it clear this was no chance encounter.

Price said, "Good morning. To what do we owe the honor of your visit?"

Henry replied, "I heard you were checking out of the condo today. Is your holiday over?"

Price responded, "Our holiday has just begun; we're just changing venues. We thought we'd do some exploring."

"I had the sense this is what you were doing already," replied Henry. "Did you not find what you were looking for?"

"We've had a wonderful time," said Mary.

"I'm curious about some things, so I hope you don't mind if I ask," exclaimed Henry. Without giving Price or Mary a chance to respond, Henry proceeded. "Yesterday, you rented a boat and went somewhere – where did you go?"

"Not that it's any of your business, but we just sailed around, did some fishing, and checked out some coves," said Price. "Why do you ask?"

"Just curious," answered Henry. "Just strange that you left with a full fuel tank and returned six hours later with a virtually empty tank, but only showing less than two hours of engine time."

Price managed not to react and said, "I cannot explain what you say about the fuel, but we were not motoring around the entire time we were gone. We anchored for much of the time, fishing, swimming, and just enjoying the day. Besides, what makes you so interested in our activities?"

"Just curious," replied Henry. "There are other things that have piqued my interest in you two, but it's obvious you're not going to clear any of these things up, so I'll just drop them for now."

"What things?" said Mary.

"Oh, your comings and goings," replied Henry. "For example, there's no record of Price's arrival in Hawaii when I first met him. There's his 'stolen' scuba gear found out near our facility. There's your recent shopping, and various expeditions."

"I didn't know we were of such interest to you," stated Price. "You could have come with us. Next time we're in town, we'll look you up. Maybe you could arrange a tour of your facility."

Henry ignored this and said, "Have a nice day," then left.

Mary said, "It's good that we're getting out of here. Officer Henry is paying all too close attention to us."

"You've got that right," exclaimed Price. "With the level of detail he's been paying attention, I suspect he'll find our exit yet another question to add to his list."

"Should we be worried?" asked Mary.

"Concerned – yes," said Price. "Worried, I don't think so. Besides, if Mahoney acts on the information we provided to him, I'd suspect Officer Henry will be quite busy."

"I'm sure that'll be true," stated Mary. "But I just have a bad feeling."

"We just need to make our exit as covert as possible," said Price. "We don't want to be seen entering the water and then not showing up again. I believe the best way to do this will be at night. I can use the remote control of the sub to maneuver it close to the shore. We can head out on a walk along the water's edge. I can have the sub move parallel to us. When we're sure we're not being observed, we'll simply slip into the water and disappear. I'd rather do this in the light, but the darkness will help cover what we're doing. Unfortunately, this means we can take very little with us. Hopefully, this won't be a problem."

"No, all's good here," answered Mary. "We shipped most everything back, other than what we put on the sub already. I'll just have a small beach bag with whatever's left to take."

That evening, everything went as planned, and they made their exit. Price had noticed they were being followed, but as they proceeded along the coast away from the Khan facility and towards normal tourist haunts, the observers seemed to lose interest. Just to be on the safe side, they stopped in at a local bar and spent some time listening to the live band. They made several more stops before they found an isolated area where they could slip into the water unnoticed.

Chapter 17

Lost and Found

They cruised very casually, spending time on the surface as well as traveling submerged. This gave them lots of time to get to know each other better and relax. Neither Price nor Mary appreciated just how stressful their situation had been until they experienced the relative tranquility of cruising the open ocean. On their third day out, they decided they should find out what was going on. They established a satellite link and telephoned Mahoney.

Mahoney informed them that based upon the information Price had provided, he'd gotten a court order and went into the Khan facility. There, authorities had found a treasure trove of evidence of wrongdoing that spread around the world. Mahoney reluctantly acknowledged that Price's conjecture had been correct. Not only had they been tapping the Internet and using the information they gleaned for nefarious purposes, they also seemed to be running a criminal enterprise that encompassed much of the trafficking – people, illicit drugs, and weapons – that plagued the civilized world.

"The bad news is that Khan and his key staff got away before we could apprehend them," lamented Mahoney. "We believe someone tipped them off, and we're looking for who it might have been. It was likely someone down in the organization, since they didn't get much warning. Someone higher up knew about the impending raid much earlier. Our success in not giving them any advance warning is how we got all this evidence. By the way, we also found a huge stash of cash."

"Glad I could help," said Price. "It sounds like this should be a real feather in your cap."

Mahoney replied, "It would have been much better had we gotten Khan and his lieutenants. With them on the loose, these activities will just start up from another base of operations. Don't misunderstand me – this was a big deal and delivered them a major setback; however, their business is far too lucrative for them to simply walk away from. By the way, where are you calling from? I've been trying to reach you."

Price replied, "We'll be staying in touch, and glad we could be of service." He then terminated the call.

"Wow!" said Mary. "I didn't realize what a big deal our recent escapade was. It feels good to have done something against evil. I think I now have a better understanding of why you do what you do."

Just then one of the alerts went off, indicating their proximity to another craft. It startled both Mary and Price. After a moment, Price realized what it was and immediately checked his various sensors and used the periscope to scan the surface. There was nothing on the surface that he could see, but his indicators were showing something less than 1,000 yards away from them. Price concluded it must be a submarine of sorts and decided to see what he might learn about it. It didn't appear the other submarine had noticed them, but they were both headed more or less on a parallel course. Price decided to position his sub in the wake of the other sub, where they would be even less detectable.

After Price had explained what was going on, Mary said, "You do lead an exciting life. I've not had this much excitement – maybe never."

"I'm going to follow it, and perhaps get closer so we might see what we can learn," said Price.

Once directly behind the other sub, Price began to close the distance to it. He wasn't quite sure what he was looking for, but he liked the adventure. When he got closer, he was able to see what appeared to be one of those luxury submersible yachts. It was a far cry from his own very humble quarters, with sleek lines – and if he remembered correctly – quite fast and agile on the surface, but not beneath the water. Additionally, unless it was retrofitted, these craft didn't have very sophisticated underwater sensors, so Price felt relatively safe from discovery.

Price was enjoying his surreptitious surveillance of his prey. He was admiring its sleek design, which he could see better with every yard he got closer to it. Price was wondering why anyone would be travelling submerged with such a vessel, which could make much better time on the surface. He could only imagine the reason had to do with the desire to be covert. When

Price had gotten as close as he dared, he understood. There, painted on its stern was its name: Khan Avenger. This must be how Khan and his top staff had escaped.

Now the question was what to do about it. In speaking with Mary, Price's own feelings were affirmed that it was far more important to get these criminals captured than it was to maintain the secrecy of his own submarine; however, what Price decided to do was facilitate their capture, but not explicitly reveal how. The answer came to him when he discovered the remnants of an old fishing net drifting along. Price broke off his pursuit of the Avenger long enough to gather up the net using his robot arm. Price reasoned that if he could stop the vessel for a long enough period of time, he could direct the authorities to the ship's location, where they could apprehend its passengers.

Price's plan, as he explained it to Mary, entailed three steps: 1) attach the net to hull of the boat ahead of the propeller; 2) let the net foul the propeller and rudder; and 3) ensure the damage won't be easy to remedy. While dangerous, Price had a sound understanding of what he needed to do with respect to the first two steps, whereas the third was less clear. Price figured he'd play that one by ear. He realized the first step was really to get the "cavalry" on the way, so he placed another satellite call to Mahoney.

"Hey, it's me again," said Price.

"Twice in one day? To what do I owe this honor?" asked Mahoney.

Price provided a latitude and longitude, as well as a course heading and speed. He then said, "Have you got that? This is the location of your bad guys, but you need to come quickly."

Mahoney responded, "Hell, that's in the middle of the Pacific Ocean. How do you know this? I can't just direct ships and planes without substantial justification."

Price replied, "If you want the bad guys, you'll get some folks to that location pronto." With that, Price hung up.

Mary seemed very leery of Price's plan, as it involved some significant risk. Essentially, they would maneuver their sub underneath the other, and slightly ahead of it. Price, in diving gear, would exit the boat and secure the net to the Avenger. He would then release the net and let it foul the prop and rudder. Price would then survey the damage, help "improve" it, and then get back into their sub. Mary's job was to control their sub to account for any course or speed changes the Avenger might make. Price had given Mary instruction on the sub's operation and given her practice at every opportunity, but this called for true expertise and not just the limited skill she'd attained. It's not all that difficult but on the other hand this called for flawless execution.

"You're kidding – right?" exclaimed Mary. "That's the craziest plan I've ever heard of. I can think of so many things that could go wrong…"

Price cut in, "It's the only plan that can work. We have no weapons, they can outrun us on the surface, and the biggest risk I see is me getting sucked into their propeller. We can prevent that by tethering me to this sub."

"What about if you get tangled up in the net?" asked Mary.

"Obviously, I'll try to avoid that, but in addition I'll bring two knives with me, both of which I'll attach to my belt so I can't drop them," said Price.

"I can see there's no talking you out of this crazy stunt," said an exasperated Mary. "At least can we spend just a little time going through it in detail, to ensure we've taken as many precautions as we can?"

They spent the next few minutes going over the plan, making adjustments as they went along and trying to make it as safe as possible. Mary would be able to watch, so they developed some rudimentary hand signals. When they started to go over old ground for the third time, Price declared it was time. He donned his dive gear, fashioned a harness which he then connected a line to, and secured it to a fitting in the airlock. He was ready.

He'd already maneuvered the sub underneath and slightly ahead of the Avenger. Now it was Mary's turn to make sure they stayed in position. Mary needed to ensure vertical separation to preclude a collision and horizontal separation so Price didn't get too close to the

Avenger's propeller. Mary was a skilled seaman, but she didn't have much experience with this submarine, or any submarine for that matter. Under more favorable circumstances, they might have rehearsed the plan a few times; however, they had the circumstances they had and needed to make the best of them.

Right off the bat, there was a problem. Price was having trouble opening the airlock hatch, which was hinged on the forward facing side; this meant the current of water was holding the hatch closed. He'd have to stop, open the hatch, and then proceed. He picked up the phone in the airlock and told Mary what needed to be done. He banged a tool he found there on the hull to signify when she could resume speed and get back into position, then latched the hatch open; otherwise, the water flow would have shut it again.

Mary demonstrated her seamanship and did a great job getting back into position beneath and slightly forward of the Avenger. Now it was Price's turn. Getting out wasn't that difficult, but as soon as he was free, he had to grab onto the handholds with all of his might to keep from being sucked backward by the force of the water. Not only couldn't he allow himself to go backward, he actually had to move forward to free the netting from the robot arm. This proved torturous. Every muscle in his arms and legs was straining; however, in due course he made it to the robot arm, bracing himself against the bow of the sub. This gave his arms and legs a brief respite, but now his body was being pummeled by the current. He looked to where one of the cameras was and gave the thumbs up signal.

One of the lines connected to the netting looked to be in relatively good shape and was long enough for what he needed it for. It was also floating back in the slipstream. With some difficulty, Price was able to pull it in and make a loose coil of it. He then looked back at the Avenger with its sleek hull and tried to find where he might be able to secure the line to. There was nothing on the bottom he could see, then he noticed a large chrome eye protruding from the forward-most part of the keel, about halfway up the bow.

Price now needed to thread the line he'd just gathered through the opening and secure it. He let his tether out a little at a time, which brought him back towards the Avenger. When he was under the right spot, he secured his tether. Now he had to rise enough to reach the coupling, this took multiple tries. He was really being beat up by the water pounding into him, and his every muscle ached. Eventually, he managed to feed the line through the opening and tie it off. He then signaled Mary, who opened the jaws of the robot arm to release the net.

Some of the net released, but other parts got caught on the arm and other parts of the sub. Price made his way back down to the sub and one place at a time started to free the net. When he was done, it was blowing like a flag from the keel fitting its lead line was attached to. Price went to that fitting and started to let the line out, which let the net get ever closer to the propeller. When it was real close, it started to swirl in the vortex created by the propeller. Then it was in and around the propeller, wrapping itself tightly around the shaft and bringing the propeller to an unceremonious halt.

Mary was doing her job and immediately throttled back so Price could get to the site of the damage. The netting was all jammed up around the propeller and the rudder. Just as Price was inspecting it, the propeller made a feeble attempt to go into reverse. This only exacerbated the situation for the Avenger; however, Price wanted to leave nothing to chance. So, he took some of the floats on the net and pounded them as best he could in a way to wedge the rudder. Then for good measure, Price took a frayed piece of line and used it to clog the water intake. This last step would cause the engine to overheat.

Price was exhausted and just felt like taking a nap, but his elation at the success of his plan allowed him to make his way back to the sub. The trip was infinitely easier without the water current pummeling him. He was back and inside the airlock in just a few minutes. Shortly after that, he made it to the cockpit, where he hugged Mary and promptly collapsed.

Price didn't know how long he was out for, but when he came to Mary told him the Avenger had surfaced and deployed a sea anchor. She also said there was no sign of the cavalry yet. These words were barely out of her lips when a Coast Guard helicopter brought a boarding party to the Avenger. Several hours later a cutter showed up, put the Avenger in tow, and headed for San Diego. They followed for a while but decided the cutter and possibly other defenses might detect them, so they made a course for Price's home.

On the way, Price called Mahoney again and asked, "Did you get anyone to those coordinates I gave you? If you did, was it worth your while?"

"Damn you, Price, you keep doing things of enormous value, but I'm certain I don't want to know how, as it was no doubt unorthodox and likely illegal," said Mahoney.

Price just said, "You're welcome," and hung up.

Chapter 18

Surprise

The rest of their journey was uneventful. It gave them a good opportunity to relax, talk, and contemplate the future. Mary was surprised herself as to how exhilarated she was by their "adventure", as she put it. It also gave her a deep sense of doing something of value. While Price was driven to it by his feelings of inadequacy that resulted in his family's deaths, Mary just felt good doing something that would hopefully make the world a better place. Mary also liked the closeness and teamwork that supporting Price in his quest engendered. She gave very little consideration to the risks involved.

For the next several months, they took turns being at each other's houses and spending some time tooling around in the sub, looking to do good. They did encounter a couple of illicit drug shipments, which they promptly tipped the authorities to. They also interfered with a troublemaker's boat that seemed to be out harassing other boaters, but none of these had the impact for Mary she was looking for; however, despite her disappointment on this front, her feelings for Price intensified. This turned out to be mutual, and surprising himself, perhaps more than Mary, Price proposed matrimony.

He didn't do this in any ordinary fashion, but instead came up with a complex plan that included Mary's daughter Melissa, who was thrilled by the relationship and glad they were going to get married. Price bought concert tickets at the Shoreline Amphitheater in Mountain View, California, for Mary and Melissa to go to while he needed to be away. Price said they could have some special Mother–Daughter time. That night, a singer of Broadway fame was doing an evening of Broadway hits. Mary had once commented how much she liked the artist. The theater wasn't very far from Palo Alto, so it was easy for Melissa to get there from her school's dorm where she lived.

 Unbeknownst to Mary, Price actually knew the artist, as he'd once done him a huge favor, and secondly Price wasn't out of town. The concert proceeded along as normal. Just before the intermission, there was a song the artist said he wanted to enhance with some dramatic interpretation, and they sought an audience participant. Needless to say, it was rigged so Mary was picked. Melissa was there to ensure that her mother's natural shyness wouldn't keep her from going onstage. It took some persuasion, but she finally made her way onto the stage.

 The artist then said, "This song is about a couple that's deeply in love with each other who decide that getting married would be the best thing either of them could do. It comes from a show where these two people had been through a lot before meeting each other. When they met, they fell in love, but because of their past they'd been slow to let the relationship reach its full potential; however, one day each realized what the right answer for them was, but they remained tentative. In this scene, the man takes a chance and asks her to marry him. Got it? What's your name?"

"My name is Mary, but this doesn't seem like something I can do."

"You're right. We need a man...sir, how about you?" asked the artist, pointing at an octogenarian sitting in the front row. "What's your name?"

The elderly gentleman replied, "My name is Frank. I don't have to sing, do I?"

The artist replied, "No, you don't need to sing, but I do need you to put on some costume pieces. So please go backstage, where they'll help you out, as well as give you instructions for your important entrance. Now Mary, we've got a cape for you to put on, and then I'd like you to stand right here and keep facing the audience."

Mary complied, albeit with great apprehension. The orchestra started, and the artist began to sing. Out from the back of the stage came a man in an elaborate costume, but it was Price, not the Octogenarian. He came up behind Mary and gently put one hand on her shoulder. Mary looked very uncomfortable but kept facing forward, as she'd been told. The artist then mimed for the man to kneel down and propose. Price came around and kneeled in front of Mary, who wasn't looking at him. He took out a ring and in a loud voice amplified by the microphone he was wearing said, "Mary, will you marry me?"

Mary took a second to realize this was Price, not the old man, and that he'd just asked her to marry him. She looked up and saw that it was indeed her David. Her eyes filled with tears, and she could see that so were his. Mary said something no one could hear, so the singer came over and handed Mary the microphone and asked her to repeat what she'd just said. By now, Mary wasn't sufficiently composed to speak a full sentence, so she just said, "Yes!"

While Price slipped the ring on Mary's finger and they hugged, the artist explained to the audience what they'd just witnessed. All were applauding, and some had tears in their eyes, and then the announcer said there would be a 20-minute intermission. The stage lights went down, and the audience light brightened. The audience filed out, as did the orchestra. The artist walked by on the way off stage and said congratulations, but Mary and Price just stood there holding each other, looking into each other's eyes. Eventually, Melissa made her way on stage and broke the spell. Melissa, whose eye makeup had run, came up and hugged each of them and said how happy she was. Together, they left the stage. As they walked towards the exit, complete strangers from the audience congratulated them. Finally, they made it to the car Mary and Melissa had come in.

"Let's go out and celebrate," exclaimed Price.

"This night is for you guys, so why not drop me off at school?" said Melissa.

Price answered, "Don't be silly. Hopefully, you think of us as a family in the making, and today is a very important day – a new beginning for us all."

"I didn't think of it like that, and I feel very special that you're thinking like that," said Melissa.

Mary spoke up. "I agree with David. Besides, with you there I'll be less tempted to kill him for getting me up on that stage."

"Did I do something wrong?" asked Price with a grin.

"No, you did right, but I think my 15 minutes of fame are enough to last me a lifetime. A lifetime with you," said Mary. "I love you so much."

"Mom, if you don't mind, what did you answer Price when no one could hear?" asked Melissa after a short while.

Mary replied, "It's about time."

They all laughed, got in the car, and drove off. Mary and Price were real quiet, each remembering the past and contemplating the future. On the other hand, Melissa just kept asking questions about the future, the wedding, and the logistics of their lives together. She received few, if any, answers, and when she was answered, it was with only one or two words.

They had a great French dinner in downtown Palo Alto, dropped Melissa off at school, and then decided to get a room rather than make the drive. They hardly spoke. Their lovemaking was tender, and they fell asleep in each other's arms. When they awoke, they were both almost giddy with joy.

On the drive to Price's house, Mary said in a somewhat subdued way, "I think there's something we should discuss. I've wanted to bring it up but could never find the right time."

Price replied, "Uh oh, is the honeymoon already over – and we didn't even get to the wedding?"

Mary quickly responded, "No, it's not about us, the impending wedding, or our new family. As far as I'm concerned, that couldn't be better. Instead, it's about your quest."

"Are you saying you don't want me to do it?" asked Price.

"On the contrary, I think **we** should continue to pursue it in a methodical and aggressive manner," said Mary. "However, ever since we got back from our Hawaiian caper, as I think of it, we haven't really done anything that I feel has amounted to much. It really felt good to have helped close down the Khan operation. We made a difference. Since then, I don't feel we have. I want us to work towards making another significant mark in the war against crime."

"What about the drug busts we helped make happen?" asked Price.

Mary replied, "They were certainly better than nothing, but lacked the psychic reward I felt in the Khan operation."

"I can't disagree, but opportunities like those aren't always readily available," answered Price.

"I bet they are," said Mary. "It's a matter of finding them. It takes time and effort. All I'm saying is that we should set our objective and then take steps to implement it."

"I'll give Mahoney a call and see what problems he's working on," replied Price.

A couple of days later when returning home from a shopping trip, there was a big package waiting at the front door. Neither Mary nor Price had ordered anything, so they were curious as to what it was. When they brought it into the house, Price read the attached note aloud.

"I caught your marriage proposal on network TV news the other night. How nice for both of you. I'd lost track of you when you left, though I could never find evidence of you leaving. Just letting you know that I've not forgotten you. I hope my instincts are wrong about you, but if not, justice will be done. – Henry"

The package contained some pieces of the dive equipment Price had taken off and hidden as he was hastily getting away from the Khan facility.

He exclaimed, "Well, I guess Officer Henry wasn't onboard the Avenger when we facilitated its capture. We're going to need to keep an eye out for this guy. I'll bring this note up when I speak with Mahoney."

"Good idea," Mary replied. "He's somewhat scary, but some of his thugs are truly frightening."

Chapter 19

Honeymoon

Price called Mahoney the next day but had to leave a message, as Mike wasn't in the office. Early the following morning, the doorbell rang at 8 o'clock in the morning. Mary and Price were awake, but hardly in a state to entertain visitors.

"Who do you think that is?" asked Mary.

"I haven't a clue, but I don't think they're going to go away, so I'll go answer the door and find out," exclaimed Price.

Price was a little miffed by the interruption, as they both cherished the time together after a good night's sleep. This time together seemed to prepare them for the day ahead.

Price grabbed a robe and yelled, "I'm coming. Hold on just a moment."

When Price opened the door, he was confronted by none other than Mike Mahoney, who said, "Good morning – I hope I didn't wake you. Just returning your phone call. I was in the vicinity and thought I'd come in person, rather than calling."

"Well, I do want to speak with you," said Price. "I just wish you let us know you were going to stop by. Would you like some coffee?

"That would be nice," answered Mahoney.

"I'll make you some," said Price. "The newspaper should be out on the driveway. Make yourself at home while I go make myself more presentable."

Mahoney got the newspaper and sat and enjoyed his fresh brewed coffee while Price cleaned up and dressed. Price reappeared in just 15 minutes.

"I feel much better now," said Price.

"Well, you're not any better looking," joked Mahoney. "So what is it I can do for you?"

Price answered, "I was calling to see if you had any projects you need help with? However, since I decided to call, I received a package from the security chief at Khan Industries. It contained a veiled – or maybe not-so-veiled – threat regarding my potential involvement with what transpired in Hawaii. Can you tell me how that all went down, and in particular what you found at the coordinates I sent you? Did you arrest Khan?"

Mahoney gave him a top-level summary of all that went on and who they'd detained or arrested. Absent from the list was Khan and Officer Henry. They may have made their escape on the Avenger, but somehow they got off before the vessel was boarded. Price knew this meant they were picked up very shortly after escaping, since he had them under surveillance for quite some time; however, Price didn't want to get into this subject with Mahoney.

"Have you got a lead on them?" asked Price.

Mahoney replied, "We don't have a clue where they are, though it appears Henry must be in the Bay Area to have seen you on TV. What we do know is they continue to be behind a number of illicit activities and criminal enterprises."

"Unfortunately, you can't correctly conclude they're in the Bay Area, since that news footage went viral on the Internet and was seen all over the world," said Price. "Can you trace the origin of the package that was shipped to me?"

"That's easy," proclaimed Mahoney. "It should be on the shipper's website. If you have the shipping number, we can look it up now."

Price did and looked it up, seeing that it was shipped from San Francisco Airport. He remarked, "They could have dropped it there while in transit to somewhere else. They could be anywhere. We're no more knowledgeable than we were before."

"On the contrary, we know a day and time they were possibly at the airport," explained Mahoney. "This identification of a timeframe may narrow the search enough to make it practical to explore all of the camera footage using facial recognition software. I'm going to get some people right on that. I'll give you a call back if I get a hit."

They bid their farewells, and Price explained to Mary, "Khan and Henry weren't picked up when, thanks to us, the Avenger was intercepted. They don't know where they are, though there's a possibility they might get a lead on them by examining security footage at the San Francisco Airport around the time the package we just received was shipped."

"What are we going to do?" replied Mary. "While I'm not so naïve as to not know there are others, it would seem that shutting down these guys would go a long way towards fulfilling your, no call it our quest."

Price responded, "I can't disagree. Hopefully, Mahoney's search of the security footage will provide some clue."

It did the next day, when Mahoney called back and said, "We traced Khan and Henry through the airport, ultimately catching a flight to London. From there they caught a series of flights, ultimately ending up in the Greek Isles. Not sure which island they went to, but it's at least a start."

"So what more are you going to do?" asked Price.

"Not much," said Mahoney. "We'll put an alert out and wait and see what happens."

"How about if I try to find them?" asked Price.

"I can't stop you," said Mahoney, "but I can't directly support you either. What you do is so outside of accepted practices that I have to keep my distance; however, I can keep you filled in on what we learn if you keep in touch. I can also try to answer questions that might arise and follow up on leads that you suggest."

"So what else is new?" exclaimed Price. "I'll see what I can figure out, but I may need some help from you."

Mahoney replied, "I'll see what I can do. Just let me know what you need."

Later, Price said to Mary, "Hey honey, how would you like to honeymoon in the Greek Isles? The Mediterranean is beautiful this time of year."

Mary and Price spent the next several days making preparations for their trip. In addition to the trip logistics, they prepared their respective houses for a prolonged absence and paid a visit to Melissa. It was Melissa who suggested that if they were going to go on a honeymoon, they should probably get married first. So just before leaving, they legally got married. Melissa was the only guest. They vowed that when they returned, they would have a huge party for all of their friends, as well as a more traditional ceremony.

Melissa knew of some of their exploits and was therefore concerned for their well being. She said, "I'm going to hold you to this – you better come back."

Chapter 20

Island Villa

It wasn't long before the newlyweds had a fight. Price wanted to take the sub to the Med by himself while Mary took more conventional transportation; Mary wanted none of this and wanted to stay with Price. Price's last argument was that he needed Mary to go over and secure a secluded home with a dock and a good size boat.

Rather than fight, Mary decided to act and called Mahoney. She asked if he could make the arrangements they needed. When he agreed to secure the house and boat they needed, Mary simply went up to Price and said, "The house and boat are secured, so I'm coming with you."

That was it. The argument was over, and the next day they left together in the sub. This change in plan took some shifting around of cargo, but Price simply took some of it out of the sub and added it to the boxed up stuff that was to be shipped once there was an address to ship it to. Having been married before, he knew when to give up. To her credit, Mary didn't gloat over her victory and instead just dealt with the business at hand.

It took quite some time to get there, as it was a very long trip, no matter the route they took. Price left with some external fuel bladders that could be folded up and stowed once empty, and there was of course the renewable electricity, all of which were needed to allow them to make the voyage without needing to stop for fuel. There was a large supply of fresh fish, which they judiciously added to their freeze dried selections, and they had a reverse osmosis device to make fresh water from seawater. Despite all of this, it was still a challenging journey. Despite the circumstances, Mary and Price found it brought them closer together as a couple. Being alone at sea with no one to interrupt, having time for both their own thoughts, and ability to interact in total privacy at their leisure but on a frequent basis all contributed to this.

They made frequent contact with Mahoney, who was quite curious about where they were, but in the end he decided he really didn't want to know. A couple of days into the journey, Mahoney advised them of the house and boat he'd rented for them. Price made arrangements to have the shipments he'd prepared sent to that locale. He also set it as their destination in the navigation system.

On the day of their arrival, Mahoney advised them that Khan had a private island that was within 15 km of where their house was. Price and Mary decided to swing by and check it out on the way to where they would be staying. It turned out to be a relatively large island, with steep cliffs on three sides and a small harbor on the South side. A large yacht, a 40 foot sailboat, and several runabouts populated it. There was a very large house on a promontory overlooking the harbor. Adjacent to the harbor was a small beach.

"Looks like they got quite the place," said Mary.

Price responded, "Sure does. There'll be more time to explore it later, so why don't we go see what Mahoney got us?"

Price set course for their place, but before the sub came fully about, he noticed a patrol boat that seemed to be circling the island. Just over an hour and a half later, they arrived at their place. It was relatively isolated, but Price had no idea if anyone was on the property, so he didn't simply want to surface without first taking a look around.

"Do you feel like a swim?" Price asked Mary. "It looks like a lovely day."

Mary nodded, and they made their way to the airlock. On the way, they put on their swim suits. They surfaced and swam ashore. There was a small beach, and they left their gear there while they went up to explore the house. When they walked around to the front door, they noted a car just coming down the driveway. It was the groundskeeper who had been expecting them. He was bringing the keys and wanted to show them where their packages were stored.

The groundskeeper asked, "How did you get here? I don't see any vehicles."

Price answered, "We were dropped off and just decided to take a swim."

The groundskeeper let the matter drop and simply gave them a tour of the property and the house. He gave them the keys for the house and the boat. The boat was a 22 foot runabout with a small cuddy cabin. Before leaving, he left his contact information and said they could call him at any time should they have any issues. He explained that he lived just on the other side of the island but could get there relatively quickly. They thanked him, said goodbye, and the groundskeeper left.

Mary and Price were both impressed by the property. In fact, it was the perfect setting for a honeymoon. They spent the next couple of days familiarizing themselves with it and getting acclimated to being back on land and not in the confined space of the sub. The fresh air, bright sunshine, and ability to walk around felt exhilarating. They also dealt with some logistical matters, including unpacking what they'd shipped and refueling the sub. The latter proved easy to do, despite the boat that came with the property being gas-powered. Their property had a big diesel generator to provide power should utility power from the island fail. The quite sizeable tank for this was near the dock with plumbing out to the dock so it could be refilled from the water side of the property. Price took advantage of this. In the darkness of night, he surfaced the sub and with the onboard pump fueled directly from the generator's fuel tank.

While technically easy, explaining why the generator's fuel tank was so depleted would no doubt be another issue; however, he would save that for another day. This was one question he didn't need to seek out, as it would eventually find him. Besides, they had much more important things to do. So Mary and Price turned their attention to their mission.

Mary and Price were outside on the patio reading some information Mahoney had provided on Khan. They were so fully engaged in this and planning what they would do next that they were totally taken by surprise when they heard a noise coming from the house. Given what they'd been doing, this frightened both of them. Price had a gun on the sub, but a lot of good that would do them now. He decided that whoever was making the noise wasn't aware of them, so perhaps he would surprise them.

Price asked Mary to stay outside while he quietly made his way into the house. Despite his request, he found Mary right on his heels. They made their way into the kitchen and heard noise coming from the upstairs. Together, they proceeded to the staircase and climbed it as quietly as they could. At the top of the stairs, they turned towards the master bedroom, which seemed to be the source of the noise. They quietly approached the bedroom, and their adrenaline had their heart rates at near maximum as they rushed into the room.

Their sudden presence resulted in three frightened people: Mary, Price, and what appeared to be a housekeeper. The woman, who had been making their bed, screamed at their sudden appearance. Indeed it was the housekeeper, who was also the groundskeeper's wife. Fortunately, she spoke English. She explained that no one had answered when she'd knocked on the door, so she'd let herself in. Her job was to clean the house, keep it stocked with food, and cook if that was what the guests wanted. If not, she could at least find out what provisions the guests wanted. She would then do the shopping and bring the stuff on her next visit. Her planned visits were Monday, Wednesday, and Friday. She explained what foodstuffs she'd brought on speculation and asked if it was OK. Mary and Price were so relieved that their intruder wasn't a threat, but instead there to help them, they just laughed and said it was fine.

In the course of the discussion that ensued, Mary mentioned they were on their honeymoon. At this point, the housekeeper insisted upon cooking them some food, which they could heat up when they wanted to eat. She also mentioned there were some small restaurants on the other side of the island but that it was better for honeymooners to eat at home. She said she would take good care of them and could come on Tuesdays and Thursdays if they wished. Mary and Price said they would let her know but that for now she could stick with her 3 days/week schedule.

The housekeeper resumed her duties while Price and Mary returned to their planning; however, the fright they had kept them from being able to concentrate. They put their papers away and decided to have lunch.

They no sooner entered the kitchen than the housekeeper came in and asked what she could make them.

Mary said, "We surprised you before, so why don't you surprise us now?"

The housekeeper responded, "But I don't know your likes and dislikes."

Price replied, "We're very flexible eaters, and I'm sure anything you make will be wonderful."

"If you say so," said the housekeeper. "Then please get out of the kitchen and let me work, and I'll serve you out by the pool."

The lunch the housekeeper provided was wonderful, and they both enjoyed the home-cooked food, especially after eating mostly packaged food during their voyage. There was fresh baked bread, Mediterranean style chicken, a wonderful salad with all fresh vegetables, and finally a berry cobbler served with ice cream. They discussed with the housekeeper some rules of engagement so they wouldn't frighten each other again. Among other things these included sticking to a schedule and communicating any change in plans. Part of the rationale they provided was that they were honeymooners. The housekeeper smiled knowingly and agreed that she wouldn't let herself in except by prior agreement. She said she would pass the word on to her husband also. They agreed to a schedule, and the housekeeper left them.

CHAPTER 21

Fortress

From the documents they reviewed, it appeared Khan was still leading a vast criminal enterprise, but at least his large scale compromise of the Internet had been curtailed; the work Mary and Price had done in Hawaii had seen to that. While that had cost Khan a major loss in revenue, he still made billions in his other illicit trades.

Mary and Price decided to take a closer look at Khan's private island. The next day, they boarded the sub and headed to the island. Careful inspection revealed some subtle but significant defenses, including lights, radar, cameras, and sentries. There were likely dogs, too, as they noted pens but didn't see any dogs roaming; they probably saved them for at night. They also scanned the water's bottom in the cove that served as the islands' anchorage and docking area. There were no nets or extraordinary cables headed to sea, but it did appear that there was some sort of instrumentation submerged near the dock. While they didn't know what it was, they knew it would be best to avoid it and hope it hadn't already detected them.

"Had we not seen their last place, one would say this is quite an impregnable fortress," said Price.

Mary replied, "It sure seems that way. The only thing I didn't see was anti-aircraft gun emplacements, but I'm sure they have shoulder fired weapons."

"No doubt," responded Price. "I think for now we can enhance the picture of this place as gleaned from overhead imagery by adding in what we can see from ground level. While this won't do anything to bring Khan's criminal enterprise to a halt, it will improve knowledge of the place if and when it comes time to act."

Price and Mary spent the next several days painstakingly annotating imagery and maps with everything they could see. They also noted sentry schedules and in a less precise way captured the general rhythm of the island. This included general movements around the island and both the regular comings and goings of boats, presumably supplies, and ad hoc visits.

They concluded they'd learned about as much as they could and packaged up their work and sent it off to Mahoney.
Mary said, "I'm not sure what else there is to do here."

Price answered, "We need to get onto the island and get an even closer look."

Mary exclaimed, "That's crazy! With all those defenses, it's almost certain we'd get caught."

"Well, let's think on it some and see if there's a plan we can come up with," replied Price.

They spent the next couple of days brainstorming and debating different ideas; however, before they could come up with a plan, they needed to think through their objective. Was it just to gather more intelligence on the island's layout and defenses, or was it to take affirmative steps towards shutting down Khan's activities?

After several days, they concluded they wanted to do something to shut Khan down once and for all. They figured the best way to do this would be to reverse the tables and tap all of Khan's communications. The only question was how to do it. This took several more days of planning, then returning to the island to see if they noticed any changes.

CHAPTER 22

Indiscriminant Evil

Price and Mary decided they needed a small break, so they set off to the other side of their island one evening to try one of the restaurants the housekeeper had mentioned. They were enjoying their dinner when who should enter the restaurant than Officer Henry? At first he didn't notice them, but with his ever scanning eyes it didn't take long. It then took him another moment to recognize them, and he wasted no time coming over to their table.

"Well, what a coincidence to run into you a half a world away from our last encounter," said Henry.

"It's nice to see you," said Price. "What brings you to these parts?"

"I could ask you the same thing," responded Henry. "This is just too unlikely to be an accident."

Mary replied, "We're on our honeymoon. We got married."

"I guess I should say congratulations," said Henry, "however, I'm troubled that our paths keep crossing. Where are you staying? How long will you be here?"

Price answered, "On the other side of the island. How about you?"

Henry absently responded, "On another island. Perhaps you should visit for lunch some day. I'll get you an invitation and arrange for transportation."

After Henry left, Price said to Mary, "Well, that should make things a little more difficult."

"How so?" asked Mary.

"He already believes we may have been in some way connected to the bad luck they had in Hawaii, so he'll be more vigilant than ever," answered Price. "It wouldn't surprise me if he put us under surveillance."

In the days following that encounter, Price and Mary continued their research and made plans to do some reconnaissance on the island. It was mid-morning on the third day when a courier arrived with an invitation to join Khan for lunch the next day at his island. The courier was to await their reply. Despite their apprehension, they agreed and were told that a boat would come and get them at their dock at 11:30 AM the next day.

In response to the encounter with Officer Henry, several days earlier they'd taken any documentation they weren't using, as well as any hardware that wasn't consistent with being on holiday, and moved it aboard their sub as a precaution. They policed the house and property to make sure there wasn't anything that might tip their hand, and Price put some tell-tales in place that would reveal if someone had searched the premises. They finished a mere 30 minutes before the boat was to show up and barely had time to clean up and dress for their engagement.

At 11:30 AM sharp, an ocean racing type of boat showed up to get them. It was a beautiful, sleek craft of 39 feet in length, and it sounded powerful. The cockpit had two bucket seats in front and a bench seat with three positions in the rear. Price and Mary got in the rear seats, and the boat's captain and his mate sat in the front. It wasn't long before Price knew the boat not only sounded powerful, it was powerful and very fast. They got to Khan's dock in just under 15 minutes.

They'd just disembarked and were catching their breath from their exhilarating trip when Khan appeared.
"Hello, and welcome to my island," he said. "I hope the trip over was pleasant. Let's head up to the house, where I trust you'll find it more relaxing. I'll lead the way."

The house was spectacular and had a lovely poolside patio, where they were evidently going to sit and have lunch. The view took in the surrounding waters in all directions, except where it was blocked by the house; however, the house's location wasn't by happenstance, but instead was chosen to block the prevailing winds so the patio was in its lee. Price really wanted to get a look inside the house, but even when he asked for a restroom, he was pointed to a poolside cabana.

Mary and Price did the best they could to see as much as they could, but it was obvious they were being restricted to the outdoors. When they settled into some chairs prior to having lunch, Price asked, "Where's Officer Henry? I thought he might be here."

Khan replied, "He had something he needed to do for me, so he won't be able to join us."

Both Mary and Price looked at each other with the same thought in mind – namely he that was busy searching their house. Instead of voicing this, Price said, "Well, that's too bad, as we were just getting to know each other."

Khan played the good host, though he had many questions regarding the Prices, as they did of him. He dwelled on what their jobs were, what they were doing in Hawaii, and how they came to be in the Greek Isles. He also hinted at some of the mysteries Henry had voiced regarding their comings and goings in Hawaii. Price and Mary kept their responses superficial and consistent with what they'd told Henry before. Khan's responses to their inquiries weren't any more informative.

After having a sumptuous multi-course lunch, it was time to depart. In fact, Khan brought it to an end by stating he had matters he needed to attend to, though it did coincide with another boat arriving in his harbor.

By the time they reached their boat, however, there was no sign of who had been on the other boat. They bid their thanks and farewells and were on their way. The trip back was just as fast as the trip over. It was a far cry from the time it took them to make the same trip on the sub.

Price told Mary they shouldn't say anything in the house, in case it had been bugged. As they made their way up from the dock, Price started checking the tell-tales he'd planted; every one of them had been tripped, signifying that someone had made a very thorough search. While they'd been prepared for this, what greeted them inside the house came as a shock.

At the base of the stairs was their housekeeper, dead with a broken neck. It had all the appearances of an accident, where she'd fallen down the steps; unfortunately, both Price and Mary knew this was no accident. They'd forgotten she would be there and no doubt had walked in on Henry and/or his henchmen, who then needed to dispose of her. Price and Mary felt very sad about this and felt responsible. They knew Khan had ruined many people's lives - in the millions. Despite this being just one life, it was someone they knew, which took it from the abstract to something more real.

Price called the local authorities, who came out to the house and spent the rest of the day collecting evidence and questioning both Mary and Price. In the midst of this, the housekeeper's husband came. He was completely distraught, and the local doctor, who seconded as the medical examiner, was already there and needed to sedate him. The preliminary finding was that she'd tripped and fallen down the stairs; nonetheless, the authorities instructed Mary and Price not to leave the island without letting them know in advance.

Mary and Price had difficulty sleeping after this ordeal, but it did serve to strengthen their resolve to do something about Khan. It was also difficult to sleep knowing your home had been violated, not only by the death, but by the bugging that was likely put in place. They were careful in the conversations they had in the house, while at the same time they wanted to seem natural. The thought that they were being surveilled also curtailed their acting like true honeymooners. Fortunately, the death could also explain their loss of ardor.

Price spent the next day meticulously searching for surveillance devices, and his efforts didn't disappoint. There were both audio and video, and even his computer had a key logger installed. The question was what to do about these. If they got rid of them, Henry and Khan's interest in them would be piqued, whereas if they left them it would be difficult to function. The key logger was another matter. Price's real computer had been in the sub, so this computer was just there for appearances and to deal with matters consistent with their honeymoon story.

They decided to get rid of the bugs, but they wanted to do so in a manner where it would be plausible that the loss couldn't be attributed to them. Price came up with a plan. All the bugs were powered from house power with battery backup. What Price planned to do was generate a huge electrical spike into their house power the next time there was lightning. Henry might believe their house's power system had been hit and "fried" all of the devices. To add credibility to this, Price would leave the TV's plugged in and let them get fried, too. He would then get them repaired or replaced in as publicly visible a manner as possible. Hopefully, Henry would find out about this and reach the conclusion that the electrical system had gotten hit by lightning.

In actuality, it would be unlikely that all bugs would get "fried" by a spike in the electrical system. So, Price configured coils close to each device that would assure their destruction on command. The trickiest part was doing this while being under surveillance. Price found a way and was ready as soon as there was a lightning storm; he didn't have to wait too long. Right after the first hit that was close by, he triggered the pulse to kill the bugs. Coincident with this, power in the house went out momentarily and resumed when the generator started. The power grid actually had taken a hit, making it all the more credible that the storm had killed the bugs. Price visited each one to ensure it was indeed dead, and they all were. One TV was damaged, which was enough. Despite this, Mary and Price kept their conversations related to Khan in the privacy of the outdoors.

They made a big deal of finding the right TV to replace the damaged one, letting virtually everyone on the island know they'd been hit by lightning. When the new TV arrived, they checked it to see if it had been bugged; it hadn't. For the time being, they felt a little more secure in their house, but they were certain that while they thought of themselves as the hunters, they too were being hunted.

They went to the funeral for their housekeeper, which seemingly had every person on the island in attendance. They not only offered their sincere condolences to the groundskeeper, they also offered him their help. They suggested that when he was ready, he should come out to the house and they'd speak. He agreed, as this was neither the time nor place for such a discussion.

Time was passing them by, and they weren't making any progress in their pursuit of Khan. A few updated and new reports came their way from Mahoney, but they hadn't contributed anything themselves other than their possibly being a minor distraction to Khan's security. The question was what they could do and what the best way to affect it was.

A week after the funeral, the groundskeeper came by. He was quite subdued, as the unexpected loss of his wife had hit him quite hard. He hadn't come out to the house for help, but instead to resume some sort of normalcy to his life; however, when they began to speak with each other, it became clear he needed someone to talk to and see if he could make any sense of what happened.

Price and Mary spoke with him for about two hours. They treated him like a guest, serving him coffee and sandwiches, and not like an employee. When he left, he thanked them and asked if it would be OK to return on occasion. Price and Mary both said, "Anytime!"

Little did they expect when they made this gesture, it would be taken up with such fervor. The groundskeeper showed up almost daily, often bringing cakes, cheese, or other items, but mostly he wanted to talk. Both Mary and Price understood loss and were happy to do their part, but beyond that they liked the groundskeeper and actually looked forward to their conversations.

During the course of their conversation, the groundskeeper said a few things that piqued their interest. First, he spoke of his knowledge of the island Khan was on. In his youth, it was a place to take a girl to or go on a picnic with a group of friends. Later, he helped with some of the work when they were building the house there now. If he'd just blurted this out, Mary and Price would have been suspicious, but it was in response to a question they'd asked about the surrounding islands. Secondly, he noted there were a couple of strangers in town who'd been there since the funeral. He said he wasn't sure, but it seemed like they knew the people who visited from Khan's island to get supplies.

Price asked the groundskeeper, "Don't you get lots of visitors to these islands?"

The groundskeeper responded, "True, but these guys are different. They're not tourists – at least they don't behave like tourists, nor do they behave like artists."

Mary asked, "What do they do?"

"They speak to people around town, sometimes handing out money in return for answers to their questions," answered the groundskeeper.

"Do you know what sort of questions they're asking?" questioned Price.

The groundskeeper replied, "I don't have firsthand knowledge, but I think the questions are about you two."

This could mean not only were Price and Mary being watched by Khan's people, now there was a chance the entire island had eyes on them. This didn't make them feel in any imminent danger, at least not any more than they had before, but they'd need to be careful.

Mary and Price decided to take a short visit to town and see if they could see their rivals. They ran into the groundskeeper, who advised them that the men he'd spoken about were in the tavern. So, that was where Mary and Price went. When they entered the tavern, they let their eyes adjust, located the two men, who stood out due to their different attire, and then sat down at the table right next to them.

When Price caught their eye, he said, "Hi, haven't seen you two around before. Are you from here? My wife and I are on our honeymoon and staying in a house on the other side of the island."

The men looked exceedingly uncomfortable and said, "Good day, we've got an appointment right now and have to leave." They then hurried out of the tavern.

Price needed to pick up some things, and Mary wanted to see what some of the tourist shops had to offer, so they separated. Some minutes later, Price was coming out of a store when the two men confronted him. They forced him into an alley, where they wouldn't be seen from the street. It didn't appear they wanted to chat; instead, it was clear they were going to rough him up, or worse yet kill him. They were big men who looked quite fit and carried themselves with an agility that told Price this wasn't likely to turn out well for him.

One of the men grabbed Price from behind with incredible strength, and the other man lined up to hit him. Without really thinking about it, Price crashed his head back into his captor's face. He could hear the nose crush and the anguished cry as the grip let him go. He moved just enough such that the crashing punch coming his way was a glancing blow instead of a direct hit. It still felt like he'd been hit by a truck. If it had been a direct hit, no telling what damage might have occurred. Price was down on one knee waiting for the encore, when instead he heard a crash and a grunt and the other man toppled to the ground. When Price looked up, he saw the groundskeeper with a shovel in his hand that he'd just used to club Price's adversary.

Both men lay unconscious in the alley. Price thanked the groundskeeper and said they could speak later, but for now he should leave. He hadn't been seen, and it was best for him if he wouldn't get associated with this altercation. So he left. One of the things Price had bought was rope. He now put it to good use and hogtied each of his assailants. He then went through their pockets, but he only found their room key and cell phones. Price pushed the redial button on one of them and was rewarded by it being answered by the unmistakable voice of Officer Henry. Price hung up. There were no other numbers on the phone.

Price counted on the men not being discovered and unable to escape for at least a few minutes, so he took the opportunity to check out their rooms. There was nothing there to help, so he made his way back to the alley. The men were still there, and a bit groggy, but the hate in their eyes told Price all he needed to know; however, Price was not a murderer, so he flagged someone down in the street and asked them to get the police. While Price wasn't a murderer, he justified to himself that taking them out of the action for a while would be a smart move. So, he took the shovel that had been left behind and gave one a broken leg and the other some broken ribs and a broken arm.

When the police arrived, Mary was right behind them. She had a look of real relief when she spotted Price, seemingly unharmed, and the two thugs hogtied on the ground.

"What happened here?" said the elder of the two policemen in accented English. He already knew they were Americans from his interaction with Mary.

Price replied, "I came out of the store, and these two men who I don't know, but did say hello to in the tavern earlier, pushed me in the alley to assault me. I don't know what the motive was and didn't wait to find out."

"It sure looks like they were inept or picked on the wrong guy," said the younger officer. "Can you tell me who you are and how it could be you could singlehandedly defeat what would appear to be pretty strong guys?"

"Simple answer is luck," answered Price. "I do have to admit to a little training, but I acted quickly and went all out, which they obviously weren't expecting. I think they believed I was an easy mark to have fun with."

"I think it was far more than luck," the officer said. "Would you please run through exactly what happened?"

Price replied, "As I noted earlier, my wife and I sat at a table in the tavern right next to these fine, upstanding citizens. I tried to be friendly and said hello. They rebuffed us, saying they had to go. A short time later, my wife and I left the tavern and ran our respective errands. For example, I had some things to pick up, which included this rope I ultimately ended up using to tie them up with. When I exited this store over here, the two of them converged on me and forced me into this alley. This guy with the flat, bleeding nose came up behind me and held me while his partner readied to hit me. I smashed my head back, crushing his nose, at which point he let me go. His partner's punch, which would have done grave damage, partially missed since I moved once released. I kept moving and grabbed this shovel, first whacking the guy trying to hit me a few times, and then I whacked the guy whose nose I'd broken. With both of them down, I quickly tied them up and then sent for you."

"Despite your respective conditions, it would seem like you're the wronged party, so you're free to go," said the oldest of the officers. "We'll get them some medical attention and then see what we can learn from them."

Price thanked the officers and then left with Mary, who asked what happened. Price explained it was all as he'd stated, except it was the groundskeeper who'd whacked the guy trying to hit him. Price explained, "I told him to get out of there, as he hadn't been seen, and that we'd speak later."

"Good idea to not get him openly involved," said Mary. "Let's go home."

"Agreed. By the way, I also left out that I tried calling the last (and only) number in their cell phones, and you'd never guess who answered," said Price.

"Who?" asked Mary.

"Why, Officer Henry of course," responded Price. "Oh, almost forgot – I searched their rooms and found nothing."
Several hours later, just before nightfall, the groundskeeper showed up. He was very excited and spoke quickly, "They're gone!"

"Who's gone?" asked Price.

The groundskeeper replied, "Those men. The police got them to the hospital for treatment before they took them to jail. Next thing you know, they were gone. Someone, likely from the police or hospital staff, must have helped them."

"Very likely," said Price. "Khan couldn't stand to have them around being interrogated."

"Why do you say Khan?" inquired the groundskeeper. "What does he have to do with this? Is he that feller on that island I was speaking of – the one where I went as a kid?"

Mary and Price looked at each other, nodded, and decided to tell him the whole story, including the likely reason his wife was killed. The groundskeeper listened, trying to remain calm, but he was a pot ready to boil. Price didn't go so far as to reveal his submarine, but he did say the best way for them to exact revenge was to work together to bring Khan down.

When Price finished, the groundskeeper started pacing the room in a state of great agitation, shouting, "I'll kill him! I must leave now and go kill him."

Price attempted to calm him down, but he had to get the rage out of his system. Price finally decided to let him rant, and he'd only act if the groundskeeper actually tried to leave. As Price had hoped, the groundskeeper calmed down and was ready to listen again.

Price asked, "Are you ready to work with us to see to it he's put out of business and jailed for the rest of his natural life?"

The groundskeeper's response was short and to the point. "I want him dead!"

"If you step outside of the law to right a wrong, the irony is that the law will protect Khan," said Price. "Besides, crushing his criminal empire and having him incarcerated for life would be far greater punishment for someone like Khan. It would also have the added benefit of not messing up your own life."

"I know," said the groundskeeper, "but he took my precious wife away from me."

"I understand," said Price. "Do you think you can work with us? We could really use your help."

The groundskeeper nodded and said, "Yes!"

"Great!" exclaimed Price. "Now let's put a plan in place to shut this bastard down."

They concluded they needed to get on the island and see what they could learn. The groundskeeper's knowledge of the island was quite helpful. He identified how as kids they could get to the island and stay completely out of sight. Millions of years of the sea pummeling the island had left some notches and caves at certain points on its perimeter. Some of these were only out of the water at low tide, but there were some that remained out of the water during the entire day, though in some cases their entrances would be covered at the peak of high tide. One in particular was a long cave that went to the center of the island. It ended there in a hidden vertical chimney that went to the surface.

Their planning was interrupted by the police, who came to say that the two people who had attacked Price had escaped from the hospital, where they were receiving treatment while in custody. The police said it appeared as though they had help and cautioned Price to be careful.

The next day as they continued their planning, the police interrupted again, this time to say that the bodies of the two assailants had been discovered washed up on a beach. They were apparently trying to swim off the island and drowned; at least that was what the police had to say.

When the police left, Price said, "That's the dumbest theory I've ever heard. Who would ever try to swim off this island? Especially with the plethora of boats to steal that are available and mostly unlocked. I believe Khan facilitated their escape and then killed them so they couldn't talk, and as a message to others that failure is not an acceptable alternative."

"That's truly ruthless," said Mary, "but I think you're right. This will make the rest of his troops more vigilant, and therefore our job much harder to accomplish."

"We never counted on it being easy," replied Price.

CHAPTER 23

Won't Stand For This

Melissa was walking to class one morning from her dorm. A man approached her and rapidly flashed some form of credentials and said he needed to speak with her. She wasn't alarmed, as it was broad daylight, on a campus she felt secure on, and with many other students around. So she agreed, which was a big mistake, because as soon as they turned the corner, she felt a prick in her neck and instantly became woozy. Her last thought as she entered unconsciousness was what she'd been taught since being a young child – never speak to strangers.

Melissa's absence didn't alarm anyone for some 72 hours, since it was a weekend; however, when she still didn't show up where she belonged, the school reached out to her mother. Mary took the call while they were having dinner, and Price could see something was very wrong.

When she hung up, Price asked, "What's wrong?"

"Melissa is missing," answered Mary. "She hasn't been to class or her room and was last seen three days ago. Something's very wrong."

"What would you like to do?" asked Price.

"I don't know," said Mary, who then began to weep.

Price held her and said reassuring things, but in the end he said he would let Mahoney know to make certain the authorities were doing all they could.

"Let's go do what we came here to do," said Price. "It'll help keep us from fretting, which won't help anything. We'll reconnoiter the island by sub and validate what we've been told. I also want to take a careful look at underwater defenses."

They decided the best way to preserve the secret of the submarine was to leave the house on the boat, have the submarine follow via its remote control, then when they were away from land, they would anchor, post a diving buoy, and go into the water and enter the sub's airlock.

It was a beautiful day, and despite the gloom they felt regarding Melissa, the sun and sea helped provide temporary respite. It was so beautiful, they hated to go below the surface and leave the sunshine behind, but they had a job to do.

They cruised at periscope depth towards the island. One of the sub's sensors indicated a boat was approaching, so Price put the periscope on the screen and they had a look. It was one of Khan's boats. It was still a ways off and heading their way, which was in fact on their way to Khan's island. Price zoomed the periscope in to see what he could make out. What they both saw made their blood freeze.

On the back bench was a large canvas bag that looked like it contained a person.

"Are you thinking what I'm thinking?" Price asked.

"Yeah, but what can we do?" replied Mary.

Price thought for a moment, then said, "If we can stop the boat, we might be able to do something."

"We can't hurt my baby," cried Mary.

"They won't stop willingly. Not with a kidnap victim on board," said Price. "There's only two ways I can think to stop them: ram them, or foul their propellers. The first would be very dangerous for us, and the second would be a real long shot."

"We don't have time to analyze it, but I think the ram idea would be a loser," replied Mary. "How can we foul their propellers?"

"We'll take our lifeboats and string them together across the path of the boat. We'll use all the rope we have," said Price. "I'll inflate the boats to sit just below the surface. When their boat comes through, it should snag the rope connecting the life rafts and pull them and the rope into the propellers. Let's just try. We don't have time for a better plan. They'll be here in minutes."

Price hurriedly exited the sub, released the life rafts from their holders, and proceeded as quickly as he could to string them together and position them across the path of the speeding boat. If it stopped, Price would approach the boat and clog its water intake, which would cause the engines to overheat and quit. Then he'd have to figure out what to do next. He'd seen three men on the boat, in addition to what they believed was Melissa. First they had to snag the boat.

For a moment, it looked like the boat was changing course and would miss the trap, but then it turned and was now headed directly for it. Price remained outside the sub, which was proceeding slowly in the direction of Khan's island beyond the trap. As the boat approached, oblivious to what lay just below the waves, Price and Mary held their breath.

At first it appeared as though they'd missed, but then they each heard some noise and Price observed the rafts being pulled together. The question was whether they would get completely tangled in the prop. They got lucky, and the propellers got totally fouled by the two rafts and ropes. They were so tangled, it wasn't clear it could be fixed without removing the boat from the water. There was also a chance the shafts may have gotten bent.

Price couldn't celebrate their luck or the efficacy of their trap, as they'd only attained step one.

Price made his way to the boat and stuck a big wad of rags and putty into the water intake. It was now a little like the proverbial dog that chased the car – when you catch it, what do you do with it?

Mary watched the periscope and saw real confusion in the cockpit of the boat. No one seemed to know what to do. Finally, one of the men started to remove his clothes and was getting ready to get into the water. Mary had no way to warn Price, and she was now very frightened for him. While the man getting ready to enter the water from the swim platform at the back of the boat was bigger than Price, he was going in without dive gear.

Price anticipated someone entering the water and where they would come from. He hid just forward and beneath the swim platform. He couldn't believe his good fortune when he saw that the man coming into the water had no dive gear. As soon as the man was in the water, Price zapped him with what amounted to an underwater cattle prod. His body tensed, and he seemed to take in a vast quantity of water. He then began to sink to the bottom. One down, two to go.

Mary had no way to know what was going on, but when she didn't see the man resurface, she felt some relief. She felt even more when she saw Price approaching. He reentered the sub, removed his dive gear, and let out a big sigh.

"I think we need to sink the boat," said Price. "It's the only way I can think of to get to Melissa."

"How are you going to do that?" asked Mary.

"By removing its sea-cocks or drain plugs," replied Price. "I could make a hole in several ways, but that would make noise. I might also be able to dislodge the water inlet pipe from the hose that carries water to the engine."

"Does noise really matter at this point?" asked Mary.

"I just want them as unsuspecting as possible, to make it easier to sneak up and incapacitate them," answered Price. "However, you may be right. I'm going to get back out there and finish this."

"What can I do?" asked Mary. "Sitting, watching, and worrying isn't helping me or getting our Melissa back."

"I have it covered, and I don't want to have to worry about you while I'm dealing with these jokers," replied Price.

They hugged, then Price donned a fresh tank and exited the sub. He went to the boat and removed its drain plugs. He also stuck a rod he'd brought with him into the now plugged water intake. He was gratified when he felt it break through the rubber hose. He cleaned out the plug he'd put in it and immediately felt the water rushing in.

Mary could see the boat was going down stern first. She saw the two men put on life jackets and all but ignore their human cargo – her beloved Melissa. She couldn't stand the waiting and watching anymore and decided she needed to be there. By the time she put on the dive gear and swam to the boat, it was already awash to its gunwales in water. One man went over the stern. Price promptly dispatched him with the shock stick.

Price couldn't see that the other man was exiting from the port bow, which was opposite from where Price was. In fact, Price had his back to him. Fortunately, Mary was in perfect position and dispatched this thug with her shock stick. She then headed to the stern to rendezvous with Price, and then to get Melissa. Price, who hadn't yet seen her, sensed a presence and almost attacked her before he recognized her.

Together, they grabbed the bag Melissa was in. She was in drug-induced deep sleep. Price gathered some of the floating cushions and life jackets and helped Mary arrange them to help keep Melissa afloat. He then went aboard the submarine in order to surface it, as they couldn't take Melissa underwater yet and needed to get her aboard.

With the three of them aboard, Price submerged and headed back to where they'd anchored their boat. Melissa didn't look harmed, but she was drugged. Mary tended to her daughter, though truthfully it was really tending to herself so she could feel she was doing something; there wasn't much to do with Melissa just sound asleep.

When they arrived at the boat, everyone got aboard and they operated the submerged submarine by remote control for the rest of the journey. They arrived back at their house at dusk. They could see someone coming down from the house to meet them and instantly became frightened; however, it turned out to be the groundskeeper, so it wasn't a threat, but they didn't wish to share this latest escapade with him. So, Price promptly turned the groundskeeper around and headed back toward the house.

Price told him he'd like to go with the groundskeeper out to Khan's island the next day and asked that he show up at the house at dusk; they would go in the dark. The groundskeeper thought this was a wise choice, and one he was fully competent for. He was looking forward to it and excitedly left.

Melissa was beginning to come to when Price got back to the boat. When she was fully awake, they made sure she drank lots of fluids in an attempt to flush the drugs from her system. She didn't have much to share in terms of the abduction and subsequent travels. They drugged her and kept her drugged. Mary was incredibly grateful she hadn't been harmed, and for their luck in finding and rescuing her.

After dark, they brought Melissa up to the house and got her settled in one of the rooms. She was feeling better, but still not 100%. They decided to keep her presence a secret from everyone. Price let Mary know he was going with the groundskeeper out to Khan's island the following evening.

"I'm really beginning to question whether we can stand up to the evil this man represents," exclaimed Mary. "He kidnaps my baby, murders our housekeeper because she was in his way, kills his own men, and apparently is behind much of the crime that's blight on our world. How can we take him down?"

"I'm frightened, too," said Price, "but I'm more afraid of not taking him down. It was likely people working for him were being chased when my family was killed. There are no doubt countless other stories of misery he's caused. I must do what I can to rid the Earth of the evil he spreads."

"I know," cried Mary, "but my baby. How could he go after my baby?"

Price hugged her and said, "Putting him out of business will go a long way to making it safe for Melissa and millions of other people."

CHAPTER 24

Time to Go Home

The groundskeeper showed up promptly at dusk, then they boarded the boat and headed towards Khan's island. Price put fresh air tanks and dive gear for two on board. He also put night vision equipment on board. The only weapon on board was a shotgun, and of course their knives. As a special measure, Price decided to have the sub follow them in case he needed it, but he still kept it a secret.

The groundskeeper took the official maritime chart for the waters surrounding Khan's island and started to draw on them. He pointed out that the official survey didn't really capture all the features, especially the ones they were interested in. Price let the groundskeeper navigate, and it wasn't long before they were in sight of the island, approaching from the side opposite where the house was.

Price used the night vision scope to see what he could make out of the shoreline. He couldn't see any of the features the groundskeeper had put on the chart. They were running with their lights off, so as not to draw attention; however, when they got within a few hundred yards of the shore, a patrol boat appeared. It hailed them and demanded they immediately turn around and leave, because this was a private island.

They left somewhat disappointed that they hadn't accomplished what they'd set out to do; however, from Price's perspective they'd learned something important: they must be using radar to detect approaching boats from any direction. He would keep this in mind, as well as look for other intrusion sensors that might be in place. Price also now had an annotated chart that had the local knowledge not in the official version.

The next day, Price decided to take the submarine over to the island himself and do some reconnaissance. The trip was uneventful, and staying submerged kept radar from detecting his approach. He wondered if there were any other sensors on the ocean floor, but he didn't find any. Given that they didn't find him, Price concluded there must not be any – at least not where he was.

True to the chart the groundskeeper had marked up, he found the cove where the entrance to the cave was. Price anchored the sub on the bottom, put on dive gear, and exited the craft. Indeed, there was a cave right where the groundskeeper indicated. Now the question was, what security did it have, and did it really come up in the middle of the island just behind where the buildings started? Price decided to find out.

Price found no monitoring equipment protecting the cave. He wondered if they even knew of its existence. The cave rose out of the water, and Price took off his dive gear, hiding it behind some rocks. He then made it to the end on foot. At the end was a tall shaft. He surveyed the shaft for a way up. It wouldn't be easy, but he found some handholds and footholds he could use and began to climb. It was slow going, with the ever-present danger of falling; however, he made it to the top and once again stopped and checked for any alarm sensors. He also listened intently for any patrols.

He climbed out and stayed still for a long time, just listening. It seemed all was quiet, so he began reconnoitering. He saw a number of buildings, a generator, and some satellite dishes. He carefully noted their locations. One of the buildings appeared to be the central hub of his network. Price needed to get a better look.

Price approached this building, and indeed it was filled with computer equipment. He wanted to get inside. Being unsure of whether there were people inside or what alarms might exist, he decided to climb up onto the roof. There, he was greeted by a large skylight. He checked it for alarms and found none. He also didn't see anyone in the facility.

Price opened the skylight and entered. He climbed down and began an examination of the computer hardware. He then sat down at the console and used the monitor to peruse the network. His guess was right that this was the hub of Khan's operations worldwide, but there wasn't much he could do that would be anything other than a temporary inconvenience. Then he got an idea.

He quickly started typing in commands and had just finished when he heard some noise outside. He made sure the console was as he found it, then climbed back up to the skylight. There was a great deal more activity than there had been earlier. It appeared they were looking for something, or someone.

He climbed down from the roof and started to make his way back to the cave; however, the shaft was now being guarded. He remembered the groundskeeper describing other paths down to the sea, if he could only make it to the island's edge. It was extremely slow going, as there were patrols everywhere. Finally, Price made it to where he thought he needed to be, but the crevice and pathway weren't there. The patrols were converging on him, though fortunately for him they didn't know it.

He was desperately trying to find the trail the groundskeeper had told him about when just ahead of him he spotted a guard. Price quietly dove for cover and rolled twice to get further hidden. On the second roll, he dropped into a shallow dip whose existence had been hidden by weeds. He slid down, and pretty soon he was in what must have been the trail downward to the sea.

When he got to the water, he noted a patrol boat shining its spotlight over where the cave entrance was, but he was clear to get to the sub. Unfortunately, he'd have to do it in a free dive at night without absolute certainty of where the sub was, and without a mask to make seeing easier. On his first try he found nothing, but on his second he found the sub and was able to feel his way to the hatch. He attached a line to it, rose to the surface, took a deep breath, followed the line down, and entered the sub.

His trip back was uneventful, but it took quite a while for his heart to slow down. He just wondered whether he'd done any good. In the meantime, he used the voyage to plan what he needed to do next. With Khan "knowing" Melissa was missing, it would seem unnatural that her mother wouldn't eventually detect something was wrong and go home to check it out. Price, who'd already explained the kidnapping to Mahoney, would have to let him know they'd found and rescued her – without the details, of course. He'd then ask for a passport for her in some other name so she could travel back to the States. He would arrange travel for Mary and Melissa back home. He'd also arrange for security for them. Lastly, he'd make his way back to the States, as he no longer needed to be on the island.

When he arrived back home, Mary, who'd been quite anxious in his absence, greeted him with a ferocious hug. Price filled her in on his escapades, though he played down the more harrowing details. He told her of his plans for them to return home. Mary was really torn about leaving Price, but she knew Melissa needed her more.

Over the next several days, Price made preparations for everyone's departure. He refueled and restocked the submarine, rented a seaplane, which he'd use to fly the girls to where they could catch a flight home, and started to plan what he'd do when he arrived home.

Price and Mary were more than a little shocked when who should appear at their door than Officer Henry?

"What a surprise seeing you again," said Price. "What is it we can help you with?"

"Several nights ago, a boat like yours was running with its lights out near our island," responded Officer Henry. "Our patrol boat chased it off. You wouldn't know anything about this, would you? Then two nights ago, you'd never guess what I found: some diving gear that I think belongs to you. You seem to keep misplacing your gear; first in Hawaii, and now here."

Price replied, "I don't know anything about what you're saying. The last time we visited your island was as Mr. Khan's guest. We haven't even been close since."

Price stared Henry down, who ultimately looked away. Then Henry said, "I told you the last time, I have a bad feeling about you and I'm putting you on warning that we don't take trespassing lightly."

"Well, neither do we, and you're no longer welcome here, so leave and stop trespassing," said Price.

Henry glared at them one last time, then turned and left. When he was gone, Price said to Mary, "I'm glad we're getting out of here. The sooner we leave, the better."

Mary nodded and said, "Amen to that," then they resumed their preparations.

The plane Price had rented was delivered to their dock. Price checked it out and practiced several take offs and landing. The plane was in pristine condition, which was a pleasant surprise. The owner was also quite pleased with Price's flying skills and feeling much better about renting him the aircraft. He'd agreed to do so initially due to well over the market sum he was to get. In his view, the much needed extra money compensated for the risk; however, now seeing Price fly, the risk he'd imagined wasn't there.

The trick now was to get Melissa onto the plane without being seen. Ordinarily this wouldn't have been too difficult, but the groundskeeper came by to say goodbye to Mary. They were both growing impatient for him to leave, yet they felt bad because this man had suffered a loss somewhat on account of them. So they were as gracious as they could muster; however, when it became clear he planned on waving goodbye to them as they flew off, they needed to find some way to encourage the groundskeeper's departure.

Price said, "Thank you so much for coming by today. It means a lot to us. You've been a very big help. I promise you, those responsible for your wife's death will be punished. Now if you don't mind, I'd like a little private time with my wife before we leave, since once we get to the airport I won't be seeing her for a couple of weeks." Price gave him a little wink.

"Oh, pardon me," said the groundskeeper. "I must be on my way." He gave Mary a hug and wished her safe travels, then winked back and left.

When they were certain he was gone, they wheeled out Melissa on a cart covered with blankets; they weren't taking any chances of her being seen. They'd also changed her appearance to match her new papers for when she'd be seen at the airport and on the plane heading back to the United States. With the loss of the boat and crew, Khan could only believe she was lost, too, and that was how Price wanted to keep it.

Melissa boarded the plane and lay down in the back. They'd already loaded essential baggage for the trip home, so Price and Mary got into the plane. Price went through the checklist, and before long they made their takeoff run and were airborne. Price decided to make a small detour to take a look at Khan's island. A small shiver ran down his spine when he saw it, recalling his experience there, and he promptly turned on the heading to the airport.

The next part of the plan was one no one liked, but it was necessary. Price would land the plane down the coast from the airport. Melissa would go ashore and make her way on her own to the airport. She'd be doing so in her new identity. Mary would see her in the airport, but there, too, they didn't want any prying eyes to conclude this was indeed Melissa. Price had no doubt Khan had observers at the airport, some of whom may even be officials there. Melissa's appearance and papers were one thing, but they didn't want to connect her with Mary, which could undo the charade.

Price found a perfect place to let Melissa off. She left without much ceremony, though both Price and Mary now were more anxious than ever to be home. Melissa promptly went ashore carrying her backpack and headed off for the airport on the bicycle they'd brought with them for this purpose. When she'd left, Price took off again and contacted the airport for landing instructions. He made one 360 degree turn to see Melissa safely peddling her way towards the airport, then entered the landing pattern at the airport.

When Price was on final approach, he noted a large plane on the tarmac. As he got closer, he could see it said Khan Industries on its fuselage. This triggered an idea, but for now he needed to get Mary safely on her way home. Price taxied to the terminal and shut down the engines. He then retrieved Mary's luggage and bid her a safe journey. They hugged each other like they might not see each other again, both with tears in their eyes as they readied to part ways.

Price finally said, "I love you, and I'll be home real soon. You be safe, and take care of Melissa."

Mary replied, "I love you, too. Please be safe, and come home soon."

With that, Mary headed off to the check-in area. She wasn't there very long before she observed Melissa come into the terminal and head to check-in. She was grateful, not just that Melissa had made it to the airport safely, but that it didn't appear as though she was attracting any undue attention. Both of them made it through the formalities and headed for the departure gate. They each boarded without incident and were soon airborne.

In the meantime, Price wanted to get a closer look at the plane he'd seen. There wasn't any extraordinary security around the plane, so he was able to walk right up to it. He made a slight change in his plans and went back to where he'd parked his plane. He made arrangements for it to stay the night, then set off to find a hotel. After checking in, he went shopping and bought some dark clothes. He also bought a laptop and some other electronics. He brought these back to the hotel, as he had work to do.

At around 2 AM, Price went back to the airport and revisited Khan's plane. Price was very careful and used a night vision scope to look for any security he hadn't previously observed; there was none. With as much stealth as he could muster, he approached the plane, climbed the boarding stairs, opened the hatch, and entered it. He then waited to listen and see if he heard anything unusual. When he was certain he was alone, he went to work. He finished a couple of hours later and hurriedly exited as sunrise was approaching.

Price went back to the hotel, caught a couple of hours of sleep, took a shower, and then made his way back to the seaplane to return it to the house. When he got there, he felt very alone and couldn't wait to depart; however, he was tired enough to doze off and slept for some time. He was awakened by the sound of the seaplane being picked up right on schedule. It was now time for him to make his exit, which he did.

He boarded the submerged submarine and set a course home. It took several weeks to get there. It was a lonely time, though he did spend much time on the satellite phone speaking with Mary. They'd gotten home safely and were anxiously awaiting his return. Eventually, he got to his house. He unpacked and then flew down to Mary's house, where he surprised her; unfortunately, it also surprised her security team, which Price had forgotten about. However, despite the momentary issue this caused, everyone soon forgot it and was just happy to be together again.

PART TWO

CHAPTER 25

Next Steps

In the months that followed their return, Melissa went back to school and things pretty much returned to normal, other than the security they had in place for Melissa and themselves. Price knew not to become complacent. From the reports Mahoney had been providing, he knew Khan was still in business, and that business was flourishing.

Price was busy working on the other end of what he'd put in place in Khan's facility. What he'd done was route a copy of all incoming and outgoing message traffic to a drop box where he could go retrieve the data. He'd also installed a key logger to show, at least on the system terminal, what was being typed. He reasoned this could help him to break any encryption Khan might be using.

From Price's perspective, the good news was that he was getting all of Khan's data, and Khan seemed to be oblivious to it. The bad news was that there was so much data, and its encryption was proving more vexing than he'd hoped. Once he got past the encryption, he'd have to start mapping out Khan's criminal enterprise to make sense of the data. Then he'd figure out how to make the best use of the data.

By American legal standards, what he'd done was an illegal wiretap, and none of the information acquired could be used to make a case. In fact, Mahoney couldn't even know of its existence, as he'd be bound by law to shut it down. What Price planned was to feed tips to Mahoney and let him make his own case from there. Even an ill-begotten tip provides for a tainted case, but if Mahoney could build an independent case whose origin was plausible without a tip, it would be able to help unravel Khan and his criminal enterprise. Besides, Mahoney's story would simply be that he got an anonymous tip he followed up on, and he had no idea of how the information was obtained.

One of the other things Price accomplished while in Khan's lair was getting a dump of the programs Khan had on his system; therefore, Price knew what encryption was being employed, he just needed to break the key. The weak link in any system is the people who operate it, and it was just such a case that allowed him to break the encryption Khan was using.

To thwart brute force attacks on a code, one should limit its use; hence, the regular and frequent changing of the key. Apparently, this was too much bother for his staff, who sent out an announcement that they weren't changing the key to the next in the sequence for another ninety days. This was very valuable to know, but even more so was that they sent out a form to be filled out. Price knew this because of his key logger, but he also had the encrypted message. When responses started coming in, they included the forms whose structure and headings he knew. With all of this in hand, it was relatively straightforward to "break" the code.

Price and Mary now began the arduous task of mapping Khan's empire based on email traffic. Whether or not this source would permit answering all questions, it was clear it had the potential to answer most anything anyone could possibly want. Over the ensuing weeks, a picture of a global criminal enterprise began to emerge. In fact, the earlier suspicions Mahoney had informed Price of were just the tip of the iceberg. Now the question was how to make the best use of what they learned, plus their real time updates.

Price decided there was no way anyone could legally use all they'd amassed. They had the entire organization chart for the global enterprise. They had regional headquarters, front organizations, banks, PIN numbers, lawyers, contract help, shipping companies and the like around the world. They'd have to think of a way to make this useful. In the meantime, there were a few things they could do that wouldn't reveal that their communications had been compromised. They could disrupt some operations and really create havoc by stealing money from it and making it look as though the perpetrator was another regional boss. To do this, they'd affect a wire transfer from one bank account to one owned by another region, then they'd open up an account in the name of that regional boss and transfer the money to it. Price figured just about anyone could follow this money trail, and given their ruthlessness, explanations wouldn't be given much heed.

To keep Khan from looking outside of his organization for the source of his problems, they'd have to show some restraint in terms of numbers and maintain perfect security. One key to perfect security is to tell no one. So, Price and Mary would keep the money shifting just to themselves. From some of the messages they got, it appeared Khan was already having some issues with his regional head in Asia; hence, Price decided to make matters worse and have him be the first "thief".

It was frightening how easy it was to transfer $100M from Khan's bank to the regional head's bank, and then again to a private account. They had the passwords and account numbers, which made it a breeze. There were two names on the private account: the regional leader, and a company. After many cutouts and other security steps, the company was actually Price's. Upon hearing of the demise of Khan's region head for Asia, Price transferred the money to an account that was well hidden in the labyrinth of shell companies.

Unfortunately, this was just a drop in the bucket, with much more to go, but it was a start. It was also a start at undermining whatever trust and cohesion might exist in Khan's organization. Price decided to call Mahoney to initiate the next step in his program. Mahoney answered on the first ring.

"Hello, Mike," said Price. "How have things been going?"

Mahoney replied, "You didn't call me to check on my well-being, so please get to the point, as I'm really busy."

Price retorted, "You try to be friendly, and what do you get? Well, I wanted to pass along a couple of things I've picked up. First, that 'businessman' who was tortured and killed in Singapore a few days ago – the story was in all the papers – was an associate of Khan. You might want to work with the local authorities to see what you can learn. Secondly, if I were to pass along a rumor I picked up regarding something that was going to happen, would you be able to act on it?"

"Is it terrorism related?" asked Mahoney.

"No, but I believe you'd want to know," answered Price.

"That's not the issue," said Mahoney. "The question is, what I could do with the information? There's no question I could disrupt whatever it is, but depending on the circumstances, I may not be able to prosecute."

"Is there some better way to receive a tip than not?" asked Price.
"Anonymously speaking," stated Price.

"Wait!" said Mahoney. "It doesn't work like that."

"Then for now, let my first recommendation stand," said Price. "Thoroughly explore that person in Singapore. Look at their associates, businesses, and other assets, such as real estate, planes, and ships. Yes, I believe he was into shipping. You might find something of interest there, like not everything being transported is legit."

Mahoney interrupted, "Stop, that's enough. Perhaps the authorities in Singapore can develop leads which I can pursue."

Price decided this was going to be real difficult and slow going. When he got back home, he reviewed the latest messages and found one he felt he could do something about. There was a ship coming into the west coast carrying a bunch of people being smuggled into the United States. They would be transferred just offshore from the ship to a smaller craft, which would take them ashore. His plan was simple and would hopefully give the U.S. authorities all they needed to investigate and prosecute the case.

Price fashioned some hardware and set sail in the sub for the rendezvous site. He timed it so he'd be on station before the other boats arrived. Now all he needed to do was wait. At the appointed time, first the big cargo ship showed up, followed shortly thereafter by a large work boat. They didn't waste much time. First they tied the boats together, then they commenced transfer operations.

Price maneuvered the sub just beneath the surface and on the side of the workboat furthest from the ship. He then made his way out of the sub with the package he'd built. It was nothing more than a marine radio, batteries, and antenna packaged together. He attached it to the workboat above the waterline and made his way back to the sub.

When he got back to the sub, he noted that pandemonium had broken out. The radio he'd placed had started sending out a distress call on the guard band frequency. Given their location, he knew "help" wouldn't be far away. What he hadn't counted on was that the ship was monitoring the guard band and heard the signal as soon as it began. They didn't completely understand what was going on, but they also weren't going to wait around to find out. The ship's captain ordered all lines connecting them to be severed and that any of his 'cargo' that hadn't been transferred to be thrown into the sea.

Price watched this in horror and felt helpless; however, the crew of the U.S. Coast Guard helicopter was also horrified by what they saw, but they were anything other than helpless; they were also catching this on video. There was a cutter and two fast boats on their way to help. The helicopter ordered both boats to stand down and put some inflatable life rafts in the water for those thrown overboard. The crews of both boats knew when defeat was inevitable, so they did as instructed.

Price had one more task to do: he needed to release the radio from the boat and let it sink. He provided for this and merely had to push a button for it to detach and fall into the ocean. No sense leaving anomalies around that would be difficult to explain. In this case, the USCG was responding to a distress call and happened upon this human trafficking operation, which also included attempted murder.

Price was feeling proud of himself; however, to gain maximum benefit he needed Mahoney to know this USCG interdiction warranted a more thorough investigation. He felt the best way was to be straightforward – at least to a degree. So, he called Mahoney and mentioned the operation. Mahoney had not yet heard of it, but he said he'd make sure to go over everything with a fine toothed comb. Mahoney wondered how Price had heard about it so soon, but he decided he was better off not knowing.

Over the next several months, Price would transfer some money to discredit one of the mob's leaders, letting nature take its course and periodically finding some means to interdict some of Khan's operations. He knew this had to be putting some real strain on Khan's chief of security – Officer Henry; however, it wasn't until he saw an article describing the death of Henry that he realized just how effective his actions were.

One day as Price and Mary were reviewing recent intercepts, an opportunity presented itself that was almost too good to be true. The intercept had incredible detail on an operation of great significance to the Khan criminal enterprise and included everything one would need to know to understand its scope and how to destroy it.

"Dave, have you seen this?" asked an excited Mary. "The keys to Khan's kingdom are all here for the taking. What do you think?"

Price answered, "Yeah, it looks real good, but too good. It seems like just the kind of bait a new security chief might try to see if their recent 'bad luck' was the result of someone reading their mail."

"What makes you say that?" asked Mary. "A successful attack on this operation looks like it could take the entire enterprise down."

"That's what's wrong," answered Price. "The level of detail is out of character of all their previous communications. I think it's a trap, not so much to catch the perpetrator, but instead to see whether their communications are the source of their problems. I think we should ignore this and not act on it in any way."

"Yeah, but if you're wrong, we'll have missed a great opportunity," said Mary.

Price responded, "You're correct. If I'm wrong, we'll have missed a tremendous opportunity, but we'll be no worse off than we are today; however, if I'm right and we're caught, we'll lose the most powerful tool anyone has to ultimately bring Khan down. I'm sure you're familiar with the story of Coventry."

"I've heard of it," Mary said, "but remind me."

"Back in WWII, the Allies had cracked the Nazi code and thus were knowledgeable of many of their plans," said Price. "The Allies became aware through one such intercept that the Nazis were going to bomb the city of Coventry in England. With this heads up, they could evacuate the city and save many lives, but if their actions were discovered, the Nazis would know their communications had been penetrated. The agonizing decision was made not to evacuate and suffer the casualties, as they'd be far fewer than the lives being saved by sustaining the secrecy of the Allied penetration of the Nazis' communications."

"That's awful," said Mary. "What a tough decision."

Price said, "One part of the Coventry story I left out is that the Allies did take some steps to mitigate the impact of the raid, but only to the extent they felt it could be done without them being observed. Likewise, we can look at whether this was a real opportunity with aspects that can be exploited later on, but only to the extent that it doesn't reveal that someone is reading Khan's mail. I don't know what that might be, but we should give this some thought while making sure to err on the safe side."

It was tough for both of them to steer clear of the information they'd learned, but in the end they stayed totally away from it. Their reward – if you could call it such a thing – was that communications seemed to resume their normal character. Price and Mary resumed their activities after the brief hiatus, but they were exceptionally careful. They never again saw any of the individuals, places, or other specifics mentioned in what they now viewed as a bait communiqué. This led them to the conclusion that they'd acted correctly and didn't forego some wonderful opportunity.

CHAPTER 26

Vital Intercept

One day, Mahoney called Price. "What the hell have you been doing?"

Price coyly responded, "Hello, Mike. How are you? What specifically are you referring to?"

Mahoney replied, "I'm speaking about all the money you've been stashing around. You haven't decided to join the criminal world you vowed to destroy, have you? I might say it appears your friend Khan has some unrest in his organization and has recently had a spate of bad luck, but that's another discussion. What I want to know is, where is this money coming from?"

"Are you speaking about the $10,000 I deposited in an account in the Caymans?" asked Price.

Mahoney angrily replied, "Don't give me this crap. I don't care about your $10,000 – that's between you and the IRS. What I'm speaking about has four more zeros; hundreds of millions of dollars."

Price realized the precautions he'd taken were evidently not adequate to defeat the banking intelligence efforts that had been significantly strengthened post-2001, and Mahoney had him. He said, "Mike, we should meet."

Mahoney replied, "I'm a little worried about being seen with a felon – and make no mistake, that's what your actions constitute; however, for old time's sake, why don't I come out and meet you at your place? Does the day after tomorrow work?"

Price said, "That'll be fine," and then he hung up.

Price told Mary of the call. She was worried, but not ashamed of anything they'd done – in fact, she was proud of it and confident Mahoney would share this same viewpoint. Price was thinking about how best to address the information with Mahoney so as not to preclude future prosecution of Khan. After much deliberation, he concluded he'd play it by ear and take his lead from Mahoney.

In one respect, the time passed slowly for the both of them, but when Mahoney knocked on their door, it seemed like Price had just gotten off the phone with him. They exchanged a few social niceties, and then Price began.

"Mike, the money and the bad time Khan is having all relate back to Mary and myself. We're happy to share any and all with you, but not sure how much you want to know. I can start by saying we've done extensive research into Khan's organization and thoroughly understand it inside and out; however, I will caution you that some of the means, as well as how some of this knowledge has been used, would likely be problematic for you."

"Problematic for me?" asked Mahoney. "I think it's a real problem for you. Not counting the danger you put yourself in, you've no doubt broken more laws than I think I can account for in a week's time. On the other hand, if ever there was someone despicable enough to deserve it – Khan has to be the one. I guess I'm going to need to know everything, and then we can figure out what to do."

"Doesn't that incriminate you?" asked Price. "Doesn't that eliminate all our information from being used against Khan in future prosecutions? Are you sure you want to go there?"

Mahoney confirmed, so Price told him how he'd infiltrated and ultimately compromised Khan's communications. Mary added how they'd carefully mapped out his enterprise and used that information to selectively pit one element against another. She explained this involved misdirecting funds and that this was the source of the money. Price was less explicit about their use of tactical information but pointed out they got the USCG to come out and catch them in the act of human trafficking. For some reason, Price still didn't want to reveal the existence of his submarine.

They took a short lunch break, and then Mary walked Mahoney through their mapping of the organization. Mahoney was incredibly impressed, since his people only had about 20% of what the Prices were able to put together. Lastly, they mentioned the bait communiqué, and Mahoney commended them for their insight.

"So," said Price, "how do we proceed from here? If one weren't concerned by the rules of evidence, there's more than enough to shut Kahn down, but that's not the world you live in."

"Quite right," answered Mahoney. "I'll need to give this some careful thought. You guys have done a remarkable job and have already hurt Khan's activities; however, that's not the goal – we want to shut them down for good."

"Agreed," said Price. "Is there some way I could provide your people with 'anonymous' tips every now and then? Assuming I can, would you be able to ensure their being followed up on without tainting the case?"

"That would be pushing it," said Mahoney, "but I'll see what I can do. If it's only occasional, it shouldn't be much of a problem. I'm hesitant to do this, but let me instruct you on how to better hide the monies you've been taking. Right now, you're starting to set off alarm bells."

Mahoney provided them some thoughts on how to hide money, and then he was gone. In less than one week, communications in Khan's network changed, and some of it became unreadable. Price wondered whether Mahoney was in Khan's pocket and had tipped him off to what they were up to.

Price couldn't believe Mahoney was a bad guy, but something had sure changed, and he wasn't about to ask Mahoney about it; at least not yet. However, there were two things Price needed to do. The first was to reinforce their security. If Khan had been tipped, it was likely their identity went with it and they could potentially be in serious danger. Secondly, Price wanted to see what he could do about reestablishing their penetration of Khan's network.

Over the ensuing weeks, there were no attacks on them or evidence that the threat against them had increased. Price worked tirelessly to renew their compromise of Khan's communications, and all the while Price continued to contemplate Mahoney's guilt or innocence. A breakthrough came one day when Price was reviewing the results of the key logger he'd installed on the main console's terminal in Khan's data center. Silly as it might seem, the full instructions were there on all of the changes being made to secure their network. The original message had been sent out using a different network not visible to Price; however, one of the key nodes on the network was having some difficulties and came back asking for help. Fortunately for Price and his efforts, the operator had sent the reply in the manner he did. Now Price had all he needed to put his surveillance operation back in business. It seemed no matter how sophisticated a system might be, it was still only as good as its weakest link; in this case, the human operator.

Price decided to be extra cautious in his activities, so as not to give any reason for Khan's people to know their communications were still penetrated; however, he still needed to know whether Mahoney was a friend or foe. A possibility that occurred to Price was that Mahoney had provided some information to a colleague in order to get some help and that it was that colleague who was dirty, not Mahoney. The problem was how to test this hypothesis.

In the meantime, Khan's criminal enterprise was as busy as ever and involved in every evil thing imaginable. Price didn't act, but he kept detailed notes on all that transpired, perhaps for some future action. He was still trying to keep from revealing that Khan's communications were still compromised – that was, until the day Mary uncovered some message traffic indicating Khan was about to sell some nuclear material to a group of terrorists. When she brought this to Price's attention, they agreed they couldn't just stand by and watch this happen. They had to act.

It turned out to be relatively easy to interfere with the delivery, and perhaps in a way that would have it appear as nothing but an unfortunate accident. Khan's people would be bringing the nuclear material on board ship to just off the California coast. There, it would be met by the terrorists in a much smaller boat, which would then take it and bring it ashore. The material was radioactive, so it was in a very heavy shipping container. The ship would use a crane to lower it onto the boat deck. It wasn't clear at all whether the boat would be stable with this load and how it would be managed once reaching land. Khan's people couldn't care less, and once loading it onto the boat, they'd be getting away as fast as they could.

Armed with the date and location of the rendezvous, Price made plans to interdict the shipment. He wasn't certain of exactly what he'd do, but he felt confident he could stop it. He knew he needed to succeed. Price planned to wait until the transfer had been made to the smaller boat. He didn't want to tangle with the ship at all.

Price and Mary provisioned the sub and sailed out together with the plan to arrive at the rendezvous point a day early. They each felt the tenseness that came with anticipation of the mission ahead, but they also shared this time with renewed closeness of their relationship. In fact, much of their discussion wasn't about the mission, but instead about their hopes and dreams for the future.

They saw very few vessels in these waters, so when a large freighter approached the position, they knew it had to be the right ship. When they could read its name, it confirmed it – Khan Sojourner. It was a typical freighter of its size, except for the extraordinary amount of electronics it had, as evidenced by the number of antennas and radars that could be seen.

When it sailed right past the rendezvous point, Price and Mary wondered what was going on, but in short order the ship turned around and headed back. When it did the same thing, except now in the other direction, Price immediately knew they were beginning a search for anything above them, below them, or around them. To keep from being detected, Price maneuvered so he was just behind them in their wake, and of course he remained below the surface. The disturbances their own passage made, including their props, made detection in this location virtually impossible. While the sub was generally quiet and difficult to detect, Price decided the extra measure was worth it.

In a few hours, the ship slowed and drifted to the rendezvous point and slowly maneuvered around it. At that point, Price stopped the submarine and quietly waited. Shortly, a boat obviously not meant to carry freight – or do any work, for that matter – showed up on the scene and tied up to the freighter. A crane on the ship was maneuvered so its cargo would be directly over the deck of the small boat. The crane then turned away, hoisted a container from its hold, and then positioned itself to lower its load onto the deck of the smaller boat. At that point, it lowered the container that was obviously too big and too heavy for the small craft. Regardless, when it was done, the ship detached itself and immediately left without so much as a wave.

Price watched as the small boat wallowed in the swells. The load had nearly pushed it down such that water was up to its gunwales and the boat wasn't very stable. Things only got worse when an occasional wave hit it and added seawater to the weight in the boat; nonetheless, the terrorists who hadn't thought things out in the first place were showing their lack of seamanship, and it wasn't long before the decks were awash with water. Surprisingly, the boat remained level just sitting ever deeper into the water.

Eventually, the boat scuttled itself and went under. The terrorists abandoned ship, and consistent with their previously demonstrated expertise, did so without any life preservers or raft. Price thought to himself that at least this gene pool will be terminated. He watched the boat travel all the way to the bottom, where it landed intact in the upright position.

Mary said, "Well, that was easy. They did it for us."

Price responded, "I'm glad this is the caliber of adversary we're dealing with – though that's often not the case. Now let's go finish the job."

Price explained they needed to reposition the container so it couldn't be found should the bad guys come looking for it. In the end, Price decided to move the boat and its cargo from the vicinity of the rendezvous point. This way, it could appear as though the terrorists had made off with the goodies.

This proved to be a major undertaking that took a considerable amount of time to accomplish; however, the boat was now well away from its original resting place. Price then destroyed it to make it more difficult to detect. They then took the container with its nuclear cargo even further away and actually found a cave to put it in. The next day, Price and Mary closed the entrance to the cave and headed home triumphant.

They'd been gone several days and had been up for many hours, so they saved tidying up for another day and just headed up to bed. As Price and Mary headed off to dreamland, they each had thoughts as to how wonderfully this had turned out. They'd killed multiple birds with one stone, not the least of which was giving Khan another big problem to deal with.

CHAPTER 27

A Mole

Several times over the days and weeks that followed, Price took his plane and flew over the rendezvous area. He took pictures to capture the identity of the boats and ships that were scouring the area. He also noted when the efforts were seemingly abandoned.

Price was increasingly becoming agitated about how to learn Mahoney's status. He concluded the only approach was a direct one, so he made an appointment to meet Mahoney after his workday ended. Price arranged to meet Mahoney in a place where they could speak, which wouldn't raise any suspicions and where Price could be adequately defended, should it come to that.

Mahoney found the request for a meeting intriguing and was looking forward to it. Unbeknownst to Mahoney, he'd been followed while en route to the meeting. Price had a team on him to see if he was alone; however, there was another person following Mahoney, which fortunately Price's team easily detected and avoided, though they did take a picture, which they emailed to Price.

Just before Mahoney would have reached their meeting place, Price called him on his mobile phone.

"Mike, we have a very serious matter to discuss, and it's come to my attention you're being followed. Do you know about this?"

Mahoney replied, "No, this is a complete surprise. Are you sure?"

Price responded, "Take a look at the text I just sent you. Do they look familiar?"

A moment passed, then Mahoney said, "That's my number one assistant. His name is Bob Martin, and he joined me a few years ago."

Price asked Mahoney to take some steps to lose his tail and then head to the meeting place. He said he'd call if Mahoney wasn't successful in getting free. About an hour later, they were face to face.

Mahoney spoke first. "What's going on?"

Price responded, "That's what I was going to ask you, but for starters, after our last meeting, did you tell anyone any part of what we discussed? I ask because shortly after we met, Khan took extraordinary procedures to change his codes and communications protocols that ultimately shut down my operation."

Mahoney started to say no, but then realized he'd made some limited mention of a source with greater insight into Khan's operations than the government had and needing to figure out how to capitalize on it.

"Yes, I made some mention, but nothing explicit."

"Was it to Bob?" asked Price.

Mahoney nodded affirmatively. "I'm afraid it was."

Price responded, "With all due respect to your associates and vetting processes, I think you have a Khan informer in your midst; if not Bob, then someone else. It's critical to know, but in the meantime I'd suggest you keep everything we discuss just between us. Can you do that?"

"Of course I can do that," said Mahoney. "Furthermore, I'll do that until I can know whom I can trust. Now can you tell me what's going on?"

Price explained how he'd reestablished the penetration of Khan's communications network, though he didn't mention how. He then went on to mention the sale of nuclear material Khan had made to some terrorists and how they managed on their own to lose it at sea. Price still hung onto keeping his sub a secret, so his details about the nuclear episode remained sketchy. Mahoney wanted more details, but Price managed to dodge the matter. He did assure Mahoney the nuclear materials were safe, both environmentally and from getting into the wrong hands. Lastly, Price wanted to know where they went from there.

For his part, Mahoney was embarrassed by his top aide, Bob, being one of the bad guys, or at least being in cahoots with Khan. He was also troubled by the ongoing menace Khan posed, with no obvious way to legally shut him down, especially given all they knew.

Mahoney was approaching full despair when he had an inspiration. The pursuit of terrorists was largely exempt from many of the legal niceties that applied in other criminal investigations. What if they approached Khan's enterprise as a terrorist entity? Then perhaps they could use much of the data that had been collected. The challenge would be to legally establish the fact that Khan supported terrorism.

Mahoney and Price discussed this approach until they were both exhausted, but without much conclusion. They decided to call it a day, then resume their discussions the following day. They did agree not to do anything about Bob, as he could come in handy as a means of passing disinformation. Mahoney left, and Price continued to ponder the matter with Mary.

Mary, who'd intermittently been involved with the discussions, had been reviewing all they knew to see if there was something that could be done regarding the terrorist angle. Implicating Khan personally wasn't looking promising, as he had others do his dirty work for him. There was no evidence of Khan directing any of these activities, though there was little doubt he was responsible for them.

The next day proved no more productive. Short of entrapment, they couldn't come up with an angle. It was extremely frustrating. They had a mountain of evidence that was rock solid in implicating Khan in a variety of illegal activities. They had the means to discover and interdict Khan's illicit capers, and they knew where his ill-begotten monies were; all were no use.

Price recounted, "Let me see if I understand. None of the evidence is admissible in a U.S. court of law. None of the information we have can be used to trigger an investigation, as whatever evidence was developed would be tainted by how the investigation was undertaken. Lastly, if Khan could be classified as a terrorist, then one might be able to bring in the evidence we have as the rules change. Do I have it about right?"

Mahoney responded, "You got it! Sucks – doesn't it?"

Price replied, "Yeah, but there's got to be some other way. I'm thinking out loud here, so bear with me – What if we provoked Khan into committing a crime and then caught him? Not entrapment. Let's say we stole all of his money and he came after the perpetrator, in the course of which he kidnapped, assaulted, and even murdered. Would he be prosecutable on those crimes?"

Mahoney replied, "I believe so. What're you thinking?"

"Nothing yet," replied Price. "But it seems like he would be easy to provoke, and then the trick would be through legal means to catch his unlawful response."

Mahoney cautioned, "The other trick would be to stay alive should he figure out who's behind the provocation."

They all realized this was like poking a stick into a hornet's nest. It would be uncontrollable. The only certainty was that Khan wouldn't turn to the law to address his loss, but instead he would use what he knew best: ruthless violence. Then the question was how to catch Kahn committing his criminal reprisal.

After much talk, the beginnings of a plan started to take shape. They would target Khan's assets worldwide, but do so in a manner such that his reprisals would be in the United States. This was the jurisdiction that would be in the States. They would seek to undermine any trust Khan might have in others within his organization. Lastly, they would try to provoke at least one response from Khan that they could legally catch him at and use that to leverage other investigations, and ultimately prosecutions, which would put him out of circulation for a long time.

CHAPTER 28

Got You

A challenge for Mahoney was to do what needed to be done without his "trusted" aide Bob getting wind of it. On the other hand, Bob had a key role to play in that he would provide the disinformation to Khan that would guide Khan's responses. This all required careful choreographing, which was why Mahoney, Price, and Mary spent a great deal of time orchestrating the entire plan.

The plan started off not being that different than what Price had been doing before. He raided Khan's accounts and transferred money to an account managed by one of Khan's trusted lieutenants; however, they then transferred the money to a new account they set up for Khan instead of taking the money and putting it into one of their own accounts. Mahoney provided an information trail to Bob that this lieutenant had created the account in Khan's name to set him up.

One might have felt bad for the lieutenant, since he hadn't done anything to Khan but were about to be punished in the severest way; however, in this case Price felt not even the slightest twinge of remorse. In this small world in which we live, Price had learned this lieutenant was none other than the criminal the police car was chasing so many years ago, when it went out of control and killed Price's family. Like so many other criminals, he was eventually captured and put in jail; however, jail didn't rehabilitate him, instead serving as a finishing school that enhanced his criminal abilities. Then due to overcrowding, he received an early release from prison. Khan's organization offered him a job, and with his newly polished skills and the ruthlessness he already possessed, he rose in the ranks, ultimately becoming a trusted lieutenant of Khan. When Price had seen the name on the organization chart they'd put together, he knew their plan should include this bastard as part of it. So not only did Price not feel any guilt about this aspect of their plan, but in fact he felt justice would be served.

Khan acted with a speed and ferocity that even surprised Price and Mahoney. Khan had the lieutenant brought to him, where he was evidently tortured. A body was found in the waters not far from Khan's island. It was unrecognizable, but they got DNA samples to validate the corpse's identity. The next thing that happened was where Khan made a mistake. He took the money in the account and illegally transferred it out of the United States. The account was already being watched, because it triggered attention when it was set up due to its size. Now transferring the money triggered yet a next level response, which both froze the asset and put a warrant out for Khan's arrest.

Khan wasn't particularly worried about imminent arrest, as the crime wasn't serious enough where he could be extradited back to the United States. This was where Bob came in handy again. This time, they let it leak that the FBI was going to go and rendition Khan back to the United States; in essence, they would kidnap him. They even went so far as to let Bob figure out exactly when this was to take place.

As though Khan were right on script, he had his airplane readied to take him away from his current lair to his next center of operations, which was going to be in South America. Their flight path left Europe and would then cross the Atlantic and fly just east of the United States east coast, continuing heading south to their ultimate destination. Khan was smugly satisfied that he'd taken the right steps and was enjoying what was thus far a smooth and uneventful flight. Plus, Khan thought a periodic change of venue was a good thing.

When the flight was just off the Massachusetts coastline, Khan's flight crew detected the first signs of something being wrong. The plane seemed to change course unilaterally and wouldn't accept any course correction, even when they tried to fly the plane manually. After realizing there was nothing they could do, they went and advised Khan of the problem.

Khan flew into a rage, which resulted in his shooting the co-pilot and threatening that the pilot was next if he couldn't correct the problem. Interestingly, Khan never considered the consequence of who would fly the plane if he killed the crew. The pilot hurried back to the cockpit but needn't have done so, as there was nothing he could do.

Price was flying the plane remotely, having installed the necessary stuff when he'd boarded the plane before heading back to the United States. Price was now aboard a government small jet that was above and slightly behind Khan's plane. He was controlling its every maneuver and currently directing it to land at Andrews Air Force Base in the Maryland suburbs, just outside of Washington, D.C.

On board Khan's plane, the pilot could only sit and watch, although as they entered the approach, the pilot couldn't help himself from responding to the controllers, as he'd been trained to do. It also helped to take his mind off what waited for him on the other side of the door, which thankfully was locked, bulletproof, and otherwise reinforced. The pilot was impressed by how smooth of a landing they made and instinctively began taxiing the aircraft as directed.

The plane carrying Price landed a few minutes later, but not before Price could see Khan's plane come to a halt and be surrounded by heavily armed personnel. As it turned out, Khan knew when to fight and when not to, and this was a circumstance to accept tactical defeat. Everyone on the plane was taken into custody and separated from one another.

The stories varied widely on how the co-pilot was shot and who did it. They hadn't had time to concoct a story for all to tell. The pilot told what really happened, while others had various tales of the co-pilot going berserk and needing to be subdued. With the exception of the pilot's version, each story had a different killer of the co-pilot, none of which were Khan. Unfortunately for Khan, the only story that remotely correlated with the forensic evidence was the true one; the one that implicated Khan directly. Khan was subsequently indicted for murder and the more minor currency violation. He was put in jail pending trial.

In the course of trial preparation, the prosecution was able, with just a little unofficial help from Mahoney, to unravel most if not all of Khan's criminal enterprise. Other arrests were made, assets confiscated, and additional charges made, not the least of which was tax evasion. Trials were scheduled for the various charges. Conviction on any of the charges would lead to Kahn spending the rest of his days in jail.

Surprisingly, Price didn't pay that much attention to the trials once they began, and Khan's effort to plea bargain by providing evidence against his lieutenants failed. The trials took place, and Price's life took a less exciting, but satisfying direction. Price felt he could finally close out the lingering previous chapter of his life and start enjoying the new one. The Prices had a proper honeymoon, and they both enjoyed normalcy returning to their lives. Price continued to tinker and consult, but he also had time to be a husband, and even a father figure for Melissa.

One day while reading the newspaper at breakfast, Price noted that Khan had been convicted and sentenced to 100 years in jail; however, while one might have expected someone like Khan to be sent to a super-max ultra high security facility, he was sent to the federal prison near Santa Barbara. It was located on a bluff above the Pacific Ocean, not too far from where

Price lived. Price read with greater interest some of the side articles related to the violent struggles within Khan's former enterprise to fill the power vacuum left by Khan's incarceration. While there were no assets remaining, there was still a lucrative business in crime, and people fought over territory and virtual franchises for different criminal activities. The lack of coherent leadership and internal struggles resulted in the enterprise being weakened and its activities being a mere shadow of what they once were. Price took satisfaction from this, which allowed him to move forward.

CHAPTER 29

Quid Pro Quo

Khan tried to restart and run his empire from prison, but he found that he had as many enemies as friends and needed to worry about his own survival first. He also had no lieutenants to turn to. Between those he'd eliminated and those lost in the takeover struggles since his incarceration, there wasn't much left. Despite his past wealth, he had access to very little money, so he was limited in what he could buy. He needed to get out of prison.

Escape became Khan's obsession. He thought about it day and night. He started capturing a wide array of observations in meticulous detail. These included detailed drawings of the prison's layout, guard schedules, procedures followed in response to different issues, details he could see of the land beyond the prison – particularly the cliff to the ocean – the schedule of the train that ran along the coast, and others. Khan hoped from all of this information he'd be able to synthesize a means of escape; yet, a viable plan was remaining elusive.

For Mahoney, cleaning up the enterprise was going OK, but not as well as expected. It was certainly true it lacked the might it once had, and traditional law enforcement efforts were being far more successful; however, Mahoney wanted to completely eradicate this scourge on humanity and had yet to accomplish this. Ironically, Mahoney concluded he needed Khan's help if he were to attain his goal. When this thought first came to him, Mahoney dismissed it as crazy; however, of late, Mahoney started to embrace the concept. Mahoney did wonder what he was willing to offer Khan that might be of sufficient interest to Khan for him to provide his help.

Mahoney was stuck on the quid pro quo issue, while obsessing over the eradication of the remnants of Khan's enterprise. So it was no surprise that during one of his regularly scheduled meetings with Price, he brought it up. "I know you're going to think I've gone crazy, but I think I need Khan's help in order to eradicate the vestiges of his criminal empire."

Price responded, "With all the information we acquired both before and after Khan's arrest, you still don't have enough? What do you need? Most importantly, why in the hell would you think Khan would help you?"

Mahoney replied, "To get his help, I'd need to offer Khan something he'd value. This is where I've been stuck. I think I know what Khan would like, none of which I'd be willing to offer. He's still a bad guy that shouldn't be rewarded for the evil deeds he's wrought."

"How about lying to him?" said Price. "You shouldn't feel some moral obligation for honesty to someone of his ilk."

"Yeah, but he'd want me to make good on at least part of the offer, before he'd make good on his part," answered Mahoney.

"I'm just thinking aloud here, so this is no doubt half-baked," said Price. "But how about you pose as a wealthy foreigner whose business activities require the information you're seeking? You offer to spring him from jail in exchange for his help. Each of you could exchange some signs of good faith prior to consummating the deal. Once you got him out of the prison, he'd have to deliver on what he owes you."

"I don't know about half-baked, but there's no question it's out of the box," said Mahoney. "No doubt Khan would like his freedom, but why would I ever give it to him? He's the very type of person I'm trying to take out of circulation – maybe the worst of the bunch."

Price responded, "This is where the lie part comes in. You get him out of jail, but once you get what you need, you change the deal."

"I'm not going to kill him, as much as I might like to," said Mahoney.

"I wasn't thinking quite that radical, but perhaps turn him over to a foreign country he might have wronged," answered Price.

The conversation went back and forth for the rest of the day. It resumed when they met again the following week. Slowly, a plan started to emerge, and Mahoney was warming to it. In addition to many details needing to be worked out, there remained the issue of what to do with Khan when they were done. In fact, this was the main sticking point of the plan – if you could call it that.

Mahoney was after the politicians and law enforcement officials Khan had on his payroll. Mahoney reasoned that presenting himself to Khan as a wealthy (crooked) businessman, as Price initially suggested, would be consistent with what he was seeking. This should make sense to Khan, since it would be reasonable for the character Mahoney was playing, as a crooked businessman, to want to avail his illegal activities of the same services Khan had. It also wouldn't threaten Khan's future use of these corrupt officials, since greed has no limits – and more importantly, because Mahoney would promise not to bring up Khan's name in his approach to them.

Both the Prices and Mahoney concluded the only compensation that would work with Khan was the promise of his freedom. They also agreed that freeing Kahn would be counter to what they were trying to accomplish; therefore, while they might promise it, they couldn't go through with granting it. There was no question they could spring him from jail; the vexing issue was what to do with him when they got what they wanted. They even knew how they would free Khan and maintain control of him while he thought he'd gotten free. They needed the answer to the question of what then, before they could move forward.

Their planning was stalled and stayed like that for several weeks. Whereas Price and Mahoney contemplated this matter, trying to find the answer in thin air, Mary took a more analytical approach. She decided to make a deeper examination of the files they'd accumulated on Khan to see if she could find the answer there. Indeed, after much searching she identified two candidate solutions. The first was to turn Khan over to a fellow criminal whom Khan had double-crossed and cheated. In this case, that particular criminal would know Khan was the source of his misfortunes and would likely welcome the opportunity to get his hands on Khan. Going with this solution was equivalent to executing Khan, as sure as if you'd pulled the trigger yourself. The second solution involved a third world country Khan had robbed in numerous ways. They were oblivious to Khan's misdeeds but would certainly take them seriously if they learned of them. They were also not too picky about the rules of evidence and would have no issue convicting him on evidence collected in illicit ways.

They all preferred option number two. Regardless of how despicable Khan was, they didn't wish to become murderers themselves. Now that the disposition of Khan was settled, the outline of their plan was complete. Mahoney would approach Khan as a crooked businessman who could get Khan out of jail in exchange for a list of who in government and law enforcement was on his payroll. Once they had the information, they would turn him over to a foreign government he'd committed a crime against. They would try him based on evidence Mahoney would provide, plus whatever their own investigation turned up. The escape part was also straightforward, since Khan wasn't in a high security facility. The whole plan seemed simple.

Mary and Price compiled the evidence against Khan in several countries, just in case Mahoney's first outreach wasn't successful. Mahoney began discussions with some countries and was successful on his second try. What proved more challenging were the negotiations with Khan. While it was clear he wanted his freedom more than anything else, he hadn't attained his level of power by not being a tough negotiator; however, in the end a deal was cut.

As a sort of down payment, Khan would give up one name and any supporting information that might help make the case against that person. Mahoney would then validate that he'd been given a good name. Once that was complete, the rest of the plan would move forward.

The team had expected Khan to rat out some low-level functionary as his down payment, so he was quite surprised with the name Khan provided to them. The name was so good, they became skeptical that it was nothing more than a fabrication on Khan's part. Mahoney used a special government unit to look into the individual Khan had named. The investigation would be ultra-discreet, both to protect the individual should they be innocent of any wrongdoing, and so as not to alert the individual should they be guilty until Mahoney was ready to do so.

It took nearly one month of putting this individual's life under a microscope before they had validated Khan's information was true. The person was extremely intelligent, which among other things was how they'd attained the level within the judiciary they had. They used this intellect to cover their tracks; however, the intense scrutiny they were under revealed little inconsistencies. Pulling on these 'threads' led investigators to greater evidence of the individual's wrongdoing. When the investigators were done, there was a compelling case against him.

Mahoney returned to Khan and let him know his lead had panned out. Not only could they validate the individual's criminal involvement, they now had the 'goods' to use against them to gain favor for Mahoney's purposes. Mahoney had to remember his role of getting names to help his own illicit activities, and not the reality that he was seeking to rid law enforcement and government from this scourge. Mahoney tried to get other names, but in accordance with their agreement this would not occur until after Khan was out of jail; however, Khan did provide an outline of what was to come. In all, he would reveal over two dozen high level names he claimed would be of the same caliber as the name he'd already supplied. Khan's parting comment was that Mahoney would be pleasantly surprised by the names he got – Mahoney was thinking it would be more like horrified.

CHAPTER 30

A Just Reward

The planning was now complete, and the time had come to execute the plan. Khan was to make his way to edge of the prison property at the appointed time. It was a cliff overlooking the Pacific Ocean. Security was relatively light in this sector, since the cliff represented a sheer drop of several hundred feet, which could not be navigated. At the bottom of this drop were jagged rocks. Prison officials were convinced this natural barrier was more foreboding than any manmade structure they could envision.

The one thing prison officials hadn't contemplated was that someone would install a virtual elevator that ran down the face of the cliff. This was what Mahoney had done. A set of pulleys had been mounted in the rock face at the top of the cliff. Threaded through the pulleys was the latest technology climbing rope. Attached to the rope at one end was a harness. Khan would strap himself into the harness and lower himself over the edge. He would then use the rope to lower himself to the bottom. There, he'd be met by a rubber zodiac, which would ferry him out to a larger craft. Mahoney felt that having Khan on the boat would give him the control he needed to get the names. Khan was told the boat would then take him to a place with an airstrip, where he was free to go where he wished. In reality, that was where Khan would be turned over to the authorities from the country that would prosecute him.

Price had no role in the escape or transfer of Khan, so he decided to take a front row seat to the activities from his submarine. Both Price and Mary cruised to right below the cliff Khan would be coming down. He had the periscope focused on the cliff wall and displayed on one of the monitors in the cockpit. Mary and Price were excited to see this plan play out and felt the anticipation a playwright must feel on opening night, waiting for the curtain to rise. They were actually enjoying this.

At the appointed time, which was near dusk, they could make out someone coming down the cliff face. All appeared to be working as planned. They could just see the zodiac approaching the shore at the base of the cliff – then all of a sudden one of the alerts sounded, scaring them nearly to death. The alarm was of an approaching underwater craft. Price changed their surveillance from the cliff towards the approaching craft. Price recognized immediately it was a non-military submarine yacht. He reasoned Khan must be planning to double cross Mahoney and make his exit on the submarine; Price couldn't allow this to happen.

The yacht had tremendous visibility out its bow but was virtually blind in all other directions; hence, Price steered to come up slowly behind the craft. He was trying to think what to do when he noticed a huge anchor lying on the ocean bottom below them. It must have been cut loose when some ship couldn't otherwise free itself. Using the robot arms he'd added to the sub, Price managed to attach a very sturdy line to the undersea yacht. He connected the other end to the anchor. He reasoned there was no way this undersea yacht could move that anchor. Sure enough, when the slack came out of the anchor line, the undersea yacht came to a complete standstill. Mary and Price could hear it racing its motors, seeking to get free, but to no avail. Additionally, the crew of the yacht couldn't see what the problem was, and so for at least the time being they were stuck.

Feeling very proud of himself, Price turned his attention back to the cliff. He was just in time to see Khan boarding the Zodiac and it heading out for its rendezvous with the cabin cruiser that was to take Kahn to the next part of his adventure. They weren't sure whether it was their imagination or not, but it seemed Khan was looking for the team he evidently arranged for to rescue him from his rescuers. With Khan's double-cross plan stuck to an anchor on the sea bottom, the Zodiac delivered Khan to the luxury cabin cruiser that would be the next stop in his journey.

When Khan stepped aboard the craft, he looked despondent as opposed to elated that he was free. Perhaps he had some sixth sense feeling that freedom wasn't really in his immediate future; if ever. He just couldn't figure out why the plan he'd secretly created didn't come to pass. He knew he'd selected reliable and loyal people to get him away from what he viewed not as rescuers, but just another set of captors. Khan figured he'd deal with those who had let him down. Similarly, he'd deal with his ostensible rescuers who got him out of prison if they didn't fulfill their promise. Khan wasn't someone to let down or try to mess with.

After Khan was thoroughly searched, he was given new clothes to wear. Once he was cleaned up and dressed, he came into the main salon, where he was met by Mahoney, who was unaware of the failed double cross.

"I trust you're satisfied with all we've done to affect your escape?"

Khan replied, "Everything appears to be going according to plan, but how do I know that once I give you what you're looking for, you won't arrange for me to be recaptured, or even killed?"

"All I can do is give you my word that you won't be returned to U.S. authorities, and my word has proven to be good thus far – has it not?" asked Mahoney. "Besides, how do I know the information you give us before we set you completely free will be good information?"

Khan simply replied, "You don't."

"I decided the risk is too high that you'll try to cheat us in some way," said Mahoney, "so I'm making a very small change to the plan. You will give us the list of names, and we'll validate them and their positions before we set you free. While I'd like to go further and actually investigate each of the individuals before setting you free, that would take too much time."

"You cannot change the plan," protested Khan. "We had a deal."

"The validation will take place while we cruise to the airstrip," answered Mahoney. "It won't add any time to your stay with us."

Khan didn't like people changing plans on him; never thinking about how he'd tried to change what transpired. Besides, Khan was going to give them a valid list – albeit only 90% of the officials he'd corrupted – and would save the best for his future work. Khan knew he'd need some assets when he set about rebuilding his empire.

After lunch, Khan provided Mahoney with 18 names and had forgotten that he'd previously agreed to provide two dozen names.

Mahoney inquired, "What about the other six names?"

Khan responded, "I was wrong when I cited two dozen. These are the names."

Mahoney said, "You will give me the other six names, or we'll turn this boat around and get you back to prison."

Khan insisted he'd been mistaken and these were all the names. Mahoney held firm, and thus it went back and forth for some time. In the midst of this debate, Mahoney left the room and had the craft noticeably change course, heading back to where they came from. For his part, Khan too held firm. They were in a stalemate.

They weren't too far from where they'd started out when Khan noticed a Coast Guard boat tending to a surfaced submarine yacht. Khan didn't appreciate its significance, nor the fact that it had been stolen and the Coast Guard was in the process of arresting its crew and commandeering the craft. Khan did wonder, however, whether his failure to be rescued had been a result of the effort being interfered with, as opposed to sheer disobedience on the part of those he'd turned to for help. Then again, it made no difference – he'd get rid of them. He had no tolerance for those who failed him, and he'd show no mercy.

When the cruiser stopped and started to lower the Zodiac into the water, Khan relented. He provided five more names to Mahoney, who asked, "Where's the sixth name?"

"OK – I'll give it to you. I just don't want to go back to that prison," said Khan.

"I've promised you and will deliver on that promise that you won't be returned to the authorities that incarcerated you," replied Mahoney. "I always keep my promises."

Khan thought to himself, *And I always keep my promises, too.*

The names, while in many cases surprising, all turned out to be officials whose corruption would benefit a criminal like Khan. Each would be investigated to see if there was a case against any of them. They now entered the last phase of the plan.

They'd cruised to an isolated cove on the Baja Peninsula. Mahoney took Khan to an airstrip where a business jet in civilian livery was standing ready to take Khan away. Khan boarded the plane and immediately gave orders as to where he wanted to go. The pilot said certainly, and the plane took off.

After they'd flown for some 30- 45 minutes, Khan felt relaxed enough to try to sleep. He was just nodding off when he felt a presence. Thinking it was a steward, Khan said he didn't want anything. The response he got was a hard punch to the stomach, then being thrown down face first to the floor, where he was handcuffed. When he was reseated, he was informed that he was under arrest for crimes he'd committed against the country he was on his way to for trial.

Khan strained at his shackles, which by now connected him to his seat. He was enraged and swore an oath that he would avenge this treachery; however, he realized he was in a serious predicament and that it might be some time before he could do anything about it.

CHAPTER 31

Missing

Investigation of the names provided resulted in indictments against all, as well as uncovering other corrupt individuals. Trials were held, with convictions and long sentences attained in all cases. When the last of the trials was over, Mahoney went to visit the Prices to give them the good news.

Khan's trial took place the day after he arrived in country, and he too received a severe sentence. He was promptly taken to the jail he'd spend the rest of his life in. Khan's rage over this matter didn't abate and manifested itself against the only targets at his disposal: guards and other inmates. There were numerous altercations, resulting in one death and several serious injuries, including Khan, who was severely beaten by guards in retaliation for an attack on one of their own. Khan felt he'd be lucky to stay alive, let alone rebuild an empire.

When Mahoney arrived at the Prices' home, he discovered both of them away. He knew he should have called first. He left a note asking them to call, then he departed. Unbeknownst to Mahoney, they were visiting with Melissa at her school. Price was feeling more driven to family than he was towards the continued pursuit of criminals. He felt he more than lived up to his promise in the aftermath of the deaths of his wife Sandy and daughter Becky. His efforts couldn't bring them back. While he helped make the world a little better, Price felt he needed to invest more in love than revenge for his family's death. The love he now felt for Mary and Melissa was a testament to the love he'd shared with his first family, not the forsaking of it. Besides, his adventures were getting less gratifying, while his time with family was proving more so.

Price, Mary, and Melissa were dining at a nice restaurant in Palo Alto. It had been a nice but low key day. They'd done some touring, some shopping and a bunch of lazing around. Mary and Melissa excused themselves from the table to visit the restroom. After a few minutes, Price started to feel anxious. He got up and checked the lady's room, which was empty. Now his anxiety increased dramatically. He went out the back door and saw no one, but a shimmer on the ground caught his eye and turned out to be one of the earrings Mary had just bought that day and was wearing that night. Price's blood ran cold.

Price did the only thing he could think of: call Mahoney. Mahoney explained how he'd visited their house and so was on the West Coast. He promised to get there as quickly as he could and asked for Price to meet him at the local airport. Mahoney managed to get one of the government helicopters to take him to Palo Alto. He connected up with Price faster than either expected.

Price told him everything he knew – which was nothing. Price then said, "What do I do?"

While there could be a number of explanations for the disappearance of Mary and Melissa, none of which were good, both Price and Mahoney tended to focus on Khan's potential involvement, if for no other reason than their recent escapades. Absent this, they had no angles to pursue at all. Even with the might Mahoney was able to bring to bear from the government, hours turned into days, which turned into weeks, and Price was frantic. There was no sign of what happened to them. Price was beside himself with grief and guilt that somehow he may lose yet another family. He resolved that as long as he had one breath left in him, he couldn't let that happen.

CHAPTER 32

The Search

Mary was awakening from what seemed like a dream. While her memory was hazy, she recalled she was having dinner with Melissa and Dave and excused herself with Melissa to go to the restroom. She felt an insect sting and must have passed out. She had vague recollections of different people and traveling, but none of it made any sense. Then she noted that despite the nice surroundings of her room, she was shackled to the bed. She also noted that she was wearing different clothes than those she had worn for dinner and had no idea what happened or where she was. When she was fully conscious, she became alarmed and wondered what had happened and where Melissa and Price were.

It didn't take long after she was fully awake to start getting some answers. Unfortunately, the answers were nearly as disquieting as not knowing.

Someone entered and said, "Good, I see you're up. How are you feeling?"

Mary replied, "Who are you? Where am I? Where's my family? Why am I shackled to the bed?"

Her visitor responded, "All will be answered in due course, but for now I can unlock you. You were only shackled for your own safety."

"What do you mean for my own safety?" asked Mary.

The visitor didn't get a chance to answer, as someone who looked vaguely familiar walked in, accompanied by Melissa. Mary hugged Melissa and was assured that she was all right. It was a tearful reunion, but when it was over Mary forcefully said, "What's going on here?"

It was then that Mary took a closer look at the person who came in with Melissa and realized she knew him. It was Officer Henry, but he was dead. This was really strange, and her face must have showed it, as the stranger started to laugh.

"I see you recognize me, and let me assure you that word of my death was greatly exaggerated. Let me reintroduce myself – I am Paul Henry, formally with Khan Industries. Today, however, I go by the name Terry Peters so Mr. Henry may rest in peace. 'Dying' served a number of useful purposes, not the least of which was getting Khan off my back."

"Would you kindly tell me what's going on? Where am I? Let me and my daughter go home," Mary stated.

"All will become clear in due time, but for now suffice it to say that your husband has proven to be quite resourceful in the past, and we'd like to put those talents to work for us," explained Officer Henry. He continued. "We were all but certain he wouldn't help without a little incentive, and that's the role you and your daughter play. Cooperate, and you'll suffer no discomfort and this will be over before you know it. I needn't go into what it could be like if you and your husband don't play ball."

For Price, hours turned into days, and those into weeks. When he'd lost his first wife and their child, he'd felt lost, but there was a reality he couldn't change, so he needed to figure out how to move forward. In this case, all he had was uncertainty and a belief that he could remedy the situation if given a chance to do so. The agonizing part was not knowing what was going on or what he could do to fix it.

Mahoney was earnestly using all of his influence to apply the resources at his disposal toward figuring out where Mary and Melissa were at and discovering what was behind their disappearance; however, he was having no success. It just didn't make sense that there wasn't even a hint of what was going on, and if it was a kidnapping, why they hadn't heard from the captors.

Mahoney came into the room Price was in and said, "I'm going to have to be getting back to the office, but I'll continue to push on every *button* I can to find them and help bring them safely back. I'll let you know the second I learn something, and hopefully you'll do the same."

"I know you will, and I really appreciate all the effort you've put into this," said Price.

"I thought I had more time to spend out here with you, but the office is calling; otherwise, I wouldn't be leaving so soon," said Mahoney.

"That OK – I know you've been trying and that your efforts will continue, even with you not being here," answered Price.

All the way back to Washington, Mahoney was wondering what crisis needed his attention so badly that he couldn't stay to help a friend. When he arrived back at his office, his team was waiting for him and explained the project that had come to them directly through the National Security Advisor's office, with an inference that it came from the President's office; however, the substance of what was being asked was seemingly not very important, but it would take a great deal of work to accomplish. While it made no sense, Mahoney chalked it up to politics in some form and turned himself loose on completing the task. This left virtually no time to apply himself to helping Price. Mahoney felt bad at first, but he was rapidly consumed, and Price's issue retreated from the forefront of his mind.

Meanwhile, it was the only thing on Price's mind. Given the lack of information, he couldn't figure out a course of action and was starting to fret and do nothing. Finally, when he was about at his wit's end, he received an email from Mary. It stated that she and Melissa were doing well but that they were being held captive, with their future well-being hinging on Price fulfilling some task he would be receiving shortly. There was a proof of life photo of Mary and Melissa with a copy of a newspaper from the day before.

Price was greatly relieved they were alive and doing OK under the circumstances. He immediately called Mahoney but could only leave a message. Later that evening, Mahoney called back and Price explained the email. Once again, Mahoney was surprised that he hadn't gotten a report of this email from his sources, as he had numerous monitors set up on Price's communications. He queried his sources and was dismayed to learn they had terminated their monitoring, believing he was no longer interested, as evidenced by his intensive efforts on the new project.

Later that day, Mahoney and his team got new tasking related to their current project. This new tasking required substantially more work, but they weren't given any relief on their deadline. Soon Mahoney temporarily forgot the Price matter and focused on the project at hand.

Price partially emerged from his slump but was frustrated that he still didn't know what would be asked of him or how he might otherwise rescue Mary and Melissa. To keep himself busy, Price went to work on a means to backtrack to their source any future emails that might come his way. Price well knew the classic approaches to doing this and their limitations. What he was seeking were some innovative approaches that might be more effective and not as subject to countermeasures.

It wasn't too long before he got to try his methods out. He received another email from Mary. It informed him that he'd be receiving a package and that he should follow the directions he'd find in it. When he applied his new techniques to the message, he discovered little other than somewhere in the path was a satellite link. While there could be several explanations for this, the most likely outcome was that the email emanated from somewhere remote or on the water; not much, but a start.

Whereas the first email sounded like Mary, this one did in parts, but in others it did not. Price made a closer examination of the text. Not having much to do until the package arrived, Price studied the email as though looking at it under a microscope. When Price highlighted the text of the email to copy and paste it into another document he could use as a working copy, he noted that the font and font size were blank. He decided to pursue this further. He examined his working copy line by line and letter by letter; what he discovered both elated him but also frightened him in terms of what might happen if Mary's efforts were found out.

Mary did two different things within the email to send a secret message. First, she changed the font of some letters within the text. Unless you were an expert, it wasn't noticeable. Price only uncovered it because he was looking one letter at a time. These letters, which were interspersed within the words of the email, spelled the following: "O - K – O – n – b – o- a - t – o- f- f – c –

o –a –s -t – n –o –t – f –a -r – l –o –v –e - y –o -u". The second thing Mary did was write in small print in-between the lines of text using white letter color. This made the text invisible unless you highlighted it and/or changed the font color or background color of the document. Price found the following hidden text: *"I think we're in anchorage near Santa Rosa Island. Yacht bigger than 50 feet. We're OK. Be safe. Love you. Mary"*

Price knew Santa Rosa Island was the second largest of the Channel Islands off the California coast. It hosted many recreational activities and was a place where a yacht would not draw attention to itself. Price decided to fly over the area without getting too close and see what he could find. As he approached the island, his pulse sped up. Not surprisingly, he found several yachts that could be where Mary and Melissa were being held captive, but he had no way of knowing which, if any, was the right one.

A couple of days went by without receiving the package or any further emails. Price was frantic that Mary may have gotten caught for sending her secret messages. Just when he'd reached a peak of anxiety, Price received another email. It told him there was a change of plan and he should pick up the package and was given instructions on how to do so. He then searched the email for secret content and only found the following: *"s- t-i-l-l-h-e-r-e-h-a-v-e-n-o-t-m-o-v-e-d".* Price felt immediate relief that she apparently had not been caught and was still alive and well.

CHAPTER 33

Ransom or Rescue

Price picked up the package as instructed. When he opened it, he found a couple of prepaid cell phones; one labeled #1, and the other labeled #2. There was a brief note:

> **Your wife and daughter are comfortable and have not been harmed in any manner. To ensure that this continues to be the case, you will follow all instructions with alacrity, and secrecy. If you inform law enforcement in an attempt to thwart our efforts, the consequences will be severe for your wife and daughter.**
>
> **At 6:00 PM tomorrow night, you are to be in the main terminal of San Francisco International Airport. Then and only then are you to turn on telephone #1. You should not turn on telephone #2 until instructed to do so. You are to wait up to 5:00 minutes for a call. If none comes, turn the phone off and repeat the next day, only 1 hour earlier- e.g. 5:00 PM.**

They were sure taking precautions with regard to having the call intercepted and their location being compromised, thought Price. He wondered why there were no more instructions, but then it came to him that this approach gave them an opportunity to see if he was following directions, specifically with regards to not involving law enforcement. If they were to reveal more and Price had enlisted help, there might be time to employ countermeasures that would undermine or perhaps completely compromise their objective. Upon further reflection, Price concluded they must not be after money, since revealing that would not pose any particular additional risk of being compromised. So they must want something they weren't prepared to reveal until they were sure about Price's cooperation. Price wondered what that might be.

Price had never mentioned the submarine to Mahoney. He was never sure why, but that same instinct told him not to inform Mahoney of that, nor to bring Mahoney up to speed regarding the latest development; instead, Price prepared to head up to San Francisco to comply with their instructions. Price flew his own plane there, and on the way he flew over Santa Rosa Island to see what yachts were present. Price used an aerial camera to image the area as he'd done the last time. Price took the train to Terminal 2. Saying "Main Terminal" made no sense, as there were 3 domestic terminals, plus international, so he picked one in the middle.

Price went to the American ticket counter to get a pass through security to visit the Admiral's Club. He felt this would give him a measure of security and a relatively quiet place to operate from. There were still several hours before he was to turn on the cell phone, so Price decided to have a look at the images he just collected over Santa Rosa Island. He had the previous pictures he'd taken on his laptop and compared them with today's set. What he found excited him, in that there appeared to be only one yacht present in both, a 65 foot Fairline. It had two decks (upper and lower), plus a fly bridge. There were up to six staterooms, plus crew quarters, all located on the lower deck. Price reasoned such a yacht could certainly house the woman securely. He would have to get a closer look, but that would have to wait for whatever today's call would ask of him.

Six o'clock came and went without a call, so he decided to check in at a hotel near the airport, since he needed to be back the next day. It wasn't until the third day at 4 PM that the call finally came. The caller said, "I hope you haven't enlisted any help and are ready to follow directions."

Price replied, "I'm all alone on this and am ready for your request."

"It is not a request!" shouted the caller. "It is an order that you will carry out as quickly and competently as you can."

"I know," exclaimed Price. "It was just a figure of speech."

"Just shut up and listen," said the caller. "I'll tell you what you're going to do."

The caller told him he would get Khan out of prison and deliver him to a location that would be provided after Khan was free. Price was to take no more than two weeks to accomplish this. He instructed

Price to dispose of telephone #1 and expect a call at 10 AM on the morning following Khan being freed. The routine was the same; turn phone on for 5 minutes, and if no calls, then repeat the next day only one hour earlier. The caller then went through the litany of threats to his family and promptly hung up.

This time Price needed Mahoney's help, so he called him. Price limited what he had to say to only that he'd been contacted and had two weeks to free Khan, or his family would be harmed. Mahoney surprised Price by cutting off further discussion and in a most cryptic way suggesting they meet in two days at 7 PM outside the location where they first encountered each other. Mahoney then hung up.

Following the phone call, Mahoney wondered whether it was brief enough to have avoided detection by whoever was involved in this entire affair. He also wondered whether he was clear enough to Price, and if intercepted, not so clear to others. Whatever was going on was clearly criminal and at the highest levels of government. It would have been the type of challenge he liked, except for the fact that the family of someone he now considered a friend was in jeopardy.

Price was very perplexed by Mahoney's manner and by the message itself. When Price first met Mahoney, he was working at TSA, whose offices were just outside of Washington, D.C., not far from the Pentagon City Metro stop. There was a small breakfast shop close by where they used to meet. It closed by noon every weekday, and they used to joke that one would not want to be caught dead in that area after 7 PM. Price considered that Mahoney's instructions were intentionally misleading to throw off any listeners and that he wanted to meet there at 7 AM. Price figured he had nothing to lose in following this theory, because if he was wrong, he could always return 12 hours later.

Price was really torn between attempting a rescue of his wife and her daughter Melissa versus seeing Mahoney. He needed to get to the bottom of this, or they'd never be safe. He imagined they would be okay at least until Khan was free, so he opted to head to Washington, D.C., on the first available flight. He made reservations to stay at the Pentagon City Ritz Carlton, which was located right at the Pentagon City Metro Station. He was not seeking its opulence, but instead the strategic location of the hotel.

The trip was uneventful, and he was in his room at the Ritz the night before the planned meet. He was unable to get to sleep because he was anxious about freeing his family, concerned by Mahoney's demeanor, and then there was the 3-hour time zone change. Price decided to scout out the neighborhood. It wasn't that late at night, but his recollection of the area was accurate. It was not a place one would like to be after all of the day's workers left it. This was especially true of some of the smaller side streets, like the one the breakfast shop was on; nonetheless, despite seeing some questionable characters, he was not accosted in any way and able to check out the area and return safely to the hotel.

During his trip, he noticed a place where he could surveil the entire scene proximate to the breakfast shop without being seen. Feeling satisfied that he interpreted the time and location of the meeting with Mahoney correctly, Price was able to drift off to sleep. While he only slept for a few hours, it was very sound and he actually felt well rested.

Price departed the hotel at 6:15 AM and took a circuitous route to the breakfast shop. He did not see anyone following him. The walk took him about 20 minutes, and he set himself up to watch the breakfast shop and its environs. At about five minutes to 7 AM, he saw Mahoney approaching the shop. Price was about to go out and greet him when he noticed Mahoney was being followed.

Price called Mahoney's cell phone, which he answered on the second ring. Price said, "I'm here watching, and you have a friend. If it's OK, scratch your head; if not, proceed to the Metro Station. I'll meet you."

Mahoney did not scratch his head; instead, he looked around and then set off toward the Metro Station. Price ran to be ahead of him. When he got close to the station, Price approached a young man and asked him if he'd pass a note to this man who was coming toward the station and would be there in less than 2 minutes. He offered ten dollars for the service. The fellow agreed, and Price found a point to watch from.

The young man did precisely as requested and got the note to Mahoney. Mahoney read its contents:

> *Suggest you go down steps from the street and then come up steps into hotel. Try to lose yourself in the hubbub of everyone going to work. Then meet me in the elevator lobby of Ritz.*

Mahoney followed the directions and even changed his appearance as he went down the stairs by removing his jacket and putting on a baseball cap he had. As best as Price could see, Mahoney's follower had lost him. They promptly got in the elevator and rode to three floors above Price's room. During the ride, Mahoney removed the battery from his cell phone, but no one spoke. When the elevator stopped, they got out and Mahoney followed Price to the stairwell and down to Price's room. They walked to the sliding glass door and stepped out onto the terrace.

"What in the hell is going on?" Price asked.

Mahoney answered, "I wish I knew, but I noted that my efforts to help you were being thwarted in a way that could only be done from the highest levels of government. Whoever it turns out being is likely very involved with Khan's criminal enterprise, and quite possibly its real mastermind. If they were able to turn off surveillance, I expect they could order that those very same resources be turned on our efforts. That is why I didn't want to have this discussion on the telephone the other day."

Price responded, "If what you suppose is right, I'd expect they would interfere with any efforts to rescue my family but help or stay out of the way of freeing Khan. So we should keep discussion of those efforts completely separate and take extraordinary precautions when it comes to my family. Here are two prepaid cell phones to use – don't turn them on until needed. I'll call you and name a time. Turn the phone on 15 minutes before the time I say, and I'll call you. We'll still keep the calls very brief and shut the telephone off in-between calls."

Mahoney replied, "Sounds right. Now what do you have in mind?"

Price explained he would take care of freeing his family and Mahoney should get Khan out of jail but, under no circumstances was he to release Khan. Instead, he should bring him to Price's home. Mahoney was uncomfortable with breaking the law but did not see much alternative.

Price said, "Remember you have less than two weeks to make this happen. Please let me know when you're going to do it so I can get my family."

"Do you know where they are?" asked Mahoney. "How do you plan to get them?"

Instead of responding, Price just said, "Please let me know when you will have Khan at my house."
Mahoney answered, "I understand and will let you know.

CHAPTER 34

Time for Action

Price had much to do in the next two weeks, so he headed straight to the airport for a flight back home. During the approximately 5-hour flight, Price went over what he had to do, what was going on in general, and speculating about how things would play out. Sometime during his deliberations, Price drifted off to sleep and dreamed of these very topics, although they were a little garbled, as dreams tend to be; however, there was one very realistic part of the dream, which was his first wife Sandy admonishing him to save Mary and Melissa.

Sandy said, "There was nothing you could do to save me and Becky, but Mary and Melissa need you to save them, and you can do it; however, for all of you to live in peace, you must eradicate the source of evil, not simply its messengers."

Price wanted to hear more from Sandy, but he was startled awake by the wheels thumping on the runway as they landed. He must surely have been tired, since the landing announcements didn't awaken him first. Atypical of most dreams he knew he had but couldn't recall after waking up, this dream was vivid and real, and he could recall in detail Sandy's admonition: "You need to save Mary and Melissa, and you can do it." It wasn't like Price needed any more incentive, but this created an additional imperative.

At a top level, Price needed to be ready for Khan's arrival, and he needed to go rescue Mary and Melissa. The first task was very mechanical. He needed a room to confine Khan in, and he needed some restraints to subdue Khan with. Lastly, he needed some sedatives to help make Khan easier to handle. On the other hand, the task of rescuing his family would take planning, perfect execution, and luck.

Fortunately, he didn't need to spend too much time making preparations for Khan's arrival. While not designed as a confinement cell, Price had built two secure rooms in his workshop. All he needed to do was empty them. Their security, originally aimed at keeping people out, would do a fine job of keeping them in. The only other preparations were to bolt a cot and chair to the floor and install a toilet. The latter took the most effort, but the plumbing was readily accessible to the room, so it didn't take that long. With the addition of a few shackles bolted to the concrete floor and walls, that job was complete. Of all things, he was able to order the restraints he was looking for online, with a 24-hour delivery. For the sedatives, he contacted a very close doctor friend, who gladly accommodated his request.

Now he could turn his attention to the rescue. He first needed to verify that the yacht was where he'd last seen it. So, he decided to go flying. His stomach sank when he got to Santa Rosa Island and the boat was not where he'd last seen it. Price was starting to panic when he saw the yacht on the other side of the island. He surmised it had moved to be less conspicuous, and possibly for weather considerations. The good news, besides the boat still being there, was that it moved to a location more accessible from deep water. Despite being all alone in the plane, Price said aloud, "Please be on that boat."

Price had everything he thought he would need on the submarine already. He added to his store of weapons a stun gun. He also decided it would be prudent for him to wear body armor in case someone discovered him and took a shot. Lastly, there were zip ties to restrain the captors. Price also carried his 9 mm semi-automatic handgun; just in case.

There were two forms of technology he added for this mission. First was a jammer so the occupants couldn't alert anyone of his attack by either cell phone or ship to shore radio. Second was a microphone he could place against the hull to pick up sounds from its occupants. With this, he hoped to ascertain the number of people on board he could not see and determine their locations. He might also get some information from communications he might overhear.

Price sailed to Santa Rosa Island and approached the 65 foot yacht. It was 4 PM on a clear and calm day, and all seemed quiet on the boat. Through the periscope, Price saw one person on the fly bridge, but no one else. Price figured he better get close to the boat or risk being observed from that person, so he got within 50 feet and 30 feet below the surface. Price engaged his station keeping system, which would keep the submarine in this same location relative to the yacht.

Price now waited and observed. About one hour after arriving at the scene, a man came onto the aft deck. When he turned around, Price did a double take – for he was looking at Officer Henry; a person he thought dead. Price was really confused as to what was going on. As his mind was swirling, he saw Henry get on his cell phone. Price quickly deployed the microphone he'd installed to the surface. This was not an application for it he'd anticipated, but he was hopeful he'd be able to pick up something. When it got into position, there was much background noise as Price turned on the sound; however, listening carefully, Price heard the following from Henry:

"I'm expecting that Khan will be freed within the next week. That guy Price has proven quite resourceful in the past thwarting us, and I expect that same skill to be working for us now that we're holding his family." There was a pause as the person on the other end was obviously speaking. Then Henry resumed speaking. "Yes, they've been well treated, but the wife knows who I am, so she will have to be disposed of after we have Khan – maybe we can stage them killing each other." Another pause, which gave Price a chance to recover from the chilling words he'd heard and puzzle over why Henry spoke about killing Khan. Henry's side of the conversation continued. "Yes, Khan's usefulness is certainly over. A pause, then, "No, your identity isn't known to anyone." Another pause as Henry listened. "Yes, I know you *killed me off* so I would be free of Khan and could more fully serve you and ultimately distract others away from you by setting Khan as the scapegoat. The bastard never caught on." A pause, followed by Henry saying, "Yes I'm well aware you can kill me off for real. I'll complete this phase successfully and consolidate your power over the enterprise within the next three months." A brief pause was followed by, "OK, one month." This was followed by Henry saying, "Goodbye." Price saw him put away the phone, then he heard Henry say, "That unappreciative son of a bitch. He sits in his ivory tower in D.C. while I take all these risks and he reaps all the rewards. I may have to see about changing that."

Price was numb and just sat staring at nothing for quite some time. The sunset and knowing he had something important to do rallied him into action. He needed to liberate Mary and Melissa, and the time was now getting critical. As a first step, Price needed to locate the women if he could. He carefully moved the microphone against the hull of the yacht and moved it from the bow to the stern. In the stern he heard Henry continuing to rant. Price thought to himself that Henry was quite miffed. This was potentially good in that he was distracted, but it could be bad if it contributed to his volatility, which could make his actions less predictable and more ruthless.

While still listening at the stern, he heard the rant interrupted when one of Henry's men must have entered the area. This would be number two of what Price was now thinking was a three-man crew: Henry plus two others. There was one on the fly bridge and one now speaking; he heard no others, but it was possible there were others who were sleeping. However, Price reasoned three was certainly adequate to man the boat and control the two women; any more would exacerbate logistics. For example, they'd need more food. Hence, for his planning, Price was going with three bad guys and the two women as the sole passengers on the boat.

Price did not hear the women, but he was certain they were there. The question was how to get control of the three men. He could not fight all three at once, and any disturbance would likely bring in help from the remaining others. He'd have to find a means of getting at them before they could alert each other. While he hadn't formulated a comprehensive plan, Price thought he had a way to thin the ranks.

Price put on his diving gear and exited the sub. He swam around the bottom of the yacht until he found what he was looking for: the cooling water intake for the on board generator. Price took a rag he'd brought with him and let it be sucked into the pipe. He then returned to the sub to watch what happened. He also activated his jammer so they couldn't call anyone for help.

He saw the man from the fly bridge come down on deck and animatedly speak with first the other man, then with Henry. They proceeded into the main bridge area, and shortly afterward Price saw and heard one of the engines start. Obviously, they were trying to get electricity, and with the main generator dead, their only other source was the generators that ran off the main engines. After about thirty minutes, it occurred to them that to have the lights, air conditioning, and other powered appliances like satellite TV running, they'd need to get the main generator back on line.

The diagnostics were all clear. The generator turned itself off because its engine was overheating. One of the men suggested they may have sucked in some debris and this was the cause of the failure. The other man told him he'd need to go into the water to validate his hypothesis, so the man stripped down to his shorts and jumped into the water. He hadn't thought much about the task at hand, though it wouldn't have mattered, as the shock of the cold water made him forget entirely why after dusk he was swimming around. He immediately made his way to the swim platform and got out.

"You idiot," laughed the other man. "This water is cold. You won't be able to see anything without a light, and you won't be able to stay under to do anything productive without dive gear on. Let's get you properly outfitted for the job at hand."

With much difficulty, he got into a wetsuit and put on the rest of the diving equipment. He was helped by the other man, which was a good thing since he did not know what he was doing. His ignorance regarding how to put the gear on was a good indicator of how well he could use the equipment. When he got back in the water, his first problem was clearing his mask. The second was getting his buoyancy compensator adjusted so he could submerge. Both Price and the man's colleague were terribly amused by the performance.

When he finally submerged, Price decided to put him out of business. He simply swung the robot arm into the man with enough force to knock the air out of him. He went still and floated up to the surface. His partner managed to grab him and drag him onto the swim platform. He did not do this out of any loyalty he felt; instead, he did it so he could get the dive gear to use. When he'd put the dive gear on, he entered the water. Price did not hesitate to put this guy's lights out for good by swinging the arm into him with a great deal of force.

Price's plan was now to swim onto the yacht. In the darkness with dive gear on, he felt he would easily be mistaken for one of the other two men. He pulled the rag out of the generator intake valve and then swam around to the swim platform. When he got there, he put restraints on the semi-conscious man on the swim platform. He then carefully made his way onto the deck. He made his way to the controls and restarted the generator. He anticipated this would bring Henry up on deck, and he'd be ready for him.

"Glad you guys got that generator going again," bellowed Henry as he made his way up on deck and headed aft towards the swim platform.

Hearing no reply, he moved towards the stern and peered over at the swim platform. There, he saw the inert figure of one of his crew. Before he could fully register what was going on, he was brutally shoved over the transom, bounced off the swim platform, and entered the frigid water. While he was unsure what was going on, he knew he must get out of the water, or its temperature would zap his energy and he would eventually perish. It was then something bumped into him. A quick look told him it was the other member of his crew; he was dead. Henry was repulsed, but he did grab the light and knife his now dead crew member had been carrying.

Price heard the thrashing in the water and figured he'd need to deal with Henry before he could find his family. Price went to the railing and saw Henry making his way towards the swim platform. When Henry went to grab it, Price hit him with a boat pole. Henry turned on the light to see what was going on. In one respect he was surprised to see Price, and in another he was not. The man had some uncanny ability to show up in places and cause trouble for him.

"Let me on the boat – I'm freezing," said Henry

"Maybe," answered Price, "but first a few answers. Like where's my family?

"They're down below in a cabin. They've been well treated. Now let me out of the water," pleaded Henry, whose teeth were chattering from the cold.

Ignoring Henry's plea, Price pressed on, "Is their cabin locked? Are they restrained in any way?"

Henry answered, "They're free within the suite, but the door is bolted from the outside. No key is needed. Let me onto the platform, and you can get them."

"Not so fast," answered Price. "Come over to the swim platform, and I'll pass you down some zip ties I want you to use to tie yourself to the railing."

"Anything," said Henry. "It's so cold, I've lost feeling in my hands and I'm shivering uncontrollably. I hope I'll be able to operate the zip ties in my condition."

"Well, you better be able to," said Price. "I assure you you won't like the alternative."

Henry did as he was asked and secured himself to the railing. When it appeared to Price Henry was secured, he cautiously reached over to check. Satisfied that he was secure, Price went below to find Mary and Melissa to free them.

It wasn't difficult to locate their cabin, since it was the only one with an exterior slide bolt. Price opened the door and was happily greeted by his family, who were both relieved and happy to see him. He hugged each of them but explained that he needed to get back to Henry, who was tied up on the swim platform.

Price returned to the aft railing, only to find that Henry had freed himself and was now somewhere loose on the boat, as he was certain he wouldn't have elected to reenter the water. Price was unsure of what to do, but the safety of his family was the most important task at hand. He returned to his family and had them come up on deck with him. Price felt they would be better off staying together than if they were separated on the boat. He gave his wife his 9 mm handgun, and together they proceeded to the helm. There, Price took steps to disable the yacht and the motors of the lifeboats. He then told his family they were going to need to swim from the yacht and enter the sub, which he remotely maneuvered to be just astern of the swim platform.

"It's really cold and dark, but Mary has done this before, and it's the best thing I can think of," explained Price.

"What are you planning?" asked Mary.

"Once you're off the yacht, I'm going to scuttle it," said Price. "I'll come to the sub, then we'll surface and wait for the proverbial rat to get off the sinking ship."

Mary was not happy with the plan. It was not the cold, dark swim, but she was frightened of leaving Price alone while Henry was on the loose. She did not have a better plan, since searching the yacht would have been perilous. They were unfamiliar with its layout and didn't know what weapons Henry might have. She and Melissa made their way to the sub. It was really cold, and when they were aboard the sub, both of them were shivering. They found some dry clothes and put them on and waited with blankets around them.

Price opened the sea cocks that let water into the yacht, then went to the engine room and broke open the water intake pipes, which immediately spewed water into the compartment at a rapid rate. Price was ever cautious of bumping into Henry, but there wasn't much he could do, so he just worked as fast as he could and dove off the yacht when he was done. Unbeknownst to him, Henry had been waiting for him on the other side of the yacht. Henry wasn't sure what was going on but had reasoned Price would come to the control room, so that was where he'd planned to ambush him. He hadn't seen Mary and Melissa leave, nor did he note Price letting water freely enter the yacht. He did, however, see Price disappear over the rail opposite where he'd been waiting. It wasn't until later that he came to understand Price was sinking the yacht, and there was nothing Henry could do to stop it.

Price made his way to the sub and was happy to see his family dry and warm and once again free. They could leave, but he needed some answers, and only Henry could provide them. His plan was to "rescue" Henry after the yacht sunk and extract the information from him.

CHAPTER 35

Helping an Old Acquaintance

Like the proverbial rat abandoning a sinking ship, Henry appeared in a life jacket on the deck of the sinking yacht. Water was beginning to lap around his legs, and the yacht's stability was starting to falter. It wouldn't be long before it slipped beneath the gentle swells. Sure enough, the stern started to go under, which seemed to accelerate the yacht's demise. Henry recognized this, climbed as high up towards the bow as he could, then leapt off into the water.

Price and his family watched this on the monitor in the cockpit that could display various things, in this case the periscope. They were frozen to the screen as this all unfolded; truthfully, more in the spectacle of seeing this magnificent yacht entering its grave than in the fate of its sole inhabitant. Nonetheless, they did see Henry escape into the sea and wondered what, if any, plan he might have. The look on his face was one of defiance, not of one who was resigned to his own fate.

Price had a plan of his own. At least he had the outline of a plan and was developing it as things moved forward. Price maneuvered the sub to within 100 feet of Henry. He had the bow pointed right at him to provide a minimum profile. Price then brought the sub up so its hatch was just barely above the water. He and Mary then proceeded out the hatch, and Price called to Henry, "Do you need a lift somewhere?"

Henry replied, "Go to hell. At least I can now see how you were able to accomplish some of the things I suspect you of doing. I never thought of you having a submarine – it looks Korean. You don't need to worry about me, as my help is on the way. If I were you, I'd get out of here and keep running for the rest of your lives, because that's how long you'll be pursued."

Price responded, "Good to know help is on the way, but it'll be too late for you. Do as I say, or I'll be forced to shoot you."

Henry raised his middle finger into the air and said, "Shoot this."

Before Henry knew what happened, that was exactly what Price did: he shot him in his hand. The good news for Henry was that it just winged him, but the bad news was it hurt like hell and he was bleeding. He wondered whether the blood would attract sharks, and while it was in truth a lucky shot, Henry was in awe of Price's marksmanship and felt it might be best to comply. He could then bide his time until his help arrived.

"OK, stop shooting!" shouted Henry. "I'll do whatever you ask. Just get me out of the water."

"Now that's more reasonable," answered Price. "Here's what you're going to do. I'll throw you a line, and you'll attach it to the life jacket harness. There will actually be two lines, and you only need to attach one of them. You'll then pull the other line to you, where at the end of which you'll find some handcuffs. You'll secure the handcuffs on your wrists, and I want them tight. Then I'll pull you over to the sub. Note that Mary has a shotgun, which won't be as friendly as the peashooter I used to wing you earlier."

Price threw the double line to Henry, who complied with all Price's directions. Price started to drag him towards the sub. When he was within just a few feet, Price instructed Henry to show him that the handcuffs were tight; they were, and Henry had the appearance of someone totally defeated. Price wondered whether he was just buying time until his help arrived. He could not take that chance, so despite his concerns, he brought Henry the rest of the way to the sub.

With Mary now training a TASER on Henry, having switched it for the shotgun so as not to hit Price if she had to fire, Price helped Henry onto the deck, where he sprawled face first with a little help from Price. When Price started to put duct tape around his legs, Henry started to thrash wildly and caught Price with a kick that got Price's attention. Mary did not hesitate and fired the TASER, which at least temporarily incapacitated Henry and delivered the message that she meant business.

With Henry still partially out of it and now trussed up in duct tape like a mummy, they brought him through the hatch and into the sub. There, they secured him to a bunk and then submerged the sub. Once underway, they gave Henry a drug cocktail Price had obtained, which would have several important results. First, it would make him more manageable; second, it would loosen his tongue; and lastly, it would block his memory of events just before and while he had the drug in his system.

It was now time to get down to the business of learning who the real villain was in this operation; however, before Price could begin the interrogation, Melissa alerted Price to the alarm indicating an approaching vessel. Price brought the periscope up and switched the screen to monitor what it saw. Despite the security he felt by being submerged, and therefore invisible to the approaching craft, Price couldn't help feeling a shiver of fright. The approaching boat was a 50 foot long Cigarette ocean racing boat, and it was moving at exceptional speed toward the last location of the yacht Price had sunk. When it reached the spot, it stopped and dropped its anchor.

Price wanted its name and registration number, which might serve as valuable intelligence in unraveling the network Henry was party to. So, he maneuvered the sub around the back of the racing boat and arrived just in time to see divers entering the water off its aft swimming platform. He was far enough away so he would be unlikely to be seen, but he'd now be even more careful. He switched the view on the monitor from the periscope to his forward looking underwater camera. He watched the divers descend and eventually come upon the sunken yacht. It was sitting in an upright orientation on the mostly level bottom 75 feet below the surface.

After making just a brief inspection, they resurfaced and got back on the Cigarette boat. Price decided he wouldn't risk getting closer to see what else he could learn – it was just too risky. He also knew there was no way he could follow the boat, so he let it suffice that he could send the information to Mahoney and see if he could do anything. Time was of the essence, so Price did take the risk of raising his small satellite dish to the surface and sending an email to Mahoney. It had the current location of the Cigarette boat, its description, name and registration. It said, "Saw a nice boat. Maybe you could find owners and where it's berthed so I can make an offer." Will see you at the party and will be bringing a guest along with my family." Price was satisfied the note would convey the necessary information while sounding innocent enough so as not to alert anyone of its true intent.

Chapter 36

Thwarted and Pursued

Mahoney received the message, but when he attempted to act on it, he found that his orders were being circumvented; not directly so, but instead by potential responders all of a sudden being diverted by higher priority tasking. On the surface this could be normal, but Mahoney had been around long enough to know when something isn't quite right. In this case, it appeared someone pretty high up was trying to protect the boat Price had asked him to track down. It could be some government operation, but unlikely since in his position he'd likely be aware of such a thing. If not, he'd be told when attempting to move in on it. No, something wasn't quite right.

In the meantime, besides being unable to do as Price asked with respect to the boat, Mahoney had sprung Khan from prison and was attempting to make his way to Price's house; however, he felt as though he were being followed. Luckily, he had Khan out of sight, so the most anyone could report was that Mahoney was going through extraordinary measures to observe if he was being watched and followed. Despite his efforts not revealing any followers, Mahoney could not shake the feeling that he was under surveillance, so he did not proceed with going to Price's home; instead, he continued to drive around in the hopes that his watchers would reveal themselves and/or he might come up with some form of plan.

It was nearing dusk, and Mahoney was starting to doubt his instincts, which had never failed him before. He knew better than to do so, but he was getting tired. The impending darkness would make his ability to spot watchers all but impossible, so he needed a plan. He reasoned that if he could not find the watchers, there either weren't any or he was perhaps being surveilled from above. The best countermeasure to being watched by a drone, airplane, or satellite was to go where they could not see, namely a tunnel or where foliage thoroughly covers a roadway. Absent either of these, a simple overpass might work.

Mahoney found what he was looking for on the map. He hoped it would turn out that what looked good on paper might in fact be suitable for his purposes. There was a place along the highway that had a series of overpasses which together might give him a virtual tunnel. As he approached the location and saw what was there, Mahoney got a boost in his morale. The site looked next to perfect.

Mahoney entered the "tunnel" and tried to think like a sniper regarding the current situation. He found a spot that was perhaps as secure a place as he could find. They could not be seen from virtually anywhere other than straight ahead or back from ground level. He got Khan out of the car, and there they sat waiting. Eventually, a truck came along. Seeing them, the driver asked if there was an issue.

"Nothing serious, but our car broke down, and we could sure use a lift," said Mahoney

The truck driver responded, "If you don't mind heading east, I certainly don't have any problem taking you to the next town."

So under the cover of the bridge overpasses, Mahoney got into the passenger side and Khan got into the cargo area. Mahoney had the sudden thought that if he was up against such a sophisticated adversary with access to the kinds of resources he typically had at his disposal, he better disable his cell phone, as he didn't want it reporting his position. He removed the battery and put both in the case he was carrying. He also needed to remember not to use his credit cards.

The driver was a quiet type, so after about only three minutes of conversation there was quiet, other than the road noise and that of the other sounds around them. This was good, as it afforded Mahoney time to think. He needed to think about who he was up against, and with no one to trust and no access to the normal help he counted on, how he would operate. Deep in thought, the trip passed quickly, and before long the driver broke his reverie by saying, "Here would be a good place for you to get out. After this, I'll be entering a highway that goes for miles without seeing much civilization."

Mahoney thanked the driver, then he and Kahn got out. It was only 45 minutes from when Mahoney said he would call Price, so they set about finding a store where Mahoney could buy several prepaid mobile phones. These phones had the benefit of not being traceable to their user. In addition, having more than one could confound someone trying to correlate call traffic to/from a particular phone number. Fortunately, there was a store not far from where the truck had let them off where they could buy the phones and freshen up. The store was located on a stretch of road straight in both directions and relatively flat so they could see who was coming. Just across the street from the store was a small wooded park where they went to sit and wait. The trees provided cover against any overhead surveillance, and they still had good visibility of the road. Their presence there would not seem overly strange, as they were drinking some coffee they'd bought and were eating.

When it was time, Mahoney took out the telephone and placed a call to Price. No one answered on the first attempt. The protocol they had worked out was to call again so many minutes later, as determined by the closest hour. For example, if it was 5:45, the next call attempt should be in six minutes. If it was 5:20, then it would be in 5 minutes, and so on. Additional attempts, if needed, would follow the same plan; however, Mahoney started to worry after the second attempted failed to reach Price. All kinds of thoughts began to enter his mind, both with respect to Price's status and what they were up against.

Just when despair was about to overwhelm him, Mahoney had finally gotten through to Price on his fourth attempt. His relief was so great, he almost missed seeing the black sedan entering the town. Khan pointed it out, and before they were noticed, the both of them sunk further back from the road into the woods. The car was an obvious unmarked car of the type favored by the federal government. It stopped in front of the store. Both occupants got out. They looked to Mahoney like stereotypical federal agents. One of them stayed with the car and was looking all around, and the other entered the store.

Coming from Mahoney's phone was Price asking, "Are you there? What's going on? Are you OK?"

Mahoney responded, "Sorry, some feds showed up where we are, and we had to move to safer ground. I think they're trying to find us but not sure where we are, so not an imminent threat. The bigger issue is exactly what we're up against."

"Did you learn anything regarding the boat I sent you the information about?" asked Price.

"No," answered Mahoney. "It's part of what has me worried. Tracking down the information should have been trivial, yet I was thwarted at every turn. This tells me we're up against an extremely well connected, high level adversary; in fact, someone that outranks my boss, and perhaps his."

Price asked, "Where exactly are you? We need to connect somewhere safe. Plus, I'd like to get my wife and daughter somewhere out of harm's way."

Mahoney replied, "I'm on the coast road in some one-horse town within 10 miles or so of your house. There's just a general store with a park across the street, and not much else. I've been very careful about being followed, but now I have questions about the wisdom of going to your place. The adversary we're facing would certainly know about our connection."

Price responded, "I know exactly where you are. Head directly west, and you'll come to the water. Depending upon the precise path you take, there's a cove that will either be to the right or left of where you come out of the trees. There's a boat house where you can hang out. I should be there within a couple of hours. We'll speak when I get there."

Mahoney noted the feds had left, so he and Khan headed for the water. Just as Price had said, there was indeed a cove with a boat house adjacent to it. They looked around for a while before breaking cover and heading to the boat house. It was open, and they went in. It smelled a bit musty, but otherwise it was just fine. In fact, there were some boat cushions and old life jackets. Khan and Mahoney each fashioned "nests" for themselves to rest. It was good that there was cover, because it started to rain. The rain was fortuitous in that it would wash away any tracks they had made.

Price decided to let his wife and daughter off at their home and have them get the car and leave for Mary's closest friend's home. They departed the boat while it was submerged through its airlock. Price watched through the scope as they entered the house, then departed shortly in Mary's car. Mary called when she arrived at her friend's house. She said all was fine and then through prearranged innocuous phrases secretly told him there was a van outside their house, apparently watching it, but they didn't follow her and Melissa.

For now, Price felt they were safe and proceeded to head to the cove where Mahoney and Khan were. The issue was not in getting them, as they were likely secure, it was where to go once he had them. He would discuss it with Mahoney.

Despite feeling they were secure, Price still took precautions. First he made sure Henry was still out and tied securely so that even if he came to that, he could not cause problems. Then Price anchored the sub just a short distance from the boat house, leaving it submerged. He did not want to risk surfacing. Next he watched the surrounding area, land, water, and sky for several minutes through his scope. He didn't see anything untoward. It was time to take the next step.

Price departed the sub through its airlock and swam parallel to the beach for a distance, then went to the shore in such a way as not to be seen from the boat house and out of the line of sight of anyone watching the boat house. Once he made it to the tree line, Price removed one of the prepaid phones from its waterproof pouch and dialed Mahoney. Mike picked up on the first ring and said, "Where are you?"

"Everything still look OK from your end?" asked Price.

Mahoney answered, a bit sheepishly, "Actually, I was napping, so I can't really say."

"Well, I have eyes on you, and all looks quiet," said Price. "I'll take one last look at the street, and if it's clear I'll come and get you."

The road was empty, and Price didn't see any strange vehicles hanging about, so he headed for the boat house, where he found Mahoney and Khan. "Where did you come from?" asked Mahoney.

"You wouldn't believe it if I told you, so I'll show you later," replied Price. "First, I think we need to talk and make some preliminary plans."

They excused themselves from Khan and found a place to sit that afforded them a view of the boat house and the general approaches to the area. All was normal, as best as they could tell. Price went first and explained, "I rescued my wife and daughter and captured Henry. In the course of doing so, Henry had no doubt called for help and an ocean racing boat arrived on the scene. This was the boat I contacted you about. By then Henry's boat had sunk, and all they found was open and empty water. Then they left. Before all of this, it was apparent from conversations Henry was having that while he might not know the true identity, he has communicated with the person in charge. That person would seem very well connected. It also appeared this person and Henry used Khan as the scapegoat, should things ever turn bad. At present, or at least prior to my upsetting his plans, Henry was feeling like he should be in charge and this other person was just a leach. This could give us something to work with in speaking with Henry."

Mahoney replied, "I really want to hear how you did all of this by yourself, but there are more important matters at hand. We must find out who the kingpin is. To do that, we'll need to remain free and safe. We'll also need to know what resources we can count on without risk of compromise. Quite frankly, I'm spooked by just how high a level this person must be operating from."

They continued to speak for over an hour. At the end of that time, they concluded that Price's makeshift prison accommodations could work if they could access it without being seen by either the van on the street outside of Price's house or by overhead assets. They also decided they really needed Mary's methodical analytical skills to help work through this. Price called her to check on her and Melissa and found they were all settled in with her friend and the streets seemed empty. This was encouraging to Price, in that there was not a chance for anyone to obtain an observation post to surveil them from, since visiting this friend could not have been anticipated. Therefore, any watchers would need to be on the street.

Price considered the possibility of continuing to keep the submarine a secret from Mahoney but decided it was time to tell him. No way would he trust Khan; he could drug Khan as he had Henry and erase any memory he might have of the sub. So he told Mahoney, who was incredibly impressed. Price then explained his immediate plan to Mahoney, who had a few questions but was overall satisfied with it. Plus, he couldn't think of any real alternatives.

CHAPTER 37

Need a Plan

They went back to the boat house and found Khan napping. Price gave him an injection of the drug before they woke him, then they explained they were going for a swim. Khan found this incredible to understand, but he was already feeling the effect of the drugs and in his new pliable state did not resist.

Price went first to ready the airlock and the sub itself. Henry was still securely restrained and asleep. For a moment, Price hoped he didn't overdo the dosage. While pliable, Khan proved to be incapable of making the short dive underwater to the sub. Mahoney finally lost patience and knocked Khan out with a quick punch to the jaw. Mahoney then covered Khan's mouth and nose so he wouldn't ingest any water, then together with Price they got him down to the airlock and into the sub.

Once they were aboard, Mahoney continued to be impressed as he looked around while getting Khan settled in. Fortunately, they could exit the sub covertly in Price's boat house so they wouldn't have to struggle with either of the "guests" to get them through the airlock; however, maneuvering limp bodies in confined spaces was still a challenge. Price gave Mahoney some dry clothes for himself and changed out of his own wet clothes. The climate system Price had added to the sub was a significant improvement from its original design, and they were quite comfortable. Price had Mahoney sit down and stay out of the way while he prepared to get underway.

Before long, Price had the anchor raised and they were motoring submerged the relatively short trip to Price's house. When they arrived, Price maneuvered into the boat house and prepared to exit the boat. In addition to the amnesiac they'd given to Khan, they'd also given him a sedative to keep him out. Once Price had secured the boat, one at a time they removed Henry and Khan from the boat and placed them in separate holding rooms Price had prepared. They were operating in very subdued light, as they didn't want to turn any lights on and possibly draw the attention of any watchers. This made the going a little slow; however, once they were inside and the door was shut, they could turn on some lights, as there were no windows. It was then Mahoney became truly impressed.

"I can't believe it," said Mahoney. "You have your very own submarine, covert docking facility, and holding cells. What next, a stealth helicopter?"

Price responded, "I'm glad you like it – and no, I don't have a stealth helicopter, but not a bad idea."

Mahoney said, "I'm impressed, but I didn't say I liked it. It's not much different from when you commandeered that commercial airliner. It is impressive, but you should be arrested; however, with that said, your actions – while illegal – certainly have helped make the world a better place. Now if only we can uncover who's hiding within the upper ranks of government and running what may be the largest criminal enterprise in history. Once we do that, I'll look into how to legitimize your arsenal and actions."

"Thanks for the compliment about making things better," said Price. "However, I'm not sure I could do what I do from a totally legitimized position. I would be most appreciative, though, if you don't have me arrested when we're through with this. Now let's see what we can do."

Price and Mahoney spent the next several hours discussing how to approach the problem, then addressed what outcome they would find acceptable. Whoever was responsible could be eliminated, politically disgraced, and/or convicted in a criminal court. The latter would involve rules of evidence they could not possibly follow. While an obvious conclusion, it made Mahoney extremely uncomfortable. Neither Price nor Mahoney were up for executing the perpetrator, which left disgrace as an outcome, which seemed so inadequate.

The discussion of what they hoped to attain went on for over an hour, with no conclusion being reached. They did agree that while finding the person did not hinge on what they planned to do once they found them, it did affect the means they used. They continued to discuss this, getting nowhere other than tired and hungry. Just when they were at their wits end, Mary showed up with food and coffee. They hadn't heard her approach, which was worrisome, but they were very happy for the refreshments and a way to, at least temporarily, get away from their seemingly intractable debate.

After everyone had wolfed down their food, not being aware of just how hungry they were, Mary spoke. "I spent a little time when I arrived listening to your debate. I have some ideas that may help that I'll share in a minute. However, first I think we need to make some decisions about appearances. For example, should Dave come home and be seemingly going through normal daily activities? Should I be home? Mike, what should your posture be?"

They discussed this and agreed that their greatest security would come from an appearance of normalcy. To act otherwise would draw undue attention, and the situation could not stand close scrutiny. They then made plans.

Mary continued. "With regard to outcome, we can all agree that we want the person removed from their criminal enterprise and to severely damage its ability to function. I fear that while it might be a nice goal to totally eliminate the enterprise, that may be a bridge too far, as someone else will certainly step into the vacuum. I believe that regardless of whether you want this person dead or alive, others will see to their demise; one way or another. Obviously, if we let their criminal cronies know, they will take action to stop the person from doing harm to the criminal enterprise, such as by trading information as part of a plea deal. Another much less extreme outcome is to reveal their role, thereby neutering their power, then let law enforcement investigate them in areas well beyond where our actions may taint the evidence. They would not need much to convict and incarcerate them for a long time. Think about Al Capone being put away for tax evasion, when that was likely the least of his transgressions. I believe a similar circumstance can happen here. Therefore, I think we need to do what matters most, and that is to identify this person and put them out of business. We should use whatever means are at our disposal and not paralyze our actions worrying about the end game."

    Price and Mahoney were impressed by Mary's assessment and after just a few challenges agreed that moving ahead as best they could was what they needed to do. Despite being tired, they decided it was time to implement Mary's first observation; namely, returning to apparent normalcy. With their "guests" secure, Price and Mahoney took the sub out and found a secluded location to go ashore. Price explained how he could remotely control the sub and return it to its berth, then made his way home and entered it in a most visible fashion. Mahoney made his way to the airport, where he stayed overnight before catching a plane back to D.C. They would each go about normal business but have daily telephone calls via encrypted phones to further their plans and investigation.

CHAPTER 38

Seeking Culprit

Mahoney had no sooner arrived back at his office when he was given an assignment by the President to perform some innocuous task that seemingly served no other purpose than to get him out of the office. Under most circumstances this would have truly aggravated Mahoney, but in this case it had two benefits: 1) it provided him with an excuse to be out of the office – in fact, to spend time working out of Los Angeles; and 2) a possible clue might be uncovered as to who was behind this assignment to get Mahoney removed from his base of power. Mahoney did not consider a third possibility, namely setting him up in a place where he could be more readily attacked or eliminated. Such actions would be all but impossible in or around the White House in D.C.

Given the assignment came from the President, Mahoney had little alternative, so it was perfectly natural that he would pack up and head to the West Coast. While he uttered some protestations around the office for appearances, he was delighted that he could be close to Price and his two "guests". Despite their proximity, Mahoney could not be seen spending too much of his time with Price, so a few visits were open, but others were covert. Most of the latter visits entailed having Price pick him up from a secluded place along the coast with the sub. Some visits were held between Price and Mahoney's location. In these instances, they each did what they could with respect to counter surveillance, but they knew better than to feel overly confident that they were not being observed. So, these types of visits were kept to a minimum.

While the problem of how they might work together being on opposite coasts in different time zones was fixed, due to Mahoney's temporary change of venue, and despite the numerous meetings, they had little to no progress to speak of. Even under the influence of drugs, Henry would not speak, and Khan seemingly knew very little. They were stuck. During a dinner at their home, Mary suggested they take a very deliberate and visual approach to the problem by writing what they knew on index cards. They would put the cards on the wall and connect them where appropriate, write questions or observations, and identify potential avenues to investigate. For example, who was in a position to reassign Mahoney, or better stated, to get the President to reassign him? Intersect that with those who could thwart Mahoney's queries into the ocean racing boat that responded to Henry's call, and it might narrow down the possibilities. Once there was a culled list, one could figure out if there was any other evidence tilting towards one suspect or another. Lastly, one could plan how to validate or exonerate those on the resulting list.

The work was painstaking and slow, but just seeing all they did know and could conjecture was much more than they would have given themselves credit for. Soon they had filled an entire wall. What began to emerge was that there were only 3 individuals besides the President who fit all the information they had. The problem was that these three individuals were beyond reproach, as was the President. Mahoney and Price just couldn't believe any of them could be involved in this criminal enterprise.

Nonetheless, they put together plans on how to test a hypothesis that it was any one of the four. Given their positions and the fact that Mahoney couldn't tap his normal resources, this was a very challenging task; however, slowly they were able to come up with plans that might help to see if any one of the four was somehow involved. They spent time reviewing the plans for not only their ability to achieve the objective, but also to make sure it would remain covert and not point back at them.

By necessity, each plan was different, but each required a great deal of effort. Given their limited resources, this necessitated Mahoney and Price pursuing them in a serial manner. They started with the President and after a thorough evaluation concluded it could not be him. They then pursued each of the other three, only to reach the same conclusion. While it was gratifying that their instincts were correct that these men could not have been part of such a criminal enterprise, they were now totally frustrated. After several weeks of careful work, they were right back where they started.

Mahoney said, "I can't understand it. I'm certain our assessment was accurate that only these four individuals could possibly be responsible for interfering with my ability to pursue this matter. Yet, I'm equally confident in our analysis that says it cannot be any of the four. What's wrong with this picture, and where do we go from here?"

Price replied, "I'm right there with you. I can't figure it out either."

Mary walked in on their conversation and asked, "What can't you figure out?"

Price responded, "From our analysis, we know it had to be one of four individuals, and yet our subsequent investigation exonerates each of the four."

"Are you sure it has to be one of these individuals, or could it instead be someone close to them?" queried Mary.

Mahoney answered, "I hadn't thought of that, but it would have to be someone real close, and someone that one of the four was willing to provide access that violated established security measures."

All three of them debated the possibility and concluded it was possible and might be the only explanation. They decided following a rigorous methodology was the best way to assess this and see if any candidates emerged. Once again, they used the wall and cards approach. They wrote one name per card and then spread them out on the wall. Then going one at a time, they started to list those close to each one. Occasionally, while putting someone on one of the lists, they realized that a like person existed on each of the lists and they went back and added their names. For example, while working on one of the lists, they realized there was a cousin who was seemingly close, which made them go to each of the lists to assess close family.

Over the next day, the wall filled up with names and/or roles. They were pleased and felt they now had the guilty party's name on the wall, and they were dismayed by the number of names. Mahoney gave voice to this by saying, "It took us weeks to assess just four people. I wonder how long it will take to check out more than ten times as many."

Price responded, "I'm open to suggestions on some alternative way to run this to ground."

After a brief debate, they realized that arguing among themselves was not getting them any closer. So, they set off to coming up with a plan. They attempted to prioritize the list, but since all the names seemed equally unlikely, or at least unbelievable, it seemed an exercise in futility. Their early analysis was equally frustrating. Some people could have been responsible for some of the activities, but not for others.

They were only part of the way through when Price said, "I just had an idea. What if each of the four principals didn't violate security? There would still be an answer, and it wouldn't be anyone whose name we have on the wall."

Mahoney said, "Well, don't keep us in suspense. Who, then?"

Mary jumped in, "I know it could be one of those people in the background we tend to forget about, who's most often invisible to us. For example, couriers or Information Technology staff would have access and have the ability to intercept and/or modify communications."

"Exactly!" said Price. "Except, I was thinking IT, not couriers, as being the source of our culprit. Further, if such a person existed, the most likely candidate would be a person with access to more than one of our four principals' accounts. I believe this to be a strong possibility and will no doubt be a shorter list to follow up on than the names we're currently pursuing. Even if I'm wrong, we should be able to validate this idea relatively quickly so not much time will be wasted."

"I'm all for this," said Mahoney. "I don't feel like we're making any progress on our current course. I believe I can get a list of IT possible candidates from Human Resources without tipping any of the candidates off; evaluating the list will be another matter."

Good to his word, Mahoney got a list without much bother and under a guise that would not cause even the most paranoid (guilty) person to worry. In addition, he made the request through a third party, which made it all the more innocuous. A quick look at the list showed there were two individuals who were strategically positioned to affect all that had been done and more. Further vetting of the list exonerated one and left the other as an extremely strong candidate. That person was the Chief Information Officer of the Executive Branch, Jonathon Taylor. In this role, he had all the access that would be needed to have done what was done and the sophistication required to understand how things got done within the Executive Branch. The one problem investigating someone in this kind of role would be doing it such that it remained a secret from them, as they held all the "keys" to the "kingdom".

     Mahoney contacted a long-term friend who was an IT expert, Martin Ginsburg, and asked him to meet for dinner. Instead of going out, however, dinner was held at Price's home. Marty gratefully accepted the invitation, though he found it a bit odd. He was admonished not to mention the invitation to anyone. He was located on the West Coast not too far from Price's home, so there were no real logistics to deal with, and the dinner was set for the next evening.

CHAPTER 39

Takes One to Catch One

Price and Mahoney spent the time until the dinner laying out a case they could make, in enlisting Marty's help, that Jon was a potential criminal who must be investigated. The second issue was how much they should tell Marty. They also discussed how to keep Marty insulated from any repercussions that might occur.

Marty showed up right on time, and despite Price never having met him before, it wasn't long before they were all like a group of long-acquainted friends having a reunion. Despite the pleasant conversation, everyone was conscious of the "elephant" in the room no one was talking about. Finally, Marty's curiosity got the better of him, so he asked, "So what's the secret hush hush matter you want to speak with me about?"

In keeping with the plan they'd concocted earlier, Mahoney said, "First, we must have your assurance that whatever we discuss here will go absolutely no further. This is essential."

Marty nodded his agreement.

Mahoney continued, "There's a very senior government official we suspect is guilty of some serious ethical breaches that could be detrimental to the administration, and at worst to the country. We need to investigate this to see if there's any merit to the allegation. Due to his position, we must at all costs keep anyone from finding out about this until such time as it's determined an indictment or arrest is warranted. Besides keeping others from finding out, we must keep the target of the investigation in the dark, which will be very hard to do given his position."

Marty responded, "So who is it, and what do you think they've done?"

Price answered, "Jon Taylor, and we think it best not to share the specific allegations with you at this time. Should we uncover more damning evidence with your help, we might share some more with you. That will be up to the President."

"The Jon Taylor? The Executive Branch CIO?" exclaimed Marty. "It will be tough keeping him from finding out he's being investigated."

"That's why we need your assistance," Price said. "We recognize the challenge, but we don't need to make a comprehensive case. We don't need evidence to convict; we only need enough information to convince the President to authorize a full investigation, should that be warranted. In fact, what we need is to see if he was responsible for certain actions to impede Mahoney's pursuits, and not of any wrongdoing itself. If as a result of this effort we get additional information pertinent to the suspected wrongdoing, that will be a bonus. Are you willing to help us?"

"But Jonathon Taylor, are you sure?" queried Marty. "He's a legend in the IT field and revered by many."

"No, we're not sure," said Mahoney. "That's why we need to carry out this investigation and to do it covertly in case we're wrong. We would not want to damage his reputation should we be wrong."

Marty agreed, and they spent some time reviewing the assessment they did, which led to identifying Jon as the source of interference in Mahoney's activities. Marty was intrigued, but even more focused on just how they could assess Jon's role in this, not to mention how they could pursue this investigation covertly.

It was real late, so they decided to call it a night and resume the next day. They said their goodbyes and each reminded Marty of the need for secrecy. He might have been offended, but he understood their concern. He respected them for trying to protect Jon until there was compelling evidence of him having done something wrong before letting word get out.

Marty showed up at 8 AM the next morning and found Mahoney and Price busily working the case. Marty immediately set about thinking how to accomplish the task at hand and how to do it covertly. Three things were causing him trouble with making any progress: 1) shock that this very public person whom he revered could be involved in any kind of wrongdoing; 2) intimidated by the capabilities Jon possessed, against which Marty felt inferior; and 3) not having a clear idea of exactly what he was looking for. Price and Mahoney were totally absorbed by what they were doing, so he didn't want to bother them.

Mary came in and said hello to Marty and noticed he looked lost and that his computer screen was blank and there were no papers in front of him. She said, "Is everything all right? Do you have everything you need?"

Marty answered, "I just don't think I'm good enough to covertly go after Jon and not get caught. I just can't think where to start. Besides, I can't believe he would ever do anything that would warrant the attention of the law."

"Don't sell yourself short, Marty," said Mary. "I'm no expert, but from what I've heard you're extremely talented and skilled. Don't let his press intimidate you. At the end of the day, he's just a person who puts his pants on like everyone else – one leg at a time. As to whether he's done anything wrong, your job is as much to exonerate him as it is to find evidence of wrongdoing. If he didn't do anything wrong, then you'll be the one to prove it. Further, you'll do so in a way that keeps it private, so he'll be untarnished should the facts exonerate him."

"That's very helpful," said Marty. "I'm here to help him, should he deserve such help. If he's done something wrong, then I won't have done anything to prejudice his case in the public eye. But I still worry that I'm not in his league – and worse yet, I'm not sure what I'm looking for."

"Like I said, don't sell yourself short," responded Mary. "What you're looking for is any evidence that he's interceded where he shouldn't have. For example, is there evidence that he sent out messages using the accounts of others, communicating as though he headed the Justice Department, or even the White House? I believe Mike gave you a couple of specific dates to look at. It would also be helpful to see if you can get a cursory look at his finances to see if they make sense; i.e., is his spending in line with his earnings? I say cursory in that a full audit will be done if there is sufficient evidence that he might have done something illegal."

"OK, I got that," replied Marty. "But I'm still having trouble thinking how to begin."

"I'll have to defer to you on the specifics," said Mary, "however, it might be useful if you were to think through how you might use other people's accounts to send directives without them knowing about it. You could also think through how you might shelter money but still be able to use it to buy things without setting off any IRS alarm bells. What defenses would you put into play? Once you've identified how you might do it, you would then know what to look for. Again, I'll have to leave the technical approach to you, but that's your area of expertise. You're one of the best."

"Thank you," said Marty. "It's very kind of you to say so. Your idea to plan how I might do it and then look for the tell-tales is a good way to start. The problem is, there are more ways than one to do these things, and each would have different tell-tales. But I know what you're going to say – if it was easy, you would have done it yourself. I think I'll get going now and see what progress I might make."

Mary left, not wanting to disturb anyone, as they were all very absorbed by the task at hand, but she felt she'd made her contribution for the morning. In fact, her contribution really took hold, as Marty was able to move forward in a productive way. Marty got so caught up in what he was doing, he missed lunch and dinner and nearly missed the fact that he needed to get some rest.

It turned out not to be nearly as complicated as he'd feared, and before the following evening Marty had designed how he would spoof others while hiding it from those whose identities he borrowed. Just like Mary had suggested, the approach left certain tell-tales he could look for, particularly since he had some specific dates to check. The only question became one of hiding, or at worst misdirecting the source of the search so it didn't show up at all, in the best case, or in the worst case didn't land at his feet. Ironically, the answer to this was to employ the same spoofing technique for the search as the one he was searching for.

Having the dates and times proved to be the most helpful aspect to the search. On the first pass, Marty readily identified where someone had acted in place of another, but the individual was not Jon Taylor; instead, it was one of the myriad Executive Branch functionaries. However, upon closer inspection one noted this person's account was spoofed, and the perpetrator was Jon Taylor. He had used a double action to shield his involvement, but Marty had seen through it.

Marty proudly reported his findings to Price and Mahoney. Now he had the more challenging task of seeing what he could learn about Jon's finances. This search was not only more difficult to do, but extremely hard to hide. It could be misdirected, but to keep it stealthy was where Marty turned his attention. He was certain all the misdirection in the world would not fool Jon for long. He needed to keep Jon from even getting a whiff that something was going on.

This pursuit proved every bit as complex as Marty had anticipated. It was days before Marty felt comfortable enough to make even a superficial probe. Even this ran into defenses, which fortunately Marty was ready for; however, it did confirm that this would be a slow process.

Slowly and very carefully, Marty picked away at the software defenses and started to make his way into the core of Jon's information. While this was a formidable task like no other he'd ever done, once inside he was stymied by the layers of corporations, both onshore and off, that obfuscated the true picture of what was truly going on. He reviewed what he'd found with the team of Mahoney, Price, and Mary, but none of them had the forensic accounting experience to completely unravel what they were seeing.

The one thing that was clear was that Jon had a great deal of wealth, some of which didn't seem to be reported, with attempts made to hide it. Most interestingly was that the source for it could not be ascertained. Mahoney made the decision to stop, since further pursuit just ran the risk of discovery, and they were not equipped to get much further in their understanding of what they'd discovered already.

Mahoney said, "I feel as though there's a compelling enough story to tell that it's time to take it to the President. It's clear that Jon drove actions in the names of key Executive Branch leaders, including the President's, that regardless of motive weren't proper. It's also clear that Jon has far more wealth and income than are reported or readily explained. Whether or not Jon is the kingpin of a global crime enterprise, it's clear this represents a scandal for the administration it can ill afford."

"I agree," said Price. "Can you get a limited audience with the President without telegraphing the subject matter you wish to discuss?"

Mahoney replied, "I think so. The Chief of Staff owes me a big favor. Let me see what I can do. In the meantime, Marty, please cover your tracks and cease your efforts. We thank you. You did an awesome job."

CHAPTER 40

Cornered and Dangerous

Mahoney was granted an audience with the President, scheduled for the following week. Mahoney, Price, and Mary spent the time they had until then honing the message. It needed to be succinct, hard hitting and separate fact from conjecture without losing the message. Lastly, it needed to clearly state what the recommended next steps should be. All that in less than the five minutes Mahoney expected he had; even less after the requisite greetings and small talk before getting down to business.

After a great deal of discussion, the following emerged as the key topics:

- During an investigation into a global criminal enterprise, some information arose that implicated someone close to the President
- While such a tie remains to be proven, further investigation revealed irrefutable evidence that Jon Taylor took steps to frustrate the inquiry by initiating actions using other people's identities; including the President's
- Jon Taylor has far more wealth than he reports or could be readily explained by his government income
- Jon Taylor may or may not be a criminal mastermind, but he must immediately be isolated and further investigated to minimize

any potential resulting scandal from afflicting this administration

They polished the words and their delivery. There were supporting sentences for each point and a page of further explanation and background that could be left with the President. Mahoney would be ready to go as deep as the President wanted to go, assuming the information was known. Mahoney was ready.

Mahoney showed up early for his meeting, which turned out to be fortunate. The President's prior meeting ended early, and he was happy to start this meeting before its scheduled time. Mahoney and the President were acquainted, so no introductions were required. There were the requisite greetings and small talk, and then the President said, "How can I help you, Mike?"

Mahoney went through his points, along with some of the background and supporting information they had prepared. It was clear the President was engaged in that he asked good questions, which Mahoney fielded. It was about three minutes from when Mahoney had begun. The President was shaking his head sadly, as he was disappointed in having allowed someone on his team that, at best, suffered from some ethical issues. The President knew and respected Mahoney's credibility and integrity and so did not doubt what he'd heard. The President asked who knew and was just about to dismiss Mahoney when the Chief of Staff entered the office.

"Mr. President, may I have a word?" said the Chief of Staff.

The President signaled Mahoney to stay in place while the Chief of Staff whispered something to the President, who then said, "Show him in. This should prove to be very interesting."

The Chief of Staff opened the door and let Jon Taylor enter the office. The President said, "Hello, Jon. Can you tell me what's so urgent that you needed to see me immediately? You may say so in front of Tom, and I'm not sure if you know Mike Mahoney."

Jon replied, "Mr. President, I feel uncomfortable sharing this with anyone other than you."

"Well, I'm sorry," said the President. "That's how we're going to do it. If I deem what you're saying to be beyond what I'm comfortable with these gentlemen hearing, I'll ask you to stop and have them leave the room. OK? Please go on."

Jon began talking about a conspiracy against him and how some people were out to damage his reputation while framing him for some serious criminal activity.

The President interrupted. "Jon, what you're saying is astonishing, and quite serious. Could we pause the conversation right here to allow me to get the Attorney General over here to hear what you have to say? It won't be long, and Tom can find a place for you to wait."

After they left, the President said to Mahoney, "Mike I want you to be here for this, but let's be careful about what's said in front of the AG, since I'm sure none of your stuff is admissible and could taint any subsequent investigation."

Mahoney nodded and said, "I understand." He then stepped out to wait. In less than 45 minutes, he and the others were being shown back into the Oval Office.

The President apologized to the AG for upsetting his calendar and then asked Jon to repeat his allegation. The AG, who was a prosecutor earlier in his career, started to ask questions that were initially fielded smoothly by Jon; however, as the questions got more detailed, Jon's responses started to be less crisp, and even contradictory.

The President looked at Mahoney and asked, "Mike, please share with this group a discussion about the email I supposedly sent which diverted a team of investigators away from what they were setting out to do."

Mahoney understood the President wanted to limit the discussion to this one incident, but at the same time bring up something serious enough so one could gauge Jon's reaction. Mahoney detailed this incident and how it was accomplished, stopping just short of naming the perpetrator. When he'd begun, Jon's face had started to redden. When it was clear he not only knew how it was done, but who did it, Jon's face turned to cold fury.

Everyone was staring at Jon, whose face was frozen in an intense look of evil. The room was quiet, and then Jon spoke in a most malevolent tone. "I was afraid it would come to this. I was afraid you wouldn't be able to let a good thing alone. Well, I'm not stupid and have taken steps to ensure my continued freedom and well-being."

"Jon," the President said in a soothing voice. "No one ever thought you lacked intelligence. Now what are you so worked up about, and what do you mean by saying you took steps?"

Continuing to rant, Jon said, "You've removed two of my key pieces from the chessboard. If you freeze my assets or arrest me, you'll lose a city.

"I don't understand what you mean about pieces from the chessboard," said the President.

"I'm afraid I do, but I think it best if we not discuss this here," said Mahoney.

"No, we should discuss it," said Jon. "The President needs to know the scofflaws he surrounds himself with."

Mahoney said, "Up to you, sir."

The President nodded, so Mahoney continued. "Two of Mr. Taylor's alleged accomplices have been a house guest of one of my friends. One is there totally of their own volition, while the other might wish to go elsewhere if given a choice. Do you want to know more, Mr. President?"

"You were right. I, and especially the AG, didn't want to know even that much," said the President. "However, what's really troubling to me, Jon, is what you said about losing a city."

By this time, Jon's behavior had deteriorated to hysteria and he was mumbling incoherently. The on staff medical doctor was summoned, and he lightly sedated Jon, as well as restrained him. In the meantime, the Chief of Staff ordered that the head of psychiatry at the local military hospital be brought to the White House ASAP. Due to it being rush hour, he decided to send the President's helicopter for her.

When Dr. Joan Phillips, head of psychiatry at Bethesda Medical Center, arrived, she was whisked to a room adjacent to the Oval Office. When she saw the President, she felt both relief that he wasn't what she was summoned for and puzzlement as to why she was there. The President explained, "First, everything you see, hear, and learn here is classified at the highest level and cannot be discussed with anyone without my specific approval. Now, we have a person who seemingly had a nervous breakdown, but not before making a threat against one of our cities. We have no idea what city, the timeframe, or the source of the threat. The context of the threat suggests that only this individual can stop it and that it's already been initiated. You need to do whatever is necessary to help us get the information we need to stop the threat. I understand you may face some moral dilemma in terms of doing no harm to this person that you'll no doubt consider as a patient. I would suggest this one life is insignificant as compared to the many innocent lives that may be lost if a city gets destroyed. Please try to keep this in mind."

Dr. Phillips conferred with the house physician and started to put together a list of what she'd need. Mostly it was medications, the means to administer them, and some monitoring equipment. She then started to tend to her patient.

The President was absolutely right about there being a moral dilemma. Some of the drugs in her arsenal might do permanent damage to her patient. Then again, he was also right about the potential large scale loss of life her effort might help eliminate. After some internal deliberations with herself, she came up with a compromise course of action that would aggressively address the threat issue, but not so aggressive as to pose a significant risk to the patient. The compromise she made that put the interest of the many over the interest of the patient was that her protocol was not completely risk-free.

Over the next twelve hours, the doctor administered one drug after another into Jon, as well as provided various stimuli. Slowly, he got to a rambling and disjointed monologue while being seemingly oblivious to those around him. Mahoney had gotten permission to bring Price in, and together they reviewed all Jon had to say. Regrettably, Jon could not be questioned. They just needed him to ramble around and hopefully say something that made sense regarding the threat.

The doctor felt Jon needed some rest or would be at risk and was getting ready to sedate him. Mahoney asked her to give them another 30 minutes. She reluctantly acquiesced. Luck was with them in that before this deadline was reached, Jon started to talk about what he'd done.

CHAPTER 41

A Plan to Prevent Tragedy

Price and Mahoney had taped everything Jon had to say, and they were now piecing it together in order to have a comprehensive understanding of the threat, as was possible under the circumstances. What emerged turned their blood to ice. Using his method of directing actions through the identities of others, Jon had commandeered a warship. Worse yet, it was a submarine armed with nuclear missiles.

Price summarized, "Jon isolated the sub from the fleet, and their orders are such that unless they get the President's order to stand down, they'll launch missiles against an encrypted target package the 'President' had sent to them. Jon let the computer pick the actual target, so even he doesn't know what city is to be hit. They were further directed to maintain radio silence and defend themselves should someone or something try to keep them from fulfilling their orders. Unfortunately, the real President can't simply order them to stand down, because Jon had the crew change their encryption, and we have no idea to what setting."

Mahoney said, "We need to go see the President right now."

Price agreed, they called the Chief of Staff, and their request was immediately granted.

"Mr. President," Mahoney began without preamble. "We know what Jon has done. We're not sure of the timeline, nor do we know the target, but to be brief, he's commandeered a nuclear missile submarine and ordered them in your name to hit a target not even Jon knows. They're to do so by some unknown time, assuming you don't rescind the order."

"Well, why don't I just rescind the order, then?" asked the President.

Price responded, "There are two issues with that: 1) they were ordered to change the settings on their communications gear, and we have no idea what settings they're using. Without the proper settings, no one can communicate with them; and 2) we have no idea what the right code is for you to have them abort their countdown and launch."

By this time, the Secretary of Defense had joined them. "I've only heard part of this, but let me understand: someone has convinced a U.S. submarine to launch missiles against some unknown target, and we have no way to communicate with them to change their orders. Is that right?"

"The only thing I'd add is that they believe the order came from the President," said Mahoney.

The President said, "I want the Chairman of the Joint Chiefs, Chief of Naval Operations (CNO) with his top submarine guy to join us in the Situation Room in 30 minutes. I expect all of you to join me there, too."

He then turned and left for the residence. He needed a shower and a change of clothes, as he'd been in the office since the situation first arose.

Like clockwork, the President and the rest of the team assembled in the Situation Room by the allotted 30 minutes. The new players looked a bit confused as to what was going on, so the President asked Price to summarize. At first they were shocked, but then they started to challenge aspects of the situation as described. Point by point, Price confirmed the situation. After further debate, the Chief of Naval Operations spoke. "If there's truly nothing we can do, then we must neutralize the sub and save the city."

"I appreciate just how difficult it must be for you to say that," said the President. "However, I haven't yet reached the point where I want to sacrifice a hundred of our finest. There must be some alternative. With that in mind, is there some indication of an impending launch we could detect, and how long between it and a launch? If there was sufficient time, that might be when I would consider taking such a desperate action."

The CNO responded, "There is, but not that far in advance of an actual launch; possibly enough time, though, if we're ready. I'll order steps to find the sub and make ready to destroy it if a launch appears imminent."

"So ordered," said the President. "No premature destruction, and make sure your actions aren't detected by the sub, because they have orders to protect themselves against anything they may perceive as hostile. In the meantime, we need a plan. Does anyone have any ideas?"

There were a number of ideas offered, including taking all steps necessary to get the codes from Jon; however, a brief discussion with the psychiatrist quickly dispelled this idea as being viable. After each of the President's team members had offered what they could, there was still nothing viable on the table for them to consider.

Price spoke up. "If I could be permitted to offer up a thought which may sound a little crazy and will need some refinement, I think I have something that would work."

When he'd finished, everyone in the assembled group agreed it was a little crazy, or perhaps to be kinder, a little unorthodox; however, they also agreed they didn't have anything better to offer. So, they started to discuss the potential issues with Price's approach. First they did this at the concept level, and then at an extremely detailed level. The biggest issues identified were that they needed to find the sub, approach it without being detected, and likewise neutralize her launchers without being found out. Then the question was whether the President could convince the crew to stand down.

The assembled group worked non-stop, not even taking breaks to eat. Food was brought in, and they ate while they worked. They also shuttled experts in and out, never revealing all of what they were working on, but just enough so the expert was able to provide meaningful input. There were candidate approaches developed for each element of what had to be done. Their approach was to develop pros/cons for each and see if an acceptable plan emerged; however, none of this would mean a thing if they couldn't find the sub, and it was clear this was becoming a source of concern to the team.

The President had much of his calendar cleared and spent a great deal of his time personally engaged with the team and their deliberations. He didn't have much to contribute technically, but his common sense helped keep the team from letting minutiae obscure their thinking. Just having to explain some aspect of the plan to a layman really helped the experts ensure their thinking was complete and sound.

Just when everyone's energy was beginning to fade and morale was dipping, an excited aide to the CNO entered the room and announced that the sub had been found. It was located just off a shelf due west of the Channel Islands, not far from Santa Barbara. This information reenergized the group, who now knew they must now come up with a viable plan.

The assembled group, led by the President, decided the best and perhaps only way to bring this threat to a successful close without the need to destroy the sub and kill its crew would be to have the President speak directly with its commanding officer. This had two issues with it: 1) the President did not know the cancel codes, which the crew would believe he gave them; and 2) with the communications systems disabled, there wasn't an obvious means to establish the conversation. The team debated numerous complex approaches, all of which were deemed not practical. Once again, despair started to affect the team.

Price spoke up. "You'll recall that in the concept I offered earlier, we'll need to clandestinely approach the sub. What if we attached a sound transducer to its hull? This would turn the entire sub into a giant speaker enclosure. The sub's responses could be simply made over their PA system and picked up by a hydrophone. Both signals can be routed to wherever the President is."

The CNO said, "I agree this would work, but how are you going to get that close to the submarine without being detected?"

Price replied, "Remember, the concept I put forth requires that we get that close anyway."

The CNO interrupted. "The entire concept you put forth was naïve and would never work. I didn't fight it at the time, since it provided some hope to the team that we weren't going to have to take out the crew. However, who's kidding who?"

The President cut him off. "I've already spoken on that account, and the last time I looked, I'm still the Commander in Chief. You seem to be having difficulty in following orders. I'll deal with that after this crisis is averted. In the meantime, you may leave."

The CNO responded, "I'm sorry you feel that way, but I would like to stay."

The President turned to the Chairman of the Joint Chiefs and said, "I must lack military bearing. As the highest ranking officer in our country, please advise the CNO to leave now. If necessary, have him escorted out. In the meantime, Mr. Price, please tell me what you propose we do, and this time be specific."

All the sounds in the room had stopped when the President dismissed the CNO, so when Price began his explanation, you could hear a pin drop. Price began. "What I propose is that we take a small submarine and park it close to the target, which we know is the nuclear submarine New York, affectionately known as the Big Apple. We then secure the missile hatches so they can't fire. We attach the sound equipment, and you, Mr. President, will give what needs to be the most convincing speech of your life."

The room remained hushed and very tense given the President's prior actions, so he decided to lighten things up a little. "Yeah, maybe I should have the Chairman give me a lesson on giving orders. Your plan sounds simple, which I like. I think I know what to say and how to convince the crew to stand down. Now, people, please tell me what's wrong with the plan."

The head of undersea warfare spoke up. "There are two issues with the plan: 1) we don't have a craft suitable for the task at hand that's closer than a week or longer of being able to be on station; and 2) not sure how one can secure the hatches."

The President asked Price, "So what is your response, Mr. Price?"

Price replied, "As Mr. Mahoney can attest, I have a submarine in nearly a perfect location for this mission. It has everything one needs for the task at hand. The question of how to secure the hatches is a good one. I simply planned to use cable to secure the latches. I don't think it will require great strength, but just enough to prevent them from releasing. Not releasing will keep the hatch mechanism from activating, and if the hatch isn't open, the missiles won't fire."

The President looked to the expert, who nodded and said, "All he says is true. As long as you aren't detected before completing your task, it should work. Now tell me more about your submarine. I'm not sure that's legal."

The President spoke, "If this works, I'll pardon him for any legal issues in connection with his sub and provide Price with the necessary approvals for the future. However, speak to me about the detection concern."

The expert explained, "Subs are always monitoring for approaching threats through the use of active and passive SONAR, magnetic detectors, and unique to U.S. subs a special signal identifying them as a friend versus foe. That is, if another vessel is detected, they could differentiate a fellow member of the U.S. fleet from some enemy vessel. However, in the current case I fear the sub's captain would treat any approaching vessel as a foe."

The President asked, "It may not be important, but what's the difference between active and passive SONAR? Also, what's the vulnerability of Price's sub?"

"Mr. President, if I may," said Price. "Passive SONAR listens to its surroundings, which would allow it to hear engine noise, propeller noise, and any other sounds emanating from the target. Often, such sounds are like fingerprints, which can uniquely identify a class, or even a specific boat, within the class. Active SONAR is like traditional radar, where a signal – in this case sound – is transmitted and the system observes reflections of that signal; if there's nothing there, then there's no reflection. As to my sub, it's a North Korean mini-sub intended for special operations. Someday if you'd like, I can tell you the story; the short story of which is that I found it. I've made numerous upgrades, many of which would come into play for this mission. My plan would be to sneak up on the sub through its SONAR blind spot. I would get no closer than 200 yards, which is beyond the effective range of its magnetic detector. Then myself and possibly one other would swim the rest of the way to accomplish the tasks that need to be done."

"Again, I may not need to know this," said the President. "Our SONAR systems have blind spots?"

"Yes, they do," answered Price. "So their own propeller noises don't interfere, most systems have a dead spot that's directly behind the boat."

"I guess what I know and don't know on all of these matters is unimportant," said the President. "What matters is that it works. Will it?"

"Yes, sir," answered Price.

The submarine expert said, "I believe if they're careful and keep noise down, they can indeed approach the sub. I'm also confident the hydrophone idea will function properly; attaching the transducer shouldn't be a problem. I'm not as confident on the plan to stop a launch. Under other circumstances, I would think some special fixture would be warranted; however, given the situation I have no better idea than the one Mr. Price put forward. However, along the lines of being a little crazy, one improvement might be to use some special underwater high strength duct tape. I'd quickly tape the hatches closed and then reinforce this with chain. I recommend using a rubber coated chain to keep the noise down, but in case they're detected, hopefully the tape will be enough to preclude a launch."

The President declared, "I believe the time for talking is over. Every minute that goes by poses a risk that they might launch. Mr. Price, I hope you're right. The U.S. military will provide you with every support you need, and I'll be standing by to address the captain.

In the meantime, you have my authorization to proceed."

"Thank you, sir," said Price. "I won't let you down. I do have two guests at my home that should be taken into custody, but they'll need your special authority since they were both apprehended without normal due process; one is an escapee from prison."

The President answered, "Consider it done. They'll be treated as terrorists until we can figure out how to best deal with them."

"Please have whomever you plan to pick them up meet me at my house as soon as I can get there," said Price.

"The Chairman will arrange a fast jet to get you home as soon as possible," said the President. "I'd give you mine, but it's not that fast and draws all kinds of attention."

Price then provided the list of what he needed to the Chairman and told him where it should be delivered as quickly as possible. Price then turned to Mahoney and said, "Are you up for a swim?"

Mahoney replied, "I wouldn't miss it for anything. Let's get on the jet provided and get out to your place."

CHAPTER 42

Making Preparations

Mahoney and Price managed to catch some sleep on the flight from Washington to the West Coast. When they arrived at Price's home, there were some mysterious Federal Marshals who identified themselves and advised that they were to pick up some "guests" from Price. Mahoney showed them to the holding area, where they restrained Khan and Henry and took them away.

Price and Mahoney were busily provisioning the sub when a military truck pulled up to the house. Mary was home and met the soldiers at the front door.

The older of the two soldiers said, "Ma'am, I have a delivery to make, but it must be some kind of a mistake."

Mary replied, "Out of the ordinary, yes, but mistake, no. What have you got?"

The soldiers answered, "We have a shipping container that contains pallets of material. We were also ordered to provide whatever assistance requested of us, ma'am. Do you want it, and if so where?"

Mary replied, "Let me get my husband." She then hurried to go find Price to let him know about the delivery.

Price asked the soldiers to unload the container and place all the pallets on the driveway. He then asked that they remove the shipping container from the premises while leaving Price the forklift. Lastly, he requested that they return in 6 hours to pick up the forklift, empty pallets, and any other pallets that were untouched.

When the soldiers had left and Mahoney came out to see what all was going on, he was shocked to see the collection of wrapped pallets sitting on the driveway. Laughing, he said, "I thought we were clear that we had a mini-sub, not a boomer. What in the hell are we supposed to do with all of this?"

They set about unwrapping a couple of the pallets in order to identify what they contained; it was obvious there were two different types. One pallet had a rubber covered chain, while the other had reels of the special underwater duct tape. The chain pallet also included a box with miscellaneous hardware that could be used to connect chains to one another.

Price said, "This is certainly the right stuff, but there's so much of it. We can't even fit one pallet of each in the sub."

They concluded they probably didn't need more than one pallet of each, but they decided they'd figure out a way to bring two pallets of each with them. They were able to lash the rolls of chain to the deck of the submarine; however, this made the sub too heavy – and besides, how would they ever get the materials from where they parked to the SS New York City? They needed another plan.

    The answer was an old pontoon boat Price had. While the weight overwhelmed the craft submerging much of it, they were able to attain neutral buoyancy with the addition of some air cells in the form of truck inner tubes. When they were ready to submerge, they simply had to puncture these to let the air out. The boat had the added advantage of having a motor that would help move the cumbersome load to the target area, as long as it stayed afloat. Without this added propulsion, they might not reach the target area within an acceptable amount of time.

    There wasn't anything left to do other than get underway. They checked once more on the precise location of the SS New York City and set course for it. Keeping their cargo on the surface and with their submarine just below the surface, they began their critical journey. It would take some time, so they set up shifts so one of them could rest at any given time.

    Price worried they wouldn't make it on time. While he couldn't control what the sub's crew might do, he had some control over his own travel, though he clearly didn't control the wind and the waves. Initially these were favorable, but as they continued their trip, the seas started to kick up some. Fortunately, the extra buoyancy they added was attached to outriggers. This helped keep the boat from sinking or capsizing.

The going was slow, but they were making progress towards their objective. Price and Mahoney took turns resting, but the stakes of what they were about to do made sleep elusive. They had no doubt that they would be heard as they approached the area. The question was what the SS New York City would make of the sounds and whether they would consider them hostile. When they were five miles from the "Big Apple", they faded their sound to virtually nothing as their sub, with its odd vessel in tow, came to a stop. They needed to make the rest of their approach quietly and from the back blind spot of the target.

While they were pretty sure what orientation the SS New York City was in due to the topography of the underwater landscape in which it was located, they could not be sure in which direction the back pointed. Price and Mahoney debated this for some time, trying to reason how the Big Apple would have approached the area. They concluded that the SS New York City would have arrived from the North, and thus its tail would be facing that direction. They had a 50-50 chance of being right, but the downside of being wrong was unacceptable.

They reached out to the situation room, which had been set up to monitor and provide assistance to them. After studying charts of the ocean bottom and the last known location of the target sub, the situation room staff concluded that the tail would be facing south. This left the team in a quandary.

Mahoney said, "Now what do we do? We can't be wrong about this."

"I agree, we must get this right," answered Price. "I think we're just going to have to get some real information."

"How?" responded Mahoney.

"I don't know," answered Price. "We don't have time to just wait around, yet we can't get this wrong."

They were lost in their thoughts about how to deal with this matter when the Situation Room called back. The message read: "Sensors picked up some earlier use of active SONAR as the Big Apple navigated into the area. Conclusion is that they approached from the North, repeat North."

"That agrees with our assessment," said Mahoney.

Price replied, "Our assessment is backed up now with some real data – no choice but to go with it."

They made their preparations and began the excruciatingly slow approach to the target. They were committed now and just willed everything to be quiet. Price recalled the saying that there are no atheists in a fox hole; he concluded the sentiment is broader than that and encompasses anyone who's in a perilous situation. While not religious, he knew he not only had his fingers crossed, but was praying. The fate of a city and crew was in their hands.

Price could also not escape the irony that his target was named for the very city where he suffered a loss that had set him on the quest that took him to the here and now. He thought about his loss while he thought about the good he'd accomplished in their honor. He also thought about the positive in his finding Mary. He felt that this, too, honored the relationship he'd had and lost. He needed to be successful and save a city, and save a crew.

CHAPTER 43

Dilemma

The orders they had received had those on the Big Apple feeling very uneasy. Captain Derek Wheeler had never had orders like this before, nor had he ever heard of such a thing; however, he validated the orders, and they were proper, albeit unconventional. His training was such that he could question, but in the end, and without hesitation, he must comply with appropriately authorized and lawful orders. These just did not seem right.

"Captain, I have a contact on the surface five miles to the northeast of our position," reported the Alert Operator.

"What is it?" asked Captain Wheeler.

"I don't know," answered the Alert Operator. "I've never heard a signature quite like it. There are aspects of it that sound like a barge in tow, yet the power plants are all wrong. In addition, as strange as it seems, there are sounds of a surface wake, yet other sounds of underwater disturbances."

"Is it hostile?" asked the Captain.

"I hardly think so," answered the Alert Operator. "By the sound of it, I'm not sure what it is, though I'm certain it isn't a warship of any kind. It also appears to be fading."

"Keep an eye on it," said the Captain.

His order was acknowledged, and the Captain went back to contemplating his misgivings about his current set of orders. He decided to discuss this with his second in command. They had the same misgivings but also felt the orders were valid and proper, and therefore must be followed.

The Captain asked, "Is there any way for us to determine the target location for the strike?"

Bob Massey, his second in command, answered, "Not by any conventional means."

"With all of these young kids we have on board, there must be a hacker among them," continued the Captain. "Maybe one of them would be able to figure it out without leaving any footprints behind. Please give this some thought and how one might be able to approach them while keeping it quiet."

Massey left to consider the task he'd been given. It certainly did not violate the letter of the orders they had, and knowing the ultimate target might help them to calm their misgivings. He already had a couple of candidates in mind and set about seeing what their respective schedules were. While he wasn't comfortable expanding the circle of those involved, he knew he should consult with the Chief. Not only would it be necessary to tell the Chief something should the duty roster be changed, the Chief also knew the men the best.

Massey summoned the Chief to the ward room. It was clear the Chief was apprehensive about the reason he was summoned, so the greetings were brief, then the Chief asked, "What can I do for you, sir?"

Massey replied, "I need a computer hacker. The very best we have, and the less you know, the better."

This request caught the Chief off guard. Among the myriad possibilities that had run through his mind, needing a hacker was not one of them. "Well, there's one young man who's certainly good with computers and talks some about his exploits who might make a good choice," answered the Chief. "It's Seaman Kyle Jonas."

Massey responded, "Can he be trusted to keep his mouth shut? You said he speaks about his other extracurricular activities."

"I believe so," said the Chief, "especially if you make it explicitly clear to him that he cannot speak about this to anyone. Jonas is a good lad."

Massey asked the Chief, "Please get Jonas and bring him to the ward room. No need to tell him anything other than he's not in any trouble, and if he keeps his mouth shut, he'll stay that way. Thanks."

The Chief left, and just a few minutes later Seaman Jonas arrived. If the Chief had shown some apprehension when he arrived at their meeting, this kid looked absolutely terrified. Massey tried to put him at ease, but he realized it wouldn't be possible – he was just called to the principal's office and didn't know what he did.

Massey felt it best to get right down to the point. "Son, we have a message that contains the coordinates for a strike. Unfortunately, we don't know what the location is, as the message is encrypted. Our launch system will know, but we won't. Is there some way you could figure this out, and quickly? You may not discuss this with anyone, and I mean anyone, other than the Captain and myself. Even the Chief doesn't know why you're here, other than to help out with some computer related matter."

Jonas replied, "You can count on me to keep a secret. What I'm less confident about is whether I'll be able to decode the message; however, I'm certainly willing to try and give it my best. I trust you'll take care of moving me off the duty roster so I can concentrate on this?"

Not long afterward, Massey set Jonas up with what he said he needed, and Jonas set to work. Hours went by without any results, although every time Massey peeked in on Jonas, he seemed busily at work. Massey had arranged to have food brought to him, but Jonas was so focused on the task at hand that he hardly touched it.

Just before the break of the new day, Jonas came looking for Massey; instead, he found the Captain. "May I speak with you, sir?"

Captain Wheeler replied, "Certainly, but let me get Commander Massey, and we can meet in the Ward room."

Three minutes later, the Captain with a sleepy Commander Massey met up with Jonas at the ward room. The Captain said, "Go ahead, son, you asked for this meeting."

Jonas began. "There was indeed a set of coordinates in the message you gave to me. What was the message for? It looked like a strike package, but it can't be."

The Captain said, "What are the coordinates?"

"They're 38.57371° N, -121.4962° E," answered Jonas. "That's the capital of California. We can't be planning a strike on Sacramento – can we?"

The Captain and Massey looked at each other, and then the Captain spoke. "Go get some well deserved rest. This was a training activity, so no, we're not striking our own country. However, remember you cannot speak a word of this to anyone. Leave us now."

With that, Jonas left and the Captain and Massey just looked at each other. Finally, Massey spoke up and said, "What in the hell is going on?"

The Captain spoke and said, "We cannot strike a city within the United States. Sacramento has nearly a half million people in it. I'd rather be put in prison than do this; however, maybe it's as I told Jonas, a training exercise. Let's stay vigilant, but unless you want to relieve me of command, we're not going to launch. With that said, I'm not sure what we're going to do."

Massey agreed and returned to his cabin while the Captain went to his duty station. Massey could not sleep, as he couldn't get the current situation out of his mind. What was going on? There was no scenario he could come up with that could explain what was going on.

The Captain asked the Alert Operator what the status of the earlier hit was. The Operator said all was quiet, except for occasional but different anomalous sounds he'd picked up. None of them correlated to the earlier observation.

"Stay vigilant," said the Captain.

CHAPTER 44

Initial Execution

Price and Mahoney had thus far successfully eluded detection and had gotten as close as they were planning, just aft of the SS New York City. Price engaged the automatic station, keeping so their sub would stay in formation with the target. Then both Price and Mahoney donned their diving equipment and made ready to perform the task of securing the missile hatches and attaching the transducer to the "Big Apple's" hull.

When they entered the water, they were more than cognizant of the criticality of their work and of the destructive power the "Big Apple" had. They were also aware of just how sensitive its defenses were and the big unknown of what the Captain would do if they were detected. These thoughts and whether their measures would work were on both men's minds as they silently set to work.

The first thing they wanted to do was make an initial pass at securing the missile hatches. To do this, they used the special underwater duct tape they'd brought along. When Price first posed securing the hatches, he was ridiculed by virtually everyone who heard it. He then explained the hatches were not designed to exert much force to open; it wasn't necessary. When the idea of using tape was suggested, the idea seemed preposterous. However, the tape would be sufficient if it adhered to the surface of the ship as promised. This was the question on Price and Mahoney's minds as they set about applying the tape to the hatches. To their great relief, it stuck without any problem. The issue they did encounter was that it was much harder to cut than they anticipated.

Both Price and Mahoney had a knife and shears attached to their belt by lanyards, but neither one of these tools was proving very efficient. Despite this, they were making progress in getting each of the hatches taped shut. However, while working on the last hatch, Mahoney lost his grip on the knife and it slipped from his hands and hit the hatch cover he'd been working on. To him it sounded like a shot, and both he and Price froze. While it was unclear what they expected might happen, they nonetheless waited several minutes before moving again. In fact, they were hardly breathing.

The sound was not lost on those aboard the "Big Apple". It was not as alarming a sound as Price and Mahoney feared, but it was still anomalous. Captain Wheeler wanted to know what it was. He said to Massey, his second in command, "Bob, we're supposed to have silence. Please find out what made that noise, and let's make sure it doesn't happen again."

Massey responded, "Aye aye, Captain. I'll go check it out and remind the crew of your order for silence."

When he returned 15 minutes later, Massey told the Captain, "I can't find the origin of that noise. It might have come from the outside. Irrespective of that, the crew has now been reminded to remain silent."

The Captain dismissed the noise and got back to work, his mind preoccupied by this crazy mission and seemingly that he and his crew were being tested. Captain Wheeler was trying to make sense of what was going on. He had aspirations to achieve flag rank, so he needed to successfully pass any test he and his crew were subjected to.

Back outside, Price and Mahoney continued to work. Now they were hauling the rubber coated chain they'd brought and using it to secure the Big Apple's propellers. This was an extremely hazardous task, because should the propellers be engaged before they were secured, they had the potential to slice Price and/or Mahoney apart; however, neither Price nor Mahoney focused on harm to themselves and instead considered the threat this submarine posed to the innocent civilians should it launch one or more of its missiles. The thought of this was what kept them going, despite rapidly approaching total physical exhaustion.

Price and Mahoney were not as coordinated or nimble as they were when they began, and they fumbled things more frequently as time moved on. Most of the time what they dropped had minimal impact, but there were several close calls of having something they dropped hitting the Big Apple. Then it happened again. This time, it was the tail end of a section of chain that got fumbled, and it hit the sub and slid off. Once again, to Price and Mahoney the sound was loud and chilling. After experiencing the fright of their lives, they did the only thing they could: they pressed ahead with what they had to do.

Aboard the SS New York City, there were gasps at this new sound, but no one could identify its source or what it was. Captain Wheeler decided he needed to move to another location. He'd stay close to where he was, but possibly enough of a move to get away from the source of these noises.

The Captain ordered the crew to stand ready to move. He then gave the order to move forward at dead slow and lower their depth by 50 feet. He certainly didn't expect the boat to be unresponsive, but that's exactly what happened.

Price had just finished securing the chains around the propellers when he noticed them trying to move. A chill ran through him when he realized that had he taken just a small moment longer, he and possibly Mahoney would now be chum. The chains had worked in securing the propellers, and Price was contemplating what to do next. He reasoned that other than pray, he needed to reinforce the previous work they'd done on the missile hatches, then attach the communications equipment so the President could address the Big Apple's crew.

"Captain, I'm unable to get us underway," said Massey. "The propellers won't seem to turn in either direction."

"Are any of the diagnostics giving any indication of what might be wrong?" said Captain Wheeler.

Massey replied, "Negative, all appears normal."

"Take us up to periscope depth using ballast only," ordered the Captain.

"Aye aye, Captain, raising boat to periscope depth using ballast only," said Massey.

The boat rose normally, and the Captain looked out at his surroundings and didn't notice anything out of the ordinary. "Try getting underway again," said the Captain.

Once again, they were unsuccessful in getting the propellers to turn. "Under ordinary circumstances, I'd surface and put a work party in the water to check this situation out; however, given our orders and the fact that despite not being able to navigate, we're safe, we'll stay put for now," said Captain Wheeler. "Take us back down to where we were."

Outside the Big Apple, Price and Mahoney were both surprised when the big sub started to rise; however, their initial fright immediately dissipated when the ascent stopped and reversed a short while later. Price and Mahoney both figured the crew had discovered their stuck propellers and were simply assessing whether they'd somehow gotten themselves stuck and would also be unable to surface. When the sub settled down, they resumed their work and reinforced their initial efforts at restraining the missile hatches.

Satisfied the hatches were secure, Price and Mahoney attached the sound transducer to the Big Apple's hull. They connected the other communication gear, checking each other's work, then returned to their sub, where they disconnected the makeshift "trailer" they'd towed their materials with and reentered through its airlock.

Price and Mahoney were exhausted from their efforts, and it took them much longer than usual to remove their gear and make it to the main compartment; however, they persevered and sent a message to the White House that all was ready.

CHAPTER 45

Crescendo

The President had been anxious for the moment when he could address the crew and hopefully bring this episode to a close. He'd been over what to say and how to say it numerous times. The words were critiqued and polished beyond any speech he'd ever given. One concern was that his words not instigate any action by the crew before he had a chance to say all he had to say. The crew had been indoctrinated with following orders, and now he needed them to be open to hear those orders countermanded. Certainly, he had the authority; however, would the crew accept that he was who he said he was?

Massey and the Captain were speaking privately about what was going on. They each had different theories. One dominant theory was that they were being tested in some way. They'd never heard of anything that went quite to this level, but they were both committed to their careers and service to their country. They were quite honestly at a loss for what to do.

Of all the things they'd been trained to expect, and of all those they were capable of imagining, what happened next was beyond anything they ever could have anticipated. A voice suddenly but clearly seemed to resonate throughout the entire ship. The Captain and Massey looked at each other to assure themselves it wasn't their imagination. Shortly afterward, the Chief knocked, seeking similar assuredness. It began:

> *"Captain Derek Wheeler and the crew of the SS New York City, this is General Marshall S. Crowley, Chairman of the Joint Chiefs of Staff, to introduce the Commander in Chief, and President of the United States.*
>
> *Captain Wheeler, I hope you recognize my voice and ask that you hear me out before you take any actions called for by your existing set of orders..."*

The Captain, Massey, and Chief looked at each other, dumfounded. The Captain was comfortable with his number two and the Chief, so he spoke openly. "What in the hell is this about? I think I now can understand the circumstance we find ourselves in and the noise we all heard earlier, but is this hostile, or is this really the President?"

"If I may speak freely," said the Chief. "We have no choice but to listen; however, I think we should follow through on our existing orders up to the point where our actions would be irreversible."

"You mean up to the point of launching, right?" said Massey.

"Yes," said the Chief.

"I agree - open the missile tubes, and prepare to launch," said the Captain.

Aboard their sub, Price and Mahoney not only heard the President, they also heard the distinctive clicks of the missile hatch release mechanisms. They immediately signaled this to the White House, along with the visual they had that all the hatches remained shut.

> *"...the orders you're operating on are counterfeit, but among other things created a situation which isolated you and prevented me from being able to correct this through conventional means, most notably to be able to properly authenticate myself to you. Part of this is that your codes were changed, but we have no idea to what, and given your orders to maintain radio silence, you're unable to resynchronize. So for now all I have is my voice as a means of authentication – though I'm open to any ideas you might have which would satisfy you. Should you wish to communicate, just use your hydrophones and I'll hear you. You don't need to worry that it will give your position away, as I know it."* He then cited the coordinates.

The Chief returned and reported, "The missile tubes unlatched but did not open. We couldn't fire even if we wanted to."

"OK, I'm open to suggestions," said Wheeler. "They've got our position, and that sure sounded like the Chairman, and this sounds like the President."

> "...just hold on, Seaman. I asked you to hear me out before you took any action, and you go and try to open your missile hatches? I'll overlook this insubordination due to this unconventional and not authenticated means of communication; however, I cannot allow the launching of your missiles and will do what I need to in order to prevent it. I implore you to somehow let us know what we can do to satisfy you that you are in fact hearing from your Commander in Chief and that this order to stand down and disregard your previous orders is the right thing to do. I assure you that it is, but I do understand your dilemma..."

The Chief said, "I think he just said he'll blow us up if we continue."

Massey replied, "Something like that is what I heard. It sure does sound like the President, although I've never met the man and only heard his voice on TV. Under the circumstances, I think we must do something to break this log jam."

"Agreed," said the Captain, "but what?"

"I have an idea," said the Chief. "I've heard rumors that these boats have a special communications system designed to connect with the national command authority in a post-nuclear strike scenario. If there is such a thing, what about using it as a first step in authenticating with whom were speaking?"

The Captain replied, "I can't deny or confirm that such a system exists, but I appreciate your thinking outside of the box, and hopefully it will further our thinking regarding potential solutions. Now if you'll leave Mr. Massey and me alone for a bit."

> "...while it won't get to this, any board convened to assess your actions won't be able to come to any other conclusion than you were faced with an intractable problem and that you needed to apply reason, and not blind obedience, to get through it..."

"The Chief's idea has merit," said the Captain. "I think we're screwed no matter what we do and should therefore choose the lesser of two evils."

"I agree," said Massey. "Shall I prepare to activate the PSAMS (post strike auxiliary messaging system)? I wonder how the Chief ever heard of such a thing. I thought it was restricted to the smallest number of people, like just you and I on this boat."

"Can't slip much past a good Chief, but they also know how to keep their mouths shut," said the Captain. "Yeah, let's use that channel. It's designed to be low probability of intercept, secure, and only connected to the national command authority. If the person we're hearing from now is the President, then

PSAMS should connect us; if it isn't, we can explain our issue and get our orders revalidated."

"Mr. President, a message has just come in from the SS New York City on the Top Secret PSAMS terminal. Shall I acknowledge?" said the Chairman.

"Of course!" said the President. "Maybe then we can get somewhere."

After that, it was relatively easy. They got their conventional set of communications on the same code baseline, and new orders were given and authenticated. The Captain took the Big Apple to the surface and began the laborious task of freeing up its propellers. They would free up their missile tubes when they were in port. He felt relieved, like he acted reasonably, so this "test" should be a pass.

The President was feeling relatively good about how this played out. He asked for an opportunity to meet with the Captain and crew of the Big Apple in secret, and he wanted to meet up with Price and Mahoney to thank them. The President's Chief of Staff made plans for a West Coast visit for the President. He needed to find an explanation for the trip, have public events, yet provide time to hold the two meetings without anyone noticing.

The President also held a meeting with the CNO, where he pointed out that the situation was resolved without either compromising a dedicated crew or jeopardizing the populace of a U.S. city. He then added, "...and if you're thinking there was insubordination, let me be clear that the only lack of following orders was from you. You have a commendable record and have served this country with distinction for many years. Because of that, I'm not going to press the point, and instead give you the opportunity to resign in order to spend more time with your family – if I'm being clear. However, any attempt to get at Captain Wheeler or mention of any of this publicly will result in your public trial. Am I understood?

"Yes, sir," said the CNO, then he left, as the President obviously was done with him.

CHAPTER 46

Commendations

Two weeks later, the President made a previously unannounced trip to the West Coast. There were a number of activities that were hastily planned, and one of the stops was at a naval base, where he spoke with Marines returning from overseas. He met with them and their families and went to the base hospital to meet some of those who had been wounded in action. There were many photo opportunities. The base commander gave a tour of his base to the President, during which the President entered a large closed hangar where the crew of the Big Apple had been assembled. The base commander was asked to remain outside.

Just inside the entrance to the hangar was a small office the President used for a brief meeting with Captain Wheeler. The Captain apologized for having disobeyed the President, and even though they were bogus, for violating his orders. He said, "Mr. President, the actions I took were mine alone. It was also my responsibility that I allowed my ship to be taken out of action. It has a great crew, and they should not pay any price for any errors I made. I'll step down and accept any punishment you deem appropriate. I just ask that you treat the crew kindly and not tar them with my inadequacy."

The President responded, "First, I'm here to commend, not punish anyone. While I'd like to think it was my persuasiveness that won the day, I know it was your good judgment and creativity that got us through this. Thank you, and your actions saved many lives, either those of your crew or the population of some U.S. city."

"Sacramento, sir," said Captain Wheeler. "I have to confess to at least one additional transgression. Given the unusual nature of the orders, I had to know the target. When we discovered it was the capital of California, I knew we couldn't launch on Americans."

The President gasped, as he hadn't been told what the target was. He said, "Under the circumstances, I believe you did right. Blindly following orders is not what we want. I also think your efforts to authenticate my orders were commendable, if not brilliant. As far as I'm concerned, you performed perfectly, but you may never speak about this, nor will your record reflect it. That said, I'm am issuing commendations for you and your crew for a non-specific action vital to national security. Also, don't beat yourself up about being taken out of action. The person who did this has a list of extraordinary feats nearly as amazing as this was. To name just one, he hijacked an airliner shortly after takeoff and landed it without ever being seen by the crew."

The Captain responded, "How'd he do that – never mind. Thank you very much, sir. Shall we go out and see the crew? They're all wondering what this is about."

They proceeded to see the crew, and the President spoke briefly to them. He commended their actions and swore them to secrecy. He then surprised them with commendations and the promotion of Massey to being the Big Apple's new captain. Everyone cheered, including Wheeler. The President began to make his way from the room, and Wheeler wondered what he'd missed. He thought all was good between him and the President, yet he was apparently just relieved of command.

Before the frown completely overtook his face, the President turned around and said, "I almost forgot something; please help me congratulate the new commander of submarine operations for the Navy, Admiral Derek Wheeler. Yes, I said Admiral. We need leaders like him to impart their outstanding judgment and wisdom to more than just one crew, but instead to the entire fleet. I know he'll do a great job. Thank you all for your service and continued excellence. I gotta run now before I'm missed."

This got a laugh as the President slipped out the door and rejoined the base commander for the balance of his tour. Both Massey and Wheeler were in a daze as their crew came up to congratulate them.

"While not intended as a test, I guess it was one," said Massey.

"Yeah, and we apparently passed," said Captain Wheeler. "I'm going to defer celebrating until I see the orders in writing."

He didn't have long to wait, as he was summoned to the base commander's office after the President left. When he arrived, he was given two packages: one with his name on it, and the other with Massey's. His contained his promotion and orders, with congratulatory notes from the Secretary of the Navy and Secretary of Defense. There were two handwritten notes from the President. One was a normal – if there is such a thing, given the source – note of congratulations. The other was direction for him, in his new capacity, to transfer command to Massey and present him with his orders and promotion.

CHAPTER 47

Recognition and Reward

Price and Mahoney were enjoying coffee at Price's house. Mary came in and joined them. They were largely spent by their ordeal, but also feeling they did a good thing. Price said, "We saved a city and took a real bad guy off the street, but until Taylor's criminal enterprise is dismantled, the job isn't done."

Mahoney replied, "Agreed that Taylor's empire must be dissolved, but that only constitutes a battle won in a seemingly endless war."

"Now that's a depressing thought," said Mary.

"No, that's the way it is," said Price. "There will always be those who don't want to play by society's rules. I set out to rid the world of this scourge but have come to understand one can only improve things. It would take a concerted effort of everyone, not just one person, to truly attain a world without criminals – I just don't see it happening. However, that's how I'll continue to apply my energies and believe it will make a difference."

Just then, there was some commotion coming from the front of the house. Price and Mahoney got up. Melissa, who had been reading in the front parlor, said, "You're not going to believe it."

Just then, two big men in suits came into the room. They were serious men who offered no greeting, but instead quickly looked about the area. Price was just about to ask what was going on when the President of the United State entered. He said, "Hello, David, Mike, and this must be Mary. I'm sorry for barging in on you like this, but I wanted to thank you personally for what you just did. You got a rotten apple out of my administration, saved many lives, and rid the world of a criminal enterprise that harmed many people."

Price said, "Thank you, Mr. President. I was glad I could help."

Mahoney added, "Me, too."

"Your modesty is honorable," said the President. "However, I hope you all understand the significance of your accomplishments. Other than conveying the thanks of this nation, and doing so in secret, I'm not sure what I could do that would measure up to what you've done."

Price started to interrupt, but the President waved him quiet and continued. "I did think of a few things. First, I issued a Presidential Order that exonerates you from any liabilities that might result from actions taken. After hearing of some of your other exploits, like one including a commercial jetliner, I extended it back a couple of years. Second, I've taken the steps necessary to grant you legal right to own and operate your sub. Third, I've made provisions to reimburse you for any expenses you've incurred.

Lastly, I've created a fund in the memory of Sandy and Becky Price that will fund both victims and those who contribute to helping rid our world of crime. I should note that I've already received matching funds from corporate sponsors, and I fully expect other countries to participate. I don't know that this will attain the prestige of a Nobel Prize, but it sure has a larger endowment and should do great things for many years to come."

Price was too stunned to speak, and besides the way his eyes were brimming with tears, it wasn't likely he could have spoken anyway. It was just as well as; the President wasn't quite finished.

"There are two things I'd like you to consider. One is that I'd like you to be the Chairman of the Sandy and Becky Price Fund and help get it operating, including making grants. Second, I'd like to have you continue to support Mike in his new role as the head of a Special Task Force reporting directly to me that oversees anti-criminal activities across the government and can undertake its own operations as needed. In some regards, he'll be a super department within the Executive Branch, where other departments will defer to his leadership and support his efforts."

At this, the President turned to Mahoney and said, "I'm sure Dave needs some time to think, so what do you think about what I've got in mind for you?"

Mahoney didn't know what to say, so the President continued, "You've already been promoted to the highest level possible, retroactive to the beginning of the year. You'll have an office in the West Wing and a suite over at the Justice Department. I've carved out a budget for a modest staff, as well as to cover operations. You needn't worry; the AG is fully on board with this, and in fact welcomes it. No doubt there will need to be some selling done to others, but I'm confident the two of you won't have any problems – but if you do, I can always help."

Mahoney's head was spinning, so all he could think to say was, "Thank you, Mr. President."

Lastly, the President turned to Mary and said, "I want to thank you also for both your direct support and for loaning us your husband. I understand your insights and overall efforts helped bring this episode to its successful end. I'd love to have you continue as you and Dave see fit."

Price finally spoke up. "Mary is quite a valuable member of this team. Any decision regarding continued support to Mike will be the product of both of us. We'll discuss it, but speaking for myself, I'm honored by your visit today and by all you've said and done. I'm especially touched by the Fund and most welcome your offer to run it; at least to get it going."

Price began to choke up, so Mary interceded. "OK. We've spoken about it, Mr. President, and Dave and I would be most pleased to support Mike, if he'll have us."

With that, Mary hugged Price, there were handshakes all around, and then the President left. The three of them, along with Melissa, looked at each other as if to say, "Was the President really just here, or was this just a dream?" It had been less than 10 minutes since he'd arrived.

The spell was broken when Mahoney said, "Is there anything stronger than coffee around here? We need a celebration."

CHAPTER 48
EPILOGUE

In the months that followed the President's visit, Taylor, Khan, and Henry were extensively interrogated and various deals made to learn as much as possible about their criminal empire. Billions of dollars were recovered, numerous cells were dismantled, with their leadership arrested, convicted, and incarcerated for very long sentences. While crime had not been eradicated from the face of the Earth, it was certainly a major victory for the powers of right.

Price began his administration of the Sandy and Becky Price Fund. Price found that evaluating applications and deciding on grants was the hardest, yet most gratifying work he'd ever done. Having this fund was a perfect way to complement his lifelong commitment of honoring the memory of his first wife and daughter – victims of crime – by helping eliminate it.

Mahoney began his new job and felt good that his efforts were helping improve the crime fighting posture of the government. He was able to get cooperation from other departments, not by exercising his clout, but instead by demonstrating value. Mahoney did this by fostering coordination among departments and an openness that was able to focus on a common objective instead of petty self interests. Mahoney also didn't believe it was necessary to steal credit where others deserved it. Where others worried about recognition, Mahoney's lack of doing so not only helped him be successful, it also got him the recognition he was due.

Price and Mary supported Mahoney's efforts, and he continued to come up with innovative approaches to further the cause of goodness. Their exploits weren't just legendary, they were also proving to be quite successful. Unfortunately, Mahoney was so busy, they didn't get to spend as much time with each other as they would have preferred.

While that was true of Mahoney and them, Price and Mary were very careful to make sure work did not detract from their private lives. On the contrary, both their working together and their family lives flourished. One key to this, besides making the time, was respect for each other's prior lives. Mary was particularly supportive and proud of Price's commitment to his previous family and how honoring their memory helped to better society. Mary never felt threatened by this and instead knew she and her daughter couldn't have a better man in their family.

Life is comprised of memories, and good lives create many happy recollections. The Prices cherished their memories and through family rituals created new ones. Despite this, Price felt something was missing. It was Christmas time, a joyous time, but also a time for Price when he remembered his loss and the committed path it had put him on.

When he suggested the three of them take a trip to New York City to see the storefronts and other festive goings on, Mary, for the first time since they met, got very concerned the past might now encroach on the present; however, she saw no graceful way to decline, so she agreed. They decided to go for four nights one week prior to Christmas.

They went out to eat and saw a couple of Broadway shows. Melissa was particularly taken by the visit, as she hadn't spent much time in New York City. With the exception of not parting ways from his family, Price wasn't haunted by memories past; however, this was a ritual of a past life, not of the one he'd forged with Mary. So on the third morning, Price said to Mary, "I've seen enough. What would you say if we left early to go to one of our favorite places?"

"Are you sure?" asked Mary.

"Yes, I'm positive," said Price.

A short while later, they were leaving the hotel. They were on the sidewalk when Price saw a young man swipe a woman's purse almost right in front of them. Price couldn't help himself and gave chase. Despite the age difference, he caught and subdued the thief, then forced him to walk back to the hotel, where Price called the police.

Mary was a bit disappointed that they'd now miss their plane, but she was also reminded Price would fight crime anytime and anywhere. He'd made a made a vow and would honor that commitment, no matter what, for the rest of his days. Mary thought about it a moment, smiled, then remembered this was an important part of what she loved in Price. He'd made a life commitment. Then she revised her thought to say, "No, he'd made two commitments – one to tirelessly work against evil, and the other to our new family." This made her happier than she ever could have imagined.

The End

Made in the USA
Middletown, DE
07 February 2018